WINDS OF THE IMMORTALS

By
Parker J. Duncan

CRANTHORPE
—MILLNER—

Cover art by Chris Panatier
www.panatier.com/home.html

ISBN 978-1-912964-15-4 (Paperback)

www.cranthorpemillner.com

Published by Cranthorpe Millner Publishers (2020)

TABLE OF CONTENTS

TABLE OF CONTENTS

For Taylor R. Thompson, the Sun, and the stars that shine beyond death

BOOK I

November 18th, 2032 - Year of the Rat

"The devil keeps man from good with a thousand machinations spewed from his belly, so that when a person tries to do good, he pierces him with his shafts; and when he desires to embrace God with his whole heart in love, he subjects him to poisonous tribulations, seeking to pervert good work before God. And when a person seeks virtue, the devil tells him that he does not know what he is doing, and he teaches him he can set his own law for himself."

- Hildegard Von Bingen, Letter to Abbot c. 1166

CHAPTER 1
EXODUS FELICITY

The moon's soft reprise brought the mercenary to the balcony. He'd never been one to admit its supernal forces could turn a person, but its disappearing silver shadow brought his hearkening a glowing fortune. His eyes reached through the cold distance to embrace its silky light in silent celestial swoon. He tipped his head back to view the cloudless sky, his weary pupils falling into the blanket of the night's depths where blue hues of dead nebula lay vast at the hearth of time, behind mezzanines of the abyss, pulling the stars ever closer. And through his troubled eyes he'd affixed on something dissolved beyond that furthest fading sun, his stare unwavering like the gaze of all men whose words cease to speak a language only surfaced blood finds fluent. His eyes fell back down to the city where a grid of flashing lights and city clamor clashed with the chaotic Columbian jungle pushing up around the concrete blocks. The bustling surface of faceless beings and noisy machines below overlapped the choir of tropical birds perched on the platform of flickering holographic billboards.

Pasto was a tourist oasis in a country still ravaged by corruption. The city stood on a graveyard of both ancient natives and modern slaves, where the memory of hardship met cartel violence and people conspiring against their communities fought those protecting it, infecting the wound. The mercenary knew these patterns of history well. This knowing was the reason he stood in such a contemplative state, his eyes shifting from the orange lights of the billboards allure and down into his whiskey drink, that mirror of dance and sudden wisdom.

Born one hundred and fifty years prior, he may have been an outlaw in Pasto, his old ghost absorbed into the land's decay. But Ezra Beller, a descendent of European nomads and Missouri mountain men, was there for a new kind of crusade. His next mission would take place in the Andes: a vast range of mystery, havoc and plunder.

Having been born on September 11th, 2001, Ezra's life began with a bang. His father insisted he join the military when he came of age and Ezra enlisted in the Army at the age of 18 as the global war on terrorism in the Middle East was spilling over into West Africa, Eastern Europe and Southeast Asia. Through years of combat experience, Ezra eventually became a contractor for a security company that took him on more missions he declined existing in than not. And while the war between Iranian puppet states and Saudi Arabia pumped out as much violence as oil, the ocean's toxicity rose in the people's negligence. The unprecedented amount of damage urged the U.N. and U.S. governments' frantic search for a solution to the poisoned seas, allowing them to conduct a worldwide environmental catastrophe initiative. Ezra's mission was to help lead a security contingent hired to protect biological researchers exploring the soils of South America in hopes of finding an organism that decomposed both radioactive and fossil fuel matter quickly. The mountains of southern Columbia and northern Ecuador and Peru were riddled with heavily armed cartels, savage gold miners, and ancient Jivaro traps. The

2

initiatives' coordinators implied that a top-notch security team was absolutely necessary for the team's safety, which was where Ezra and his group came in.

Ezra laughed at a faint but happy memory as he stood in solitude, smoking his cigar away from the commotion of his fellow contractors in the hotel room. Some scientists had come to socialize with the mercenaries. One of them bought cocaine and began dicing up lines on the table. Ezra laughed and shook his head. As a veteran of ten years active military duty and twelve major deployments, there was little social interaction that brought excitement to Ezra inside civilian life. He only knew how to keep running on, and his coagulated emotions kept him distant from his friends and what was left in his family. Still, his bargaining with the moon was a subtle omen reminding himself of an entity outside his haunting. He flicked the ash from his cigar over the balcony and watched the grey flakes fall slowly against the building's mirror clear windows, spiraling to the ground hundreds of feet below. He grasped his scotch and took a drag from the cigar before gulping the fiery liquid. He turned around to a woman striding toward him. She smiled. He blinked and muttered good evening. She slowed and approached him.

"Hola, senior. Fuego?" she asked in gringo Spanish. Her eyes were an emerald mirror against the fading orange horizon as she spoke with the voice of a morning dove. And she had raven hair, long and belligerent in its wild beauty. Her hoop earrings rounded her upper jaw, a swinging frame to her cheek freckles as if they were flakes to a comet's tail. She smelled of vodka and lemongrass, and looked at Ezra uneasily as though she could see the rage inside him.

"Sure. And you are..."

"Ingrid McAdam, assistant micro-biologist for the mission. We met only once during orientation. Ezra Beller, if I'm correct?"

"Right. I remember now," Ezra said as he flicked his lighter, pressing his face closer to hers and lighting his cigar and her cigarette at once.

"So I was thinking about something... If you're a contractor and kill for money, doesn't that make you an assassin, in a sense?" she asked. She began to fix her hair before kicking off a pair of uncomfortable high heels and leaning against the balcony. She looked blankly at him for a moment and shook her head. "I'm sorry. I didn't mean to offend."

"Well if I was an assassin, I wouldn't be able to tell you anything," Ezra said, smiling from the corner of his mouth.

An awkward silence ensued.

"Well we're here!" she said. "Are you excited to go into the Andes?"

"Although I usually enjoy central and south American assignments, not so much this time. Seems like a waste of time and resources, but who's to say," Ezra said, looking away slightly.

"We're to save the planet from dying," she said, sipping her electric lemonade.

"I'm not sure if this world can be saved."

Ingrid sighed, then focused for a moment before speaking with fortitude.

"Benign are the consequences of man's misgivings until his inability to adapt lapses his inertia."

"What?" Ezra chuckled.

"This planet is like Medusa, the Gorgon mother who devoured her children. Eventually we will outnumber our

4

resources, but there is some time for us. And I believe for every greedy man there is an enduring mother giving the world back what it gave."

"We'll get what's coming to us."

"I don't disagree, but I remain an optimist," Ingrid said, squinting her eyes. "In the face of innumerable toxicities; physical, psychological, spiritual... we must have hope. If our team can be a part of the movement to rid the world from the buildup of pollution and waste, then I can die happy. With the prospect of discovering a new species of fungus that eats away waste, we can begin to build steps in restoring our planet to a more natural, biodiverse state, and hopefully-"

"Hope is a conspiracy," Ezra said, cutting off her speech and spitting over the railing.

"Well it's good that some of us have some left, or else we'd all be screwed," she said, perturbed. "Have a good night, Mr. Beller," she said as she walked away abruptly.

On her way back inside she bumped shoulders with a gorilla of a man. The middle-aged brute looked back, only to see Ingrid storm out of the party. The man approached Ezra and smiled.

"You still scaring women away?" he asked.

Ezra recognized the man and shook his head and smiled. It was Major Sergio Rodriguez, one of Ezra's former commanding officers and close friends in the desert wars of northern Mali. Sergio was a tall Hispanic masterpiece of good genes combined with military ingenuity. He was part of an experiment for the government when the department of defense began injecting older soldiers with super-steroids that improved their performance in the field. Sergio was in his late forties but could out-run and out-lift almost anyone half his age.

"What are you doing here Rodriguez?" Ezra asked, joyfully surprised. They hugged for a good few seconds. Back inside, the paranoid contractors quickly hid the cocaine under the table, laughing as they did.

"I had a chance to get out of the office for a minute," Sergio said. "The DOD has me pinned down pretty good. But I needed to burn some leave before year's end. Heard you were gonna help the team get in and out of the jungle? Should be an easy assignment for you, huh cowboy?"

"Easy is my name."

They shared a laugh and Sergio asked, "So when do you head out?"

"Weathers been shifty. Could be as soon as tomorrow."

"On-call, huh?"

"Yeah we will see. Once we set up camp, the mission should go fairly quickly and smoothly."

"Why the urgency?"

"If I had to guess... the boss is hoarding resources in preparation for something," Ezra shrugged.

"Well I want to let you know, firstly, that I'm really proud you've made it so far in your career, Ezra. The potential success of this mission is not only a huge feat for you, but for all of humankind, in a way. You know, my cousin worked for the nuclear fusion energy crisis program. They had made leaps and bounds during the oil wars. He was confident that it would all pan out, and the seizure of the refineries would end, along with our campaigns across Saudi Arabia. Then their reactors proved faulty and poisoned the whole god damned ocean. And America's exodus is just the beginning. All those people on the coastlines being forced into the mid-west right now? It's gonna be a mess. The cartels are thriving from it too. Their business

6

hoop is getting smaller and yet they have more access than ever. We don't have enough agents to cover the border AND the coasts!"

"The government justifies the exodus as a matter of national security. Several other countries have done the same. Ironic isn't it?"

"Yeah. And just yesterday POTUS deployed the homeland security army to California to start pushing people east. They're gonna get lit up once they arrive to the private militaries defending west coast timber and tech companies. I'm just glad you're here and not there, because uh..."

He hesitated, and then said quietly, "There's a reason I came here in person. As you may have guessed, things aren't looking too good through the panel right now."

Ezra turned toward him and pulled the battery and the SIM card out of his phone before leaning in.

"What do you mean?"

"Well I can't talk about it much, obviously, but when you get back to the States, I suggest you get off the grid. Somewhere secluded. It's gonna be the way to go for a few years, maybe longer. I gotta ask you, as a friend, not a senior intelligence officer... does the name Vishnu mean anything to you?"

Ezra oriented his body into a more rigid figure and looked at the Major with quivering eyes. Ezra's pupils shrunk as if cowering back into his own skull.

"Never heard of him," Ezra said, looking into his drink evasively.

"If you had heard of him, I'd tell you to be extra careful. Word through the panel is he's looking for you. Not the kind of person you want tracking you. He's a Nepalese contact that worked with the CIA but broke off a few years ago. He's considered highly dangerous and has an unknown wealth of assets. Most of its beyond what our Intel can offer, but the FBI's identified him as the mastermind behind the Vatican assassinations last month."

"No shit? And here I was thinking it was the Serbs."

"He had contacts inside the church who used swords and knives to kill twenty-two people. The armed guards were found dead in a heap and the one surviving witness says Vishnu cut the pope's hands off at the wrists and kissed the pope's ring before beheading him."

"He's bringing back romantic terrorism. No wonder the details weren't in the news. Sensationalists will love him. Have there been any arrests relating to the assassinations? Any of his cohorts detained?"

Sergio shook his head.

"The French military is working with authorities in France, Germany, and Italy to find him or anyone working with him."

Ezra laughed. "Good luck. Trying to find a Nepalese man in Europe is like finding a needle in a haystack. A quarter of Europe is a refugee camp."

"Please heed my words, Ezra. You don't have to tell me how you know him. Just don't let him find you."

"I'll keep my wits about me," Ezra said, turning his cheek.

"Anyways Ezra, the overall point is that this is the height of your career and I just want to see you end it on a good note. You're a damn good man. That out of the box thinking you got... you fight war like its meant to be fought. As an art."

"Thanks Sergio, that means a lot. You know, I've been thinking about retirement," Ezra said.

"You have? I think that would be good-"

Sergio saw Ezra start to laugh and realized he was being a wise ass.

"Don't bullshit me. You could use a break, brother. I know because I was with you for almost your whole service. Hell, I started way before you, but some of my best and worst were with Special Forces."

"Oh yeah how old were you when you joined SF again?"

Sergio laughed. "Fuck you. I had already gotten half my ass blown off in Afghanistan and was relearning to walk when you still had training wheels on your bike."

Ezra laughed, and Sergio continued, "But I've seen it with too many of my best men, Ezra," he said. "You gotta quit before this contract work before it breaks you. It's not the same kinda shit we did. In a world full of crooks you'll lose sight of justice. Anyone can pay for private military nowadays. And when you left for the private sector, I didn't even get a chance to talk to you. Just remember man, eventually you got to keep what matters close to you and leave this crazy shit behind. It's usually just a matter of time before the darkness catches up to you."

"Who says it hasn't already?" Ezra asked. "Sure... I have my moments. But I can assure you I'm confident about who I am and what I'm doing. Thanks though, Serg."

Sergio quieted and nodded slightly before asking, "Do you mind if I grab a drink real quick?"

"Yeah, go ahead. Grab me one too, will ya?"

"Sure thing E-Z-B."

Ezra turned and looked at the ice cube in his drink turn over like a capsized ship. As the Major walked away, Ezra couldn't help but slip into a strange place of nostalgia from the wild times he and Sergio had shared. They'd navigated a stolen tank named Castro in Nigeria, who's failing engine started a brushfire that ended up cutting off the advancing army of machete wielding children chasing them. They'd been caught in the middle of pitch-black shoot-outs between Indonesian rebel groups in the depths of jungle caves, where mounds of guano and bat bones served as a nesting ground for the lingering arachnids.

Ezra's hand quit trembling for a moment and he had a moment of peace and clarity. As his mind settled, a slight nervousness grew from the temporary neutrality of his emotions. He suddenly realized that he was about to embark on was a mission that would potentially solidify his retirement. It paid enough, and he didn't have any other incentives to stay if what Sergio said was true. What would he do? Where would he go? The thought frightened him more than jungle dangers themselves, which were many. Once in the mountains they had to be wary of land mines, booby traps, armed cartel groups, feral pumas, snakes with neurotoxins, tissue eating parasites and dormant diseases. But the rules were simple: protect the research team. If any violent scenario unfolded whatsoever, the mission's objective would immediately transfer command to Ezra and his unit.

How bad could it be? Ezra thought, as he looked up toward the stars again, a feeling of both wonder and fear catching him by the neck. That's how he'd always felt, as if someone were holding the tip of a sword to his throat. He couldn't remember the last time he knew what it was like to feel alive without fighting. Most of his closest comrades were either dead or retired, giving him little to protect and die for, since the people in his home nation were largely ungrateful and hung by a thread of their own, and almost all the communities he'd liberated in those war-torn countries would eventually fall victim to the recurring power vacuum. What actual purpose he felt was dwindling from a single fiber of hope that one day a feeling happiness and purpose could displace his divine madness.

Sergio returned with Ezra's drink, and the two of them spent much of the evening reminiscing of old times. Eventually after a fair amount of liquor, they succumbed to the party's wild knife games.

Ezra walked up to one of his subordinates and motioned for him to hand Ezra his knife. Thompson gave Ezra the knife back and licked his thumb where he'd cut himself playing five finger filet. Someone turned the music down.

Ezra looked at the piece, lost in its treasured reflection. His eyes followed its edge like a serpent's tongue.

"Hey Ezra, why does it say E.E.B.?" Thompson asked, taking a swig from a tequila jug.

"It was my grandfather's knife, Eugene Ezra Beller. He got it as a gift from his father before his second deployment in Vietnam. It's made from a railroad spike. See the twisted handle? He told me that when he detailed with the Army studies and observation group, they'd do long distance recon missions and end up far behind enemy lines. See my grandfather grew up in the Ozark's, poor, and far from any town. He was an avid hunter from a young age and his family relied on his hunting and trapping skills to bring food to the table. When Eugene was sent on a long campaign into Laos and Cambodia, and having already partook in a vicious deployment once before, he began hunting the NVA during his patrols as if they were game. He'd seek them out, stalk them, kill them, and study their habits from afar when not engaging. Sometimes he'd hide in the trees and pounce on them like a cat. He said he'd cut the ears off his enemies and keep them as souvenirs on a necklace, all with the edge of this

11

knife. So Thompson, you're not the first to draw blood from its blade, and you probably won't be the last."

A few of the scientists made sour faces and quickly lost interest in the game.

"That's a beautiful story, Ezra," Thompson said smiling from his drunken cloud, setting the bottle down and retracting his fingers with his handkerchief wrapped hand, "Beautiful...Thank you."

The next morning, Ezra awoke to a sledgehammer beating his skull in the form of a tequila hangover. The warm, rising sun burnt through the curtains and pierced his squinted eyes. His lips were as dry as a hot stone. He looked around, wondering when and how he got back to his own room of the hotel. After standing up, the pulsing between his temples worsened, and he grasped a cup of water and chugged it. He looked in his pockets. His phone was in his left pocket while the battery for it was in his right. After connecting them, he turned it on as a wave of messages and voicemails rolled in.

"Oh fuck," he said, clearing his throat, "and that's what I get for following OPSEC standards. Ugh."

Ezra jumped into his clothes, slipped on his boots, and put on his beret before running to the hotel conference room for briefing. He wasn't in the mood, and he'd hoped that everyone else felt as hellish as he did in his still half-drunken state.

While marching down the hall, Ezra watched a disheveled Ingrid walk out of her room. She fumbled with some folders and straightened her glasses.

"You the last one?" she asked, smiling nervously.

"Not if I can help it," Ezra said, quickening his pace.

They both raced down the hall as Ingrid beat him to the door. She opened it. The entire room looked at the two team members.

"Nice of you two to join us!" yelled Daniel Gomez, the Operations Chief.

Ezra walked in first as everyone looked at him.

"My apologies sir. My phone's been causing me some trouble," he said tapping on the perfectly functional device.

"Your excuses are tiring. While you and Miss McAdam here were sleeping in, we've been waiting to discuss today's operations."

"And just so you know… we weren't…uh… sleeping together or anything," Ingrid added as she quickly took her seat. "I just need to make that clear."

The Operations Chief looked at her and then at Ezra.

"I don't care," he said, "There's the coffee. Drink it. Wake the fuck up."

Ezra shook his head as if trying to get something out, and the rest of the group awkwardly situated themselves in their seats.

"So. We just got the forecast and the mission is a go. We leave at 1300 today. Our supply cache is almost done loading, but I'll need a few of you to help get that squared away before our transport ship comes in. Ezra, are your men and their gear ready to go?"

"Affirm. The mobile armory was transferred from customs to the cache yesterday. Our load-outs have been finalized."

"Then we just need to get the ecology team's gear inventoried and we're ready. As for everyone as a group – nothing much has changed from our previous plans, which you should all be thoroughly briefed on by your supervisors. So the idea is that once landing the ship, Ezra's forces will set up a perimeter and clear an area for an optimal extraction sight, which needs to be big enough for a transport ship. Once we've established our base camp, we need to be ready to leave quickly and in an efficient manner in any emergency situation. In terms of your personal gear, I suggest bringing everything you think you need, because there is always a chance we could be there longer than just a few days and our aerial support would be limited at that time if the weather isn't being cooperative. Any questions before we wrap this up?"

"I know you guys still had a few different locations in mind, so where and what elevation will we be landing at again?" asked Ezra.

The officer whistled quietly and thought, then said, "We will be at just over 8,000 feet in a valley near some east facing mountain slopes of the Peruvian Andes, eighty miles east of Cajumarca. I'll give you the GPS coordinates when we're finished here."

"What's the topography and terrain like?" Ezra asked, writing down notes.

"High mountain jungle. We will be nestled in a high valley so conditions may vary. Bring your rain poncho."

"Have you seen satellite images of this area? Are there good look-out positions near our landing zone?"

"Uhhh... I'm not sure. That will definitely be looked at though."

"It would be good to get eyes above the canopy. Maybe three sniper teams with wide vantages-"

"What do you think this is, a shooting spree?" Ingrid interrupted angrily from across the table.

14

"I'm just trying to protect that pretty face of yours, Miss McAdam. So why don't you let me do my job, and I will let you do yours," Ezra said calmly. Ingrid quieted and pursed her lips as she shook her head in anger.

"Settle down, it's too early for that shit," the officer said.

"All I'm saying is it would be nice for us to be able to get eyes on the whole area and allow everyone a little bit more breathing room. The narcos still monitor those mountains and a ship coming in is good way to draw attention."

"Hey, you got it Ezra, I'll see to it. Now are there any other questions?"

Dozens of people raised their hands, all with more scientific questions about the foreign plot they'd soon delve into. Ezra leaned back in his chair and drifted back to sleep. He did not want to act excited. He felt this would be no joyride, no matter how badly the scientists wanted to make it one. To him, it was just one of those uneventful security details to make some company feel safe. Ezra's premonitions for such assignments were rarely faulty, but once in a while he'd get proven wrong in a big way.

A quiet anxiousness was in the air as Ezra looked out of the plane window. For quite some time he sat gazing, if at nothing else but the constantly shifting mist between the Andean peaks. Blackish grey clouds swirled and licked the sky with the ebb and flow of the wind. The flight took hours, as heavy turbulence came in waves that had Ezra gripping his stomach in his fluctuating state of dizziness. Tips of spiny peaks poked above the river of clouds that the ship seemed to follow downstream.

The tail wind saved fuel, but didn't help those already doped up on Dramamine or quickly trying to cure their hangover.

Ingrid looked back from her seat and locked eyes with Ezra for a moment. She quickly looked away, and Ezra noticed how scared she was.

"Suit up and prepare to land!" yelled Gomez as he went to check on landing conditions with the pilot.

The scientists watched out their windows all aglow and filled with the curiosity of children. The security team faced the floor, loading their firearms and packs.

Gomez came back to the cabin in a whirl.

"Ezra, it looks like the ship is burning through its fuel faster than we had thought. Some leak in the fuel line likely. The drop point we had hoped to reach will be out of our range."

"What's the new drop point?" Ezra asked.

"Some small valley about fifty miles out from the original zone of operations. We're about to descend."

"What's the new location like?" Ezra asked.

"The Nebula One Space Station is relaying a topographic map to us, but a solar flare caused a delay in the readings."

"Motherfucker," Ezra said. "Just one shit storm after another."

"I'll give you the new coordinates."

"Copy that," Ezra said, pulling out his GPS and inserting the new numbers handed to him.

"I know how fucked up this is, and I'll be the first to write a report. I wasn't expecting them to load us onto some old piece of junk. They must need the modern models for something more important."

"I wonder why that could be?" Ezra asked, shaking his head.

"I know you're pissed at Leonard for being a penny pincher but the guy is between a rock and hard place with everything going on right now. It's a strange time for private military owners. Anyway, once we get on the ground it should be a cakewalk," Gomez assured him, turning away and walking toward the flight cabin.

"Here we go," Ezra whispered.

After Gomez came back, he looked even more distraught.

"Everyone listen up! I just got word from the pilot. Because of some issues we're having with the ship, we're going to have to adapt a bit to get you all safely on the ground. We're descending sooner than expected so prepare yourselves for landing. Let's make this easy, simple, and safe, and we won't have problems. We drop in ten!"

An anxious bustling in the cabin of the plane grew steadily. Ezra felt a lurch in his stomach and puked into the baggie in front of him. The tequila was affecting him more than it used to in his younger years, but he shook it off. He stood up and took a long drink of water before dropping to the ground and cranking out diamond push-ups in the center aisle. People watched in amusement, but he paid no attention. His heart thumped like a bass drum revived in the memory of Incan sacrifice. His hands steadied. His mind felt at ease. He thrived on the coming fear. Fear was his ally.

Ezra sat back down and went through his kit again. A charcoal stained patch sewed to the side of his pack read, 'I don't believe in anything, I'm just here for the violence'. He turned and talked to one of the overhead members on his security team.

"You got the radio frequencies I gave you, with Alpha on priority, and then cloned the teams?"

"Yes sir."

"Are you carrying non-lethals?"

"That's standard, right?"

"Leave them and bring more grenades. Grab like, six or so and tell Thompson to do the same."

"Roger."

"Where's your head at Cooke?"

"Feeling good, sir!"

"Good!"

Ezra yelled, "Just so you all are aware, Cooke will be your commanding officer in case I'm not around and have to go out on patrol. Initially, Alpha squad will set up a perimeter for Bravo squad. Bravo will reinforce that perimeter. Only once all I've just said has been executed, will the Foxtrot and Echo bio-teams assemble. We'll have a communications and operations briefing on the ground. For now, let's focus on safety and getting on the ground until these issues have been remedied. Gomez and our operations chief back on the USS JFK are the ultimate authority here unless communications fail or we are involved in a hostile situation requiring immediate action. Then I am. Is that understood?"

Everyone acknowledged with a yes, or yes sir.

"This is a simple mission, but with many dangers. These are the mountains that give way to the Amazon we're talking about. They could just as easily take your life as well as become the subject for your Nobel prize winning thesis. So stay close, be mindful of the terrain and wildlife, and always stay in contact through your radios and superiors. Am I clear?"

With Ezra's words the whole crew buckled up and prepared to land. A massive drop in altitude made some people scream as the ship's engines began sputtering. The bay door behind them suddenly opened without warning. Cool, moist air shot in. The temperature gauge on Ezra's watch dropped significantly as he clipped his M4 rifle to his pack securely and felt his chest rig for any loose gear items. The wind slapped his face as he put his pack on and stood up, grabbing a parachute from under his seat on the way up. Then the clouds suddenly opened up for a moment and a fierce cliff could be seen only a few hundred feet away from them. Everyone gasped. Up in the cockpit, Ezra could see the emergency landing light began blinking red like a terror strobe, followed by the screech of an alarm to match its abrasive warning. Gomez turned to him and yelled an order he didn't think he'd ever have to execute.

The ship started shaking from the disturbance, then dropped a few hundred feet with another heart pounding second of weightlessness before catching on a wind current and jolting the crew around. People screamed and began to panic.

"Everyone get your parachutes out!" Ezra yelled. The crowd began to fumble with their emergency parachutes and after the security team had fastened their own they initiated helping the scientists. Ezra looked around and saw everyone being helped but Ingrid was struggling with hers because her hands were trembling so violently.

"Here I got you, I got you," Ezra said as he began clipping the straps. She dropped her pale hands and looked at him.

"What's going on?"

"This plane is about to crash."

He stepped away and put his hands up.

"Everyone listen up! We're going to line up single file, clip into the static line, and jump out of the bay in increments of four seconds. Pull your cord only two seconds after you jump because we're pretty close to the ground as you can see! I'll be your Jump master and guide you through everything. Just stay calm and we will get through this!"

The nervous team lined up but before Ezra could tap the first person to go, a massive spire came into view just below them, this time close enough to touch. With a thunderous crash of splitting wires and crunching metal, the massive plane was torn apart by the merciless Andes. Those close enough to the door fell, their bodies lurching and tangling in their half opened chutes. Those unlucky enough to be on the ship were either engulfed in burning fuel or pulverized as the battered cabin tumbled down the steep canyon, plunging thousands of feet below the inversion, becoming a falling steel coffin. Ezra tried to pull his ripcord after being thrown from the door, but he had no spare moment. He hit the ground with a violent crack and rolled a ways before stopping on a small outcropping, just inches from the edge of a seemingly bottomless cliff. Pieces of the burning craft could be seen trickling down the peak like flipping candles, dimming as they fell into the thick grey fog below.

The fall hadn't knocked Ezra out, as he later might have wished. Instead, Ezra's first moments on the Andean peaks were spent wiping blood from his eyes as a gash on his forehead poured like a sieve. His body and skull were immediately sore, as if he had been beaten with a baton. His helmet had been thrown off of his head. His rifle and gear were gone. He gasped but his lungs sucked at the thin air in vein.

Ezra pulled glass shards from his slashed face before opening the canteen that dangled from his pants. He took a long swig of water from his shaking hand, and then doused his face so he could see through the coagulation. As quick as he could get the blood from his sockets they would refill. Ezra started panicking and that's when he noticed the moss dripping above him, except it wasn't like any moss he'd ever seen. He stepped back to view the deceitful organism. On the overhang above him a black tangled plant dripped large red dewdrops on his face. He began to realize what was happening. There was something in the algae, he thought, something that changed the water's color, because the rain itself was clear., but once it touched the soil it ran deep crimson. Turning about and seeing this all around him delivered Ezra into a new phase of horror. He'd been in crashes before, but never so far from extraction teams. He'd been in survival situations, but never alone or in such isolated country. He felt dizzy and began hallucinating from his head injury.

Ezra tried to convince himself he wasn't in as bad of a situation as he truly was. He leaned back against a rock to put steady pressure on his forehead and took several deep breaths. As his heart rate slowed, he felt a strange sensation in his arms. He looked down and saw his skin slowly morphing into the texture of lichen. The feeling crawled up his fingers and limbs with a prickly sensation. He tried to peel off the strange plant, but his flesh became overrun by the lichen. The feeling changed to that of acid burns growing hot from his fingertips to his torso's center like he was being dipped into a corrosive mine-lake. His entire body began boiling, and with each blink he envisioned himself soaked in a bath of gore; wrapped in human gristle, guts, and bleeding tenderized muscle. He felt he was in hell; this mountain was his hell. Thus he felt beyond death at last, rotting in that terrible realm as his third eye spewed blood to match the river's hue in his existence wrought with suffering.

He started screaming and tearing at the black moss around him, but the plant would grow several inches more each time he pulled it. Then it jumped at him. He could not tell if it was his imagination or not. As his rage grew, the moss grew back twice as long with every pull, but he kept tearing, for it infuriated him. The moss was his enemy; such a simple creature yet invincible to even the most deadly warrior. Ezra wanted the plant to suffer, like himself, but it fed off his violence. The plant grew and grew, snaking its way up and out in a coil formation, surrounding Ezra and subduing him. He took out his knife and sliced wildly at it until a massive sized nest of the disgusting organism spiraled above and around him. It caged him in and constricted any movement he so attempted. He could see through the roof as there was a small hole to the sky's blanket of light grey wash. Rain would catch on the plant's small crooked fingers on its way into his tomb. The red water gushed in faster, submerging his head.

After all the bullets and grenade shrapnel he'd managed to miss all his life, all the evaded captures and close calls with explosions, Ezra's fate was to drown alone in a cocoon he made for myself. He couldn't grasp any real memory. Panic and fear swept him, as that was all that remained in his being. He became paralyzed as the acidic lichen spread into his mouth and blossomed down around the inside of his throat, generating little mushroom caps that shot up out of his mouth as they weaved into the moss. The moss and the lichen had a partnership and Ezra was their prey. The falling water continued to fill the cage further to just under his fear-swept eyes. He held his breath, trying not to choke on the filthy fungus. A faint feeling of confusion struck the back of his neck and nausea ensued. With every small exhale into the watery tomb, his throat closed further, and the foreign invader grew and meshed within itself. Once his entire head was submerged, he opened his eyes. Small particles danced in the water around his seeping blood, a few shades darker than the crimson rain, and appeared as a smooth moving smoke below the pool's turbulent surface. He prayed, as any dying man might pray for mercy once his own efforts cease to save him. In a bubbling mess, Ezra regurgitated through his fungal infected esophagus before blacking out and submitting to the rancid enclosure.

The slow climbing fog had reached Ezra's perch by the time he awoke. The day had become no darker, yet the cloak of grey around him masked his sense of time with ambiguous light. Dull tones of savage winds aloft combed the stratus beneath them, all too quiet behind the rain's soft percussive pouring. Ezra had suffered a concussion and a few gashes from the crash, but everything else was gone as if it were all a dream: the cage of wrapping fractal moss, the fungus, the drowning, apparently all of pure hallucination. Ezra managed to stand up and check his gear. There was little equipment he possessed. A half canteen of water, his grandfather's knife, a pocket trauma kit, watch, compass and radio. His pack and rifle had fallen into oblivion. His chute was shredded.

Ezra sucked in a large breath through his nose. The smell was pungent. Though dank and sparse, the high elevation flora was highly detectable. The unusual organisms clinging to the rocks gave out a strong scent of severed flesh and bowels. Ezra felt dizzy again and puked up some bile. The radio on his belt managed to still be in one piece. He turned the device on and adjusted the frequency knob carefully before attempting to contact command.

"Curtis, Beller on Command."

Silence.

"Curtis, Beller on Command. Can you hear me? I'm requesting an immediate rescue! Hello?! *HELLO?*"

He tried more channels. Only the wind permeated beyond his echoes swallowed whole by the dense clouds' descent. As his battery light faded, so did Ezra's hopes of being extracted. The thumping on his forehead worsened as he reattached the device to his belt. He looked over the edge. There wasn't a single way to climb down. Thousand foot drops separated overhangs and small platforms between the dire chutes. High mountain raptors favored the pantheon of ruthless ascent, where gravity was its weapon of choice.

Ezra put his hand through his hair. Perhaps, with ropes and climbing equipment and the world's best climbers it was doable, but even then, a descent in such conditions could be fatal. He stared solemnly into the abyss. Short, anxious breaths ensued. Ezra sat unmoving as he contemplated and calculated his situation. He looked at his arm. The red water mixing with the dirt on his wrist appeared as Jupiter's great red storm. He gazed at it until it gave him a strange sense of déjà vu. The Jovian planet was always his favorite as a child. He remembered watching films in school of the storm moving around the planet with gentle waves of orange and tan ribbons rippling silently along its edges. Yet, he was told, inside its current winds of over three hundred miles per hour raged constantly in an area that could swallow three Earths. Beautiful from above, hell from below. Ezra thought perhaps this was the curse of the planets; and even a paradise like Earth, designed slowly by our solar system's imbalances and imperfections and given the gift of life, eventually succumbed to the exploitation of its own atrocities hidden beneath the soil. Ezra meditated for some time, and decided he needed to move past his isolation: through death, pain, whatever transfiguration came first. He needed a way to move through, and submitted himself in prayer. Not a prayer to God, but rather the kind of prayer that reflects inward, and concentrates all longing on that one sublime source of matter, energy and mysterious divine within; the kind of promise found inside a wedding vow, or a blood pact among close friends, perhaps not as often the final thoughts of a man on the brink of suicide.

Ezra stood up and walked slowly to the edge of the cliff. So slowly, one wouldn't even know he was moving. His breathing deepened. The rain fell on his hair and face. The cool air tightened his pores. The quiet, arrhythmic sound of puddles forming kissed his eardrums softly.

For the first time in seven years, his right hand shook no more as he held it up to his face. What scarred, beautiful hands they were; made for a pianist but used for feathering triggers and stacking skulls. Wrinkles between his finger webs connected strange outlines of lacerations and lengthy stitch work like an old map of train tracks and winding roads.

"I will never take another human life," he said quietly to himself.

Before Ezra had the chance to betray this oath one last time, a voice steered him.

"Ezra. I have a parachute."

He dared not turn for fear of the voice's origin. He did not trust his own mind as he once had.

"Senior Officer Beller," the woman whimpered.

After another moment of hesitation, Ezra turned to see Ingrid standing behind him near the cliff; frightened, shivering, cold and wet. She took deep breaths to calm her nervousness, for her climb to him had been slippery and exposed.

"Are you okay?" Ezra asked.

"What does okay mean in a time like this?" she asked.

She seemed sane enough, which was Ezra's largest concern after his own schizophrenic episode.

"Have you encountered any other survivors?" asked Ezra.

Ingrid shook her head. Her long black hair curled and dripped with rainwater.

"Why don't you have the algae on your face?"

"The what?" Ingrid asked. The rain had begun falling harder, and the wind swept faster through the high spires.

"The algae! It turns the ground red!"

She walked closer to him and dropped the parachute at his feet before telling him, "I don't really care about documenting algae right now. I don't know..." She lurched in anguish and started tearing up. "I don't know what I'm doing here. Just please... save me from this wretched place!"

The words crept into Ezra's ears and blanketed him, and he suddenly felt a warm aura amidst that cold world, that maybe if his life truly no longer held value perhaps hers did. Ezra would be her shield. This undiscovered sense of purpose struck Ezra and caused him to slowly put his face closer to hers and say, "My one and only assignment right now is to get you and me off of this mountain, and to safety. Now do you have a radio with full batteries?"

"Yes, but I must have had it on the wrong frequency or something-"

"It's fine. We'll use that when we get to a better location. There's still a good chance we'll make it out of here alive."

"But there could be cartels, or mine fields awaiting us. We don't know what's down there." Ingrid shuddered.

"We're about to."

Ezra began fitting the straps to Ingrid and himself. Luckily, some of the gear fell near Ingrid, and the parachute was a double harness. She also had found a handgun, which she handed to him reluctantly.

"Are there bullets in it?"

"I didn't check."

Ezra took the pistol and checked the firearm's chamber promptly. It was empty, with the magazine missing as well. After sliding the pistol in his waist band, he then turned Ingrid's shoulders, so she faced away from him and pulled her in close.

"Ah!"

"I just want to make sure you are properly secured."

"Yeah I bet you do," she snapped. Then she sighed, "I'm sorry I've been so-"

"You don't have to apologize. We're in a survival situation. We are now a unit that depends on one another. Bygones be bygones."

"Yeah but I depend on you far more than you depend on me."

"We'll see if that's the case *by the end of this*," Ezra said as he fixed the last strap. As they approached the cliff's edge, the butterflies erupted inside Ingrid's stomach.

"Okay, so all I need you to do is when I say 'three' you've got to lift up your legs so I can take a few steps to get us far away from the cliff."

"Okay!" Ingrid said, her lip quivering.

"Don't worry you're going to do fine! You ready?"

Ingrid shook her head.

"Here we go. One... Two...THREE!"

Ingrid snapped up her legs as Ezra took the two strongest steps he could muster. He lunged off of the cliff, the fog disappearing above them as they dropped into a clear-cut inversion. As the adrenaline sped through their bodies, they saw the entire valley for a few seconds, shaped like an enormous bathtub and dropping thousands of feet into the river bottom. Lush tropical forest stretched to the valley's northern end while curtains of thin waterfalls dove into the vein-like creeks, whose watersheds hid behind gargantuan trees. Ezra pulled the chute and Ingrid gave a sigh of relief as the air's resistance floated them slowly downward to the jungle. Ezra closed his eyes for a moment, wishing it were a falling dream; that he would wake between cotton sheets in his room at his parents' house in Missouri; the smell of blueberry muffins baking in the oven, the sound of his dog barking at deer on their farm, his mother's sweet voice, so rarely heard. The simple pleasures of yesteryear seemed so distant from the Andean madness, distant enough to be only a dream. Doom became transparent through a sense of longing and transcendental hunger; a desire only measurable by blood and time, and felt by both Ezra and Ingrid, as each forward movement brought them closer to the dreadful reality of their powerlessness, but also to each other.

Leaves and sticks split and snapped; hanging like ornaments in the upper branches from the aftermath of the bombing duo. The lush canopy absorbed most of their speed, and they had managed to splash into a mud pit four feet deep and as thick as molasses.

A few gurgling bubbles surfaced from the swampy pool. In a huge burp, Ezra came up from the goo gasping as he unbuckled himself from Ingrid. He pulled her to her feet as Ezra smiled and wiped the mud from his face.

"Hard part's over!"

"Right. That's very optimistic. However, I think we should get out of this potential quicksand."

"After you," Ezra said.

They pulled themselves from the bog and para-cord entanglement. Ingrid stood on the mushy ground and looked up and around in amazement. Ezra felt his spine shiver and pores loosen as the thick atmosphere weighed down upon him; the temperature was noticeably warmer. After he wiped the muck from his face and opened his eyes wide, he could hardly believe what he was seeing.

Monstrous trees towered over Ezra and Ingrid as their rows stood like ancient monoliths above the green forest. Plants and mushrooms of countless variation sprouted at their bases in every hue their eyes could cast. Birds of all different species spoke in strange chirps and caws. Multiple layers of overgrown fungus grew from dead logs, stretching out and up towards the dark sky that was split by the tall trees leaves. Their branches were like scaffolding for elusive primates that hid in shadows and knots. Vines as wide as Ezra's arms snaked around each trunk as a thick pitch poured like red honey over the trunks' slimy texture. The rain collected in the cups of mushrooms and large leaves and the soil propagated large ferns, some being the habitat of dark orange lichens that were then home to a colony of insects and so on as the mass of blossoming jungle spewed in all directions. Far away, a howler monkey's cretaceous rasp signaled their arrival.

"Look out!" Ingrid yelled.

A large spider with legs like black knives slowly tried to latch onto Ezra's shoulder from a nearby tree. He couldn't help but yell in fright before swatting it and stepping aside.

"What's the matter, afraid of a little spider?" Ingrid asked, laughing.

"That wasn't 'little'."

Ingrid was speechless at first. She took a moment then gushed with interest.

"I've been to a lot of jungles, but never one quite like this. I can see why they sent us here. It's so untouched. The biodiversity is astounding! What a wonderful mix of fungi, plants, and root systems acting as a highway system for all the creatures."

"Fuck these plants. What about us? What should we be wary of?"

"Oh you know, spiders, as you know, parasites, bright colored frogs, the millions of species of bacteria. If we were to enter the right area at the right time, one of the thousands of more lethal variations could destroy our bodies in a few days so as to optimize their domain."

"And which of these species should we stay away from?"

"I was just appointed as a field researcher on this assignment, so with my boss not around it's hard to tell. This environment is so foreign to me. I'll let you know though. Anything that resembles a poisonous organism I'll make sure to warn you of. Don't approach any spore ejections, anything sharp or resembling thorns, and no drinking any water, since we don't have a filter. Sorry, but I've none of my instruments nor colleagues to make any distinctions beyond that."

They both stood in silence for a moment, trying to grasp their stark reality behind the steeping forest.

"How long has the Amazon been developing, to the best of your knowledge?" Ezra asked.

"Most scientists agree that it's 2,000 years old. And with little human disruption in this part of the mountains, it's been able to thrive. There are thousands of species still undiscovered, which is why we're here. Some of them could maybe cure diseases or heal our sickened oceans. The possibilities are endless. It's sad to me that everyday humans bulldoze dozens of these species into extinction without ever knowing their true potential, if not at least preserving their function as a key player in this valuable ecosystem. With phytoplankton being killed off in the ocean because of the pollution, we're losing oxygen at an incredible rate. That combined with deforestation and carbon emissions, we're going to suffocate the whole world in a matter of a century at this rate."

"Damn. That's depressing," Ezra said.

Ingrid lowered her voice and said sadly, "You were probably right when you said hope is a conspiracy. I'm becoming doubtful there is a way to fix this horrific phenomenon. We were born into this age of industry and atomic power... it's like being born with a gun to your head. How could one possibly reverse this pattern of ruination?"

She approached Ezra, eye to eye, and brushed off some tiny particle spores that had collected on his head. She handed him the radio and shivered as if hearing nails being scraped along a chalkboard. With this she walked down the hill a ways in front of Ezra. He promptly started hiking behind her and turned on the radio as he did so. He turned about his area for a location with better reception. As he did, his eyes wandered up to where they had just been, then back down. The peaks were so massive that even after the several thousand-foot drop, they were yet to be off of the mountain. The hills gradually became less steep but he knew that they were following a drainage, which Ezra had expected would eventually lead to an opening of some kind. Anywhere that could give them a signal would be fitting. Ezra caught up to Ingrid.

"Why is it so hard to breathe?" she asked.

"Higher altitude than you're used to. Being hungover doesn't help either."

"Oh yeah," she said, rolling her eyes.

"I got a bit toasted last night myself. Here take these."

Ezra's hand extended to give Ingrid some pine needles.

"Ohhhhh no you don't. We can't eat anything local!"

"It's not local. I airlock fresh spruce needles with me on all my missions. I like the taste. Reminds me of home when I'm in some god forsaken shit hole."

"But you'd get a better affect from Vitamin C capsules, wouldn't you?" Ingrid asked.

"Why don't we eat all of our food in pill form, huh?"

"Right, like you're a naturalist," she said sarcastically.

"I am a purist," Ezra corrected her.

"But you're a killer," Ingrid accused.

"Nothing is more pure than death. And I am a killer. As we all are to more or lesser degrees."

"I'm not!" she yelled, and then stopped to argue with him.

"You had something killed before you ate last didn't you?" Ezra asked.

"I'm a vegan!"

Ezra laughed, "Something had to die so you could live."

"So what, just give up and don't eat?"

"I'm just saying there is no way around the sacrifice of hunger. It is the means in which we gather or hunt our food that makes the sacrifice warranted. And yes I've taken human lives too, for a far different kind of sacrifice."

"I shouldn't have said that," Ingrid said, shaking her head.

"Said what?"

"That you're a killer."

"But I am! I'm damn good at it too," Ezra said, walking ahead of her. She remained skeptical.

"So killing an animal is for dinner and killing a radical Muslim is for protection, simple as that?"

"Well... the extreme Muslims, yes. I have nothing against the Islamic faith. In fact I've fought more alongside Muslim irregulars as an advisor than I have with allied personnel. Listen, I understand your frustrations with these wars. I don't agree with a lot of what's happening either, but it's not like we can go back in time and reverse the invasion of the Middle East or the way we handled foreign policy following 9/11. You know, there was a British photojournalist who traveled with us when I was a Ranger in Syria. He never took any pictures of us giving water to babies or treating wounded civilians, but he would capture images of us when we'd step over dead bodies or the inevitable fist bump after a successful air strike. The side the media gives you isn't the full picture. But what I've learned is that there are two kinds of violence, Ingrid. The destructive kind, like when an asteroid crashes into a planet. Then there's also creative violence, like when a mother gives birth to her child. And if an asteroid crashed into a planet and spread minerals into its soil capable of making life, there becomes a marriage of elements blind to *the existence* of principle. And when countrymen seek to undergo revolution, his virtues may fail him, and there is a confusing time of hate and sorrow mixed with compassion, and if the latter does prevail, an enlightened civilization may come about at the bargain of social political elasticity and the inevitable return to tyranny. The world's flux of violence allows life to thrive as we know it, as war is often a tool for spiritual cleansing. Even without religion, poverty, famine, and greed... I think the only way peace on Earth could truly exist is if everything were dead."

Before Ingrid had a chance to speak, the radio sprang to life with a voice all too familiar to Ezra.

"This is Colonel Curtis of the United States Army attempting to contact Operations Chief Gomez! Can anyone hear this traffic? Hello! Is this damn thing even on? Where are all our new radios? This piece of shit looks like it was in Iwo Jima!"

Ezra scrambled for the radio.

"Curtis this is Security Supervisor Ezra Beller along with Ingrid McAdam. I read you loud and clear!"

"Finally! Good to hear we found someone. Where the hell are you two? Are there any other survivors you've found?"

"Negative sir, we are the only known survivors. We are at the base of the mountain where the crash occurred, southeast of the crash site."

"We have the coordinates of the crash site so give me a moment to find your position. Standby," the colonel said.

In a warm, dry room on an aircraft carrier a few hundred miles away, Curtis pulled up a screen to see two shivering humans near one of Peru's many stream bottoms.

"Okay, I can see you now on the SAT images. I wish we could send a ship down right away but it's going to be at least until morning. There's a nasty storm headed your way and the other ship had to turn around due to bad weather. My advice is to duck down away from the storm. I know it will be a bitch, but your best option would be to find a cave or shelter of some kind. Just make sure it's nearby where you're at now. Turn off your radio until 0600 to save the battery life."

"Copy that. Hey, send some cigarettes down with the boys, too, will ya?"

The radio's red light faded behind the refraction of drizzling raindrops.

"Well at least he knows where we are," Ezra said.

"We're going to live! " Ingrid yelled excitedly and hugged him.

Ezra tilted his brow, but laughed and realized having high hopes wasn't the worst way to be. Ingrid laughed too and looked at Ezra with tears of happiness streaming. She wrapped herself around him and didn't let go. After she parted from him, Ezra looked at her with an awkward expression.

"What?" she asked.

"I just haven't had one of those in a while."

"One of what?"

"A hug," he said, chuckling.

"What about your friend last night?"

"I meant... from a woman," Ezra said, blushing, realizing how stupid he must have sounded.

They continued on with a bit of a skip in their step, and Ezra wanted to distract himself from his racing thoughts by asking Ingrid about herself.

"Do you enjoy your work?" Ezra asked.

"Yes, thoroughly. It may lack the intensity of your occupation, but I've had some pretty wild adventures myself.

After college I studied in the Indonesian tropics for two years with a research team to try and find out about the cause for the disappearing wildlife. To our dismay, they were being mutated and killed off from a leaky old nuclear facility in China that was polluting the seas north of the islands; causing widespread Empty Forest Syndrome."

"Damn. That's a real thing?"

"Yep. One part of the food chain disappears, and all the large mammals move out."

"So what did you do?"

"We tried to raise awareness back in the states. We had articles going out, hired street workers asking for donations, and support from organizations to shut down the plant. Unfortunately none of it worked and we had limited funding, so we had to take matters into our own hands."

"Hmm Eco-terrorist huh?"

"Ha, no not quite. We didn't have the intention of harming anyone physically. We just needed to hit them where it counted: in the pocket. We started blocking every other shipment to and from the plant, sabotaging electric power boxes, and always changing our strategy so they couldn't pinpoint the headquarters. We lost a few good scientists who were probably imprisoned or killed. Those poor souls... Eventually we won because it finally got the United Nation's attention and they urged China to clean up their mess."

"Wow, that's incredible. You then returned to the rainforest I am guessing?"

"Yes, and much had recovered. But the image of those deformed monkeys always stuck with me. Massive sections of the forest were cleared of everything: insects, plants, mammals, and amphibians. It's as if humans are always performing a holocaust somewhere. And we've pulled plants and animals into our blood bath."

"Well look on the bright side. We're away from all that nonsense for a while. I have to admit... this is kind of soothing," Ezra added.

"Crashing a plane in the wilderness of Peru is soothing to you?" she asked.

"No, but being away from humans is. I mean, I'm stuck with a granola, but I guess it could be worse."

"Shut up," she giggled.

"So you're not too distraught to laugh, that's good. Look at us: yin and yang, working together."

Ingrid smiled and rolled her eyes. Her happiness heightened Ezra's spirits, which was a relief, but he knew all too well that they were not yet out of danger.

They walked for a ways in silence, their thoughts racing. Ezra drifted deep into his subconscious. He pondered life and death and what it would be like to see the Earth from a broad outward perspective. He thought of every person, and what they were doing right then at that moment. With all the peace, war, cities, towns, festivals, markets, churches, prisons, schools, parties, funerals, students, workers, gangs, politicians, prostitutes and all the other social distortion happening within those busy nests of civilization, it all just seemed humorous to him. He looked around at the protruding plants and trees. It was no less violent of a place, but most of the organisms' battles and partnerships happened on a microscopic level. To be in the presence of the breathing forest was invigorating. Ezra found it harder to gather his more distant memories as he let the present sink in.

As the wind began to pick up, the large trees bent and hissed with the aggressive gale. At the first lightning strike, Ingrid suddenly jumped in excitement. A python slithered between their legs without noticing her frozen pose before diving down under the lowest levels of foliage.

"I guess that's better than being struck," she said.

Ezra nodded in agreement.

The oncoming storm had all the monkeys, birds, flying squirrels and other creatures scuttling toward cover under the broad leaves. A colony of ants retreated back to their mound. To Ingrid, no phenomenon was as fascinating as that moment. A nocturnal shift brought the animals to shelter as if they were coming home from work.

Day waned to night as they followed the drainage looking for a good place to take cover. Several other tributaries converged into a large stream where the trees were as tall as five story buildings. The branches swayed with tremendous flexibility and released small helicopter-like seedlings that fell in groups.

The crisp, clear creek seemed pure enough to drink, save the yellow bacterial foam slopping on its shores. Mud held together by moss looked like bloody livers splashing from rock to rock. The creek's smell was that of rotting carcass and fecal matter, which was presumably from the stinky bacteria. This didn't stop either of the humans from feeling hungry. Their stomachs were being torn from no food or water, but eventually they were distracted from the fact when they found sanctuary in a cave. It lay nearly hidden behind the root structure of a massive fallen, decaying tree: old enough to be one of the first trees in that ancient place. As they ducked out of the rain, lightning was touching down every few seconds in the distance as the storm drew closer. A mass of black clouds gathered above them.

"Oh my God," Ingrid said faintly.

To her amazement, small glowing specks started to illuminate the air like tiny fireflies. They drifted together, changing shape with the wind like a massive flock of birds. Every once in a while, they would spin into momentary Borromean rings that seemed perfectly choreographed to some mathematical scrutiny.

"I don't think we have to worry about cartels or booby traps anymore. Something tells me humans have never been here," Ezra said cautiously as he pulled a space blanket from his pocket.

"They must be some kind of bioluminescent fungi spores. Beautiful, aren't they?" Ingrid said, astonished.

"Yes, they most certainly are," he said in a low voice, wary of the organism's intent.

They both snuck a good twenty feet into the cave and laid down on the blanket to separate them from the ground. Ezra threw a second space blanket over them. Ingrid lay sideways and sunk into relaxation, closing her eyes at first then peering through slits when she didn't think Ezra could tell.

"Does your throat hurt?" she asked.

"No its fine. Does yours?"

"It feels scratchy," she said before coughing a few times.

"Just try to get some sleep and breathe under the blanket if you can. The smell of our muddy bodies may not be so pleasant, but it's better than being poisoned," he reassured her.

Lightning and thunder rolled in, and what glorious sky hemorrhaging it was. Pulsing shock waves echoed through the mountains then back again with a sonic boom. The lightning diminished behind rain and clouds, with small flashes lighting up the area around them dimly, exposing the storm's electrifying collusion with the land. Even with the monsoon, temperatures became relatively cooler. But it was the spores Ezra feared, not the conditions. Another dose of fear swept him. He hadn't had that emotion with such a vibrant sting since his last combat mission. He knew why, too. He didn't want the beautiful creature beside him to share such a terrible fate. After all the comrades that had fallen beside him, sometimes in his arms, he suddenly couldn't stand the idea of losing another person under his command. Ezra turned to look at Ingrid, who had pulled him closer to herself for warmth. Her closed lashes caught beads of water that moistened her young complexion. She had the smoothest skin he'd ever felt. Her body was a temple of Goddess proportions. Subtle, perfect breasts mounted her beating chest; a strong heartbeat indeed, as he could feel its vibrations through the blanket even with the storm wailing outside. She opened her eyes just as Ezra was looking at her chest. He quickly looked away.

"How many people have you killed?" she asked.

Usually Ezra would not respond to that kind of question, but his vulnerability and current predicament allowed him to talk and be open without feeling judged.

"I'm not sure. I have 82 confirmed kills but it's definitely more than that. In many cases, you never know if you've hit your target, because all you can see is return fire ceasing. They could have retreated. Some enemies are consistent about taking their dead and wounded with them, too."

"So they could have been children?" she asked.

"War is hell, Ingrid. The enemy often forces children into their ranks."

"You have a very peculiar view of things Ezra."

He wiped the water from his hair then said, "I'm just trying to avenge the oppressed and destroy the malevolent. When I was young, I read a disturbing story that took place in a civil war in Africa, and it struck a chord. I knew then that I wanted to hunt these men who had turned into demons..." He closed his eyes and thought for a few seconds. "In time it makes you a bit of a monster yourself, but that's inevitable. There has to be every kind of man, no?"

"Maybe you were a gifted Centurion warrior in a former life or something."

He sighed and turned to her and said, "Maybe."

They both smiled slightly and laid there for a moment looking into each other's eyes. When they realized what they were doing, they stopped and looked away.

"When you saw the glowing spores earlier, was that the most incredible thing you've ever seen?" Ezra asked.

"Yes. Undoubtedly. Was it for you?"

"Close, but no."

"What was it then?"

"It's not a fun story, but it goes back to your comment about children in war. I had an escort mission several years ago in Bangladesh. There was a huge protest outside the embassy against the country's resource negotiations. An oil company accidentally spilled-"

"Negligently," Ingrid interrupted.

"Sure... negligently spilled two million gallons of petroleum into the sacred river, Ganges."

"Oh I remember hearing about that."

"Needless to say, the locals were unhappy. Our 'client' was in the embassy, so we were ordered to quell the resistance by whatever means necessary. My squad was ordered to hold traffic on the main street and start turning people around. We started taking small arms fire after about an hour. When the provocation increased, we got our client and pulled back to the river. Three of my men, in an effort to help a trapped family out of a building, were hit and killed by a rebel RPG. Something up there had been flammable, and the building burned down right in front of me, along with the family."

"Good God!" Ingrid said, frowning.

"The only survivor of the attack was a boy, no older than twelve, who ran shrieking by me, his clothes and skin aflame. I lunged to stop him, but he jumped in the river. The water was half oil. Charred him in seconds. He lit that entire section of river. A river of fire. The smoke rose high into the sky and turned the sun red. In the black smoke, I saw the devil's face for the first time, snarlin' at me. Maybe I was sleep deprived, but I'd never seen anything like it."

Ingrid showed a saddened expression, then Ezra continued, "I guess what I'm saying is, I've seen darker worlds than this. I've seen humans turn into feral, rabid creatures as the evil nature of humanity reveals itself through the sudden absence of civilization. I no longer think about the deep questions that I used to ask myself. I don't believe in a merciful God as I was raised to believe. I've given myself to the impersonal hostility of the universe and to the men I'd call brothers. Here I am, still a part of the chaos, still living by the sword until I most certainly die by it."

She coughed again then said, "I don't think you're a terrible person actually."

"And you did before?" Ezra smiled.

"Well, let's just say I wasn't fond of you, but I don't think you are a war machine deep down. I believe there's a compassionate side of you that you choose to dismiss out of habit. Have your noble actions toward me not redeemed you for what damage you may have done?"

"No deed could pardon my trail of bloodshed. If there is a hell, I'm going there," Ezra said, chuckling. He went on, "Should you and I survive this mess and return safely to the U.S. however, I'd much like to live far away from this world's endless torments. And they are endless."

"Will you be able to quit?"

"Yeah. I have an open contract. I can retire whenever I please. I'm just here because I have no idea what the hell I would do in the civilian world."

"You should just fish, hunt, climb mountains, and challenge yourself like you would in the military, just on your own terms and for the sake of your own wellbeing."

"That's a good idea, Ingrid. There might be hope for me after all."

With that she smiled and shut her eyes. Ezra temporarily felt so warm inside he could hardly contain it. It was a relief to tell someone of his pain, to let out his demons into the thin mountain air. He closed his eyelids, exhausted from the insanity of the day. As his body decompressed and his mind wandered into sleep, he unwillingly thought of something rather bizarre, his mind projecting some rare vivid image. This was one of the side effects to his night terrors and their onsets. This time however, it felt different to him.

A recurring scene played over and over in Ezra's head: those dancing spores with their mysterious glow below merciless black clouds. They swirled down and around Ingrid's curved naked body. Her eyes were closed, but she smiled in ecstasy. She was floating in the air but moved slowly and sensually as if suspended underwater. Her skin was green and bright, an absinthian queen glowing with psychedelic moonlight against the sterile purple gloom. Mushrooms began slithering up and around her legs and she welcomed their intimate touches. Lichens reached toward her as she spun their noodling edges in her fingers. Licking the air, Ingrid squirmed as the spores began fluttering over her body, tickling her. More plants and vines began caressing her body until she was enveloped in the forest, becoming part of it. The foliage got thicker and thicker until Ezra's slumber deepened and the vision dissipated.

Ezra awoke suddenly when a lightning bolt struck near. The flash gave way to complete blackness. Outside the cave, the storm roared as leaves whipped and branches hissed in autumn's awakening, and the wind and cumulous siphoned through that monsoonal corridor a tide of heavy sky. Sitting upright, Ezra felt a fever spreading rapidly through his skull, his eyes pulsing alternately as his temples clenched.

"This is bad," he said aloud, "this is really fucking bad."

Ingrid was also awake but seemed *undead*. She bore half her face in the mud, tightening her muscles and moving her limbs haphazardly in indescribable anguish like a seizing zombie. Screams and gargling noises erupted from her drooling mouth.

"Make it stop, DEAR GOD MAKE IT STOP!" she cried.

Ezra tried to contain her fit of torture, but she wailed with tears streaming. He felt her forehead and it was hot to the touch. As if to cry for help she moaned then locked her fingers tight around Ezra's wrists. The sickness was growing in him too, as his hands started stinging and burning as though his skin were being pealed back slowly. He could not have imagined a stranger fate; to die of poisoning in a psilocybin-infested cave deep in the Amazonian rainforest. And he contemplated how long and painful this death would be. Ezra felt he had to act but he had no anesthetic except for the cool brown water that pooled around them. *Of course!* he thought, *the most plentiful of cures. Maybe it would at least help us vomit.*

Having not had any water to drink since before the crash, Ezra decided to quench his body's desperate phase of dehydration. He had no way to test it, nor did he bear doubt, for he knew he had to find some way to pull himself and Ingrid out from that vortex of pain given to them by that mysterious spore. It may have been a torment he deserved, but *she did not.*

Ezra unclenched Ingrid's hands. Her grip was like a python's strangle. He cupped the water, looking at its bubbling color with murky mushroom vision, drinking as much as a man could in such delirium and he let the cool water absorb into his mouth and body. Ingrid would not partake, though he managed to pour some into her mouth as she squirmed for freedom from the sickness. The fever rushed through every aching molecule within them. Imagining the lichen taking over his flesh again, Ezra shut his eyes as the unsparing thought of suicide came unto him. He imagined keeping them closed, and slitting Ingrid's throat before burying his knife into his own innards as one final gesture for damnation's welcome. All of the most wretched thoughts coagulated in Ezra's mind, creating a knotted mess induced by the rhizosphere's invader and magnified by a soul-splitting sense of guilt.

"My lineage is spoiled from origin," Ezra decided at last. *But maybe it's humankind that has been cursed all this time*, he thought quietly to himself, confused as to what he was saying versus thinking. Something still fighting its way through him did not give up, however.

Ezra's vision flipped and rotated with vertigo. The absence of light dominated his reality. Bolts struck in radial view giving him momentary sights of Ingrid flopping and slinging mud. He looked back into the dark corner of the cave's depths. His knees buckled in an awkward phase of spinal depression as his hallucinations climaxed. He began seeing black demons swirl around him, their bat wings wet with acidic blood. He looked away from the light and further up into the tree's roots. There, at the tree's heart, at the center of its root system, the devil's face had emerged. Once he'd seen its face in flame, now in rotten wood, with its sexual ambiguity, its candid eyes, and malevolent grin. Ezra began making his way towards the singularity of the chamber in an attempt to gamble with the devil for one last chance. He could not walk nor crawl. To the rhythm of a crippled snake he spun, a wounded spirit succumbing to the great sabbatical spiral that pulled him through a plane of dissonance like no other. The demons laughed and taunted him before evaporating one by one. Ingrid's cries and moaning filled the cave with a haunting reverberation. Yet further he crawled, deeper still, and he went until all light faded and only his mind's eye could project what wasn't there. He opened his eyes from behind that realm of sealed darkness and saw just that. Nothing. There was no up, nor down, and his vision was suddenly deprived of all reference. Ezra was seeing fractal images through the small bursts of electricity pulsing inside his eyelids blood canals. As his face lay in the muck, he started tearing at the mud, trying to rip open the seal to hell. He ripped the rocks and roots, his fingernails splitting, his forehead thumping wildly. He dug until he sensed a spongy texture. Ezra looked up to a faint light, his pupils as dark as the musty tomb swallowing him up.

"What are you?" Ezra asked. He'd unearthed something peculiar. The organism resembled a half halo of lichen protruding from the mineral soil, glowing with a bright bioluminescent gold sheen, illuminating his maddened face. Ezra pressed his quivering, cracked lips to it and started biting the plant, praying that it would give him some kind of release, be it life or death. The ancient taste matched his fit of disgust, which only drove him to eat more. Ezra gnawed at the organism like a rabid animal and devoured the slimy yellow gills with great appetite.

"TAKE ME!" he screamed.

He swallowed as much as he could without vomiting. After eating the last bit, he slumped, the lichen's gooey remnants stuck in his teeth and gums. Everything started going into slow motion for Ezra, and suddenly the lingering taste of the plant gradually became bearable. What started as gargling sewing needles turned into a nectar so sweet that his taste buds wished for more. Then the most significant moment in Ezra's life occurred.

There was suddenly no fever, nor pain, nor feeling even, as if all fear and hope dropped away like soap and dirt in perfect union with water. And yet he was neither paralyzed nor dead, as he could perceive five shades of silence replacing his senses. Every atom within him dispersed into the absence. As he lay dying painfully inside that dark cave, Ezra found what he had been missing all his life. Love. Not a general sense of love and kinship for all things, but a specific kind of love. So rare and divine one wouldn't ever want it if they knew what it ultimately bestows. Ezra had waited for such a light. For what seemed a million years, maybe ten billion, he became awakened in this state of limbo. For what seemed enough time to construct a species, cross its faith, and drift into a legacy lost, but in those few moments riding the crest of his unfolding, Ezra did not become a God, nor did he find 'God' in any Earthly connotation.

His loss of entity flooded his mind and allowed for his imagination to flourish and his soul to commit to nothing and everything. Something golden bloomed within him. Ezra had waited for his true guide, and Ingrid was the key. She was his cosmically abandoned counterpart, and he, hers. They had been for all time, waiting to clash like planets whose gravity knows no obstacle.

As if the sun itself had exploded outside the cave, Ezra blinked wildly and snapped out of his euphoric daze. He looked out and saw a wall of fire draping the root-laden entrance. His wounds remained but neither bled nor impaired him. Wrapping the torn cloth tight around his forehead, he looked out between the plumes and saw men with guns and fire extinguishers. With alarming vitality Ezra stood, relieved and relaxed. He felt healthier than ever. He could see straight and breathe easy, his body a flume of energy. He walked up to Ingrid who lay seemingly lifeless and felt her dragging pulse, looking carefully at the freckles scattered over her blue virescent skin like the constellation of salvation. Ezra smiled and whispered into her ear, "It's time to go home, Pavonis."

He picked up her limp body and trudged onward through the flames. The fire swirled around him and washed his face of all organic particles. The combusting oxygen and chemicals cleansed his skin rather than burn him as he held Ingrid's curled body close. Ezra walked out unscathed to a blazing sun that he cared not to shield his eyes from. He nodded at the rescue team. Curtis's soldiers were putting out a fire started by the ship's exhaust but paused and stood in awe as Ezra walked toward them. Across the valley, storm clouds were receding to an open view of the great forest around them. The bright yellow sun pierced his being with the warmth of a trillion rays, each one causing a new sensation on his thirsty skin.

Ezra laid Ingrid down on the medical stretcher that had been rushed to them. She barely opened her eyes for a moment to look at him before two men put an oxygen mask on her and lifted her toward the ship's safety. Ezra rose slowly with a body transformed as he refused medical assistance with a light gesture of his hand. He opened his arms to greet that heavenly body of light, its ancient hymn combing him. Flakes of his skin peeled in the breeze like the ash peeling from the Earth's surface around him.

Ezra could see in the reflection of the men's face shields that he had black glossy eyes with dark red retina stretching from lid to lid like some vicious nocturnal beast. The soldiers stepped opposite Ezra, trembling at the sight of him. And what a sight he was; covered in dried mud and laughing in delight through heat waves of early morning napalm refraction. He'd been cultivated in the womb of Mother Nature and super modified by the rays of their closest star. Ezra felt enlightened through his new mind and body. He simply felt *no longer human.*

Colonel Curtis had come out with the rescue team and approached him with a fierce grin on his face.

"Well if it ain't the Worm himself! This will be one for the debriefing room, huh Beller? Sorry about the wild fire. Dropped the bird in low and caught some brush with the exhaust. Hard to believe this shit can even burn with all that fuckin' rain!"

"That's quite all right sir," Ezra said calmly.

"I bet you could use some grub son. Let's go, we're pullin' the fuck outta here."

Ed Curtis was an outlaw officer of military prowess, vitality and spectatorship. He was an old school Green Beret, with short grey hair that lightly covered a Buddhist head tattoo inked long ago when operating within the central Asian tribal network. Curtis was a Grandfather figure and mentor to Ezra, but even that would change in time.

"Sir," Ezra tried to get his attention. They made their way to the hovering ship and Curtis raised his voice to be heard above the droning engines.

"We'll go back to the Kennedy where there's gonna a routine medical and pathogen examination. They've got to make sure you're not going to cross contaminate with anyone before we sail back to the states, seeing how Miss McAdam got the bug so badly. But don't worry about her, they're pushin' fluids and she's got anti-toxin serum already coursin' through 'er body. She's gonna be all right. A little fever but we can heal 'er, that's the easy part."

"Then what's the hard part?" Ezra asked.

"She's gotta have clearance to head back to the states, and judging by the looks of ya', so do you. If there's any conflict with that, however, I'll handle it."

Curtis looked him over as they stepped onto the ship.

"The hell happened to your eyes?"

"Allergies, likely. Hey, did you bring those cigarettes?"

Curtis threw him a pack. Ezra took a cigarette out and lit its end to a single bent, burning mushroom on the ground just as the helicopter began rising off the ground.

"Well, we can write that one off as a failed mission and never have to come back," Curtis said.

Ezra took a long, deep puff, too large for even a seasoned smoker. The sweet nicotine might as well have been black tar heroin as it ran through his circulatory system. A quarter of the stick turned to ash: a deadly satisfaction.

"No. I think we got what we came for," Ezra said. He smiled and tossed the butt through the closing hull.

The doors slammed as they accelerated quickly away from the jungle, and as the fight between the gravitational pull and the ship's upward thrust caused resistance in the air, Ezra felt only relief. He looked out of the window, gazing at the strange place he would never drop into again, and would never want to. It gave him a gift, and an answer that he'd been waiting for. But returning to the States seemed daunting suddenly, as if it would not be the same after the transformation of his body's chemistry. He closed his eyes and relaxed, envisioning Missouri's evening skies, of how the sun sank early in the clouds like egg yolk spilling over the horizon, and how the smells of autumn and evening stove smoke reminded him of that place in the Ozark Mountains where some say you can hear the cry of many a woeful soldier.

Ezra awoke to the beeping of a heart monitor. The aluminum walls in the large room around him were covered in medical posters and military memorabilia. A doctor in a white coat leaned over him and chuckled.

"Looks like you dozed off, Ezra. Some much needed sleep, I'm sure. This means you're waking up right in time for dinner. But before I send you off there are a few things we need to go over."

"Okay."

Ezra was curious but remained observant. He was back on the aircraft carrier, and glad to be heading home, albeit rather slowly. He peered out the small, circular window. The Pacific's deep blue waves kissed the fast setting sun and glistened against a cloudless open sky. Ezra felt a warm breath within his chest; it was so pure and satisfying that his eyes closed for a moment to enjoy the invigorating sensation.

"My name is Doctor Parsons and I've conducted an analysis on you as ordered by the administration. Obviously, you had some minor injuries too, but some of the higher ups decided I should go more in depth just in case their subject had been tampered with."

"I'm not sure what you speak of."

"Ezra I know your involvement with the genetic enhancement program with the military is confidential, but I've been informed. And I've dealt with many like you. With a combat record like you have... Let me guess... You've been experiencing nerve damage, headaches and chest pains... visual and auditory hallucinations... perhaps flashbacks of home?"

Ezra looked up at the man with obsidian eyes. The purple sunset pouring through the window erased his irises.

"Well? How do you feel?" the doctor began in a calm voice.

"I feel high," Ezra mentioned, his new body awakened in the brilliance of the now.

The doctor laughed.

"Well yes, your medical records said you weren't allergic to narcotics so I gave you a very small dose of morphine while I hemmed your injuries, but that should wear off in a short while. But I mean, are you feeling sick or in pain... at all?"

"No, I'm fine. Never better."

"Good. That's very good. You have no blurry vision, loss of appetite, stomach sickness, breathing issues?"

"Well Doc, I can see fine, all I can think of is dinner, and my lungs feel like I started smoking yesterday. Doesn't mean I'm going to quit though."

The doctor smiled and continued, "Very well then. Let's begin on the surface. First off, your forehead gash you seemed to have gotten during the crash will heal just fine, and besides that there are just a few cuts I stitched up for you that you must have suffered from the crash. Here's where it gets strange though: the stitches... they already need to be taken out. This I noticed when treating a wound on your Achilles. The wound, it... it sealed before my eyes."

Curtis' shadow could be seen pacing in the hallway. Ezra heard his steps but paid no more attention.

The doctor continued, "The poisonous fungus recently documented as Amanitas Mercidious Silvus, the only organism archived in this disastrous mission, was not present in your system, as it was in Ingrid's. However, after extensive research over the last few hours, I have found that none of your red blood cells contain any original human DNA data."

"I don't understand," Ezra said, confused.

"Was there anything specific you came into contact with I should know about? Anything unusual?"

"Well *everything* was unusual. But I can tell you that I was very sick and needed an anesthetic. I drank some water, which could have contained anything I suppose, then in the cave I found a bioluminescent...thing. Maybe lichen or something buried in the mud. I ate it."

"You ate it?"

"The illness had a hold on me. I just felt as though it would either save me or kill me. Either way I wanted it to be over."

"Interesting," the doctor said as he scribbled some notes in his book. He went on, "Well in this case, you've seemed to have won the biological lottery in your recklessness, because it has done far more than just save you. After an in-depth microscopic viewing of your cells through nano-videography following an acute mitochondria analysis, I can tell you even in this short amount of time since your exposure, you are something else; perhaps a physical being capable of constant genetic metamorphosis and regeneration. I'm talking about immortality, Ezra. We will have to come up with a new species name just for you."

"But I'm still human," Ezra said, looking at his hands.

"I would have to disagree. Look closer," the doctor continued, taking his glasses off and staring at him. "Your skin tissue more readily blocks toxins while replenishing itself in thin but strong hexagonal oriented layers. Behind your skin, your muscles have developed a distinct nerve pattern that allows for a split reaction time. This I realized when you reacted to scalpel coming toward your skin. The moment the blade grazed a single hair your arm lurched in the opposite direction. I've also discovered a thin webbing in your lungs, starting inside your trachea, which contain a plethora of ultra-efficient capillaries that discard unwanted molecules in the air while absorbing recycled oxygen and other needed elements. Also when you look into the mirror later, you will see the retinas in your eyes have expanded to the whole area of the visible eye, which appear to be dark red from a distance, but are actually aubergine purple—to be most specific—having over 70,000 sensitive rods. That is nearly 20,000 more than an owl's. Your visual spectrum has expanded to see colors that no one else even knows exist."

Doctor Parsons shook his head in disbelief before continuing.

"I'm not sure how this change occurred or what kind of organism you came in contact with, but the species is unidentifiable as it's now woven into your genes and transformed them. You *are* the species, Ezra, or more explicitly, an inhibitor of its mutating capabilities."

A tickle ran up Ezra's spine and he smiled before asking, "So what does this all mean exactly?"

"I have to do some more tests, but as long as you feel okay, you're okay. You should live a long healthy life, just not as a human. I mean, whatever this is evidently made you evolve above and beyond the average pace, and there's nothing caustic or contagious about your condition that I've encountered thus far. Let's hope that people are compassionate toward their new hybrid relative. You're going to be a world-wide scientific phenomenon. Maybe even a celebrity. I hope you're ready for that."

"Thanks Doc, but I doubt the fireworks will go off just yet. I'll be anxious for more test results."

"This is the most exciting research I've ever been a part of. I will be working most the night on them. Thank you, Ezra. You are dismissed."

Ezra shook the doctor's hand and walked out to meet Colonel Curtis still pacing in the hallway.

"How do ya feel son?"

"Great."

"Glad to hear it."

"Have the teams found any other survivors?"

Curtis shook his head.

"We found the bodies. Flying 'em back to the States tomorrow. Givin' me all medals and all that shit. What a fucking waste. Wish I could bring that engineer back to life so I could kill him."

"You could just kill my boss. That would solve a lot of issues."

Curtis laughed and pulled out a flask and tipped it toward Ezra.

"No thank you sir."

"Suit yourself. It's long way to dry land," he said before walking in and talking to the doctor. Ezra watched them for a moment, then went back to his quarters. He took a shower and stood there bewildered, trying to get used to the idea of his 'new body', which felt pretty good to be in. He felt comfortable, sexy, muscular, and efficient in all physical and mental aspects. After cleaning off the mud, he looked in the mirror and noticed something else of his was enhanced. Ezra looked down, then back into the mirror, then back down again.

"Wow...uh... okay," he said to himself.

Ezra got dressed in some fresh clothes and headed to the dining hall. The clop of his combat boots slowed as he entered the room. Everyone quieted at his arrival. He nodded awkwardly to the sailors and contractors, who muttered things to each other and looked away from his dark eyes. The cooks had made a feast of prime rib, pastas, pies, garlic bread and delectable fruits and salads. The mood at the mission's operations table was somewhat uplifting even though a great tragedy had just occurred. They greeted Ezra and shook his hand. Many of the scientists were practically cheerful at their discovery of Ezra's interesting transformation.

To begin the evening, they all gave a toast to those who had lost their lives. They ate quietly but Ezra attempted to break the solemn silence by talking to them about anything but his body's transformation, though if someone did want to talk, that was the only subject on which they spoke.

He looked at the table adjacent to them and there sat Ingrid; healthy, clean, gorgeous, and ever so happy to be safe and secure. She put down her wine glass and walked over to Ezra. It was good timing because some of the scientists were so eager to study his condition that they were crowding closely around him with invasive bifocals.

"How are you feeling?" he asked her, his words having barely caught her within sound's reach. The scientists dispersed reluctantly, and Ezra rose to meet her.

"I passed out for a few hours. I feel fine now, though. It sounds funny saying this, but I practically owe you my life. I can't imagine surviving without your help through that horrible mess. Thank you, Ezra."

She hugged him and kissed him on the cheek, and he blushed. The sailors hooted and whistled behind them.

Ezra ignored them then countered her appreciation with his own. "If there's one thing I've learned about all this, it's that you saved me. I'm the one that is thankful."

They both smiled in recognition of each other's graciousness.

"That was some trip," she said. "I ate mushrooms in college but that was like ten times crazier!"

Just then one of Ezra's subordinates hollered out to Ingrid, "Hey don't look too hard into those eyes, you might just fall in!"

"Start pushing, Nerison," Ezra ordered as the rookie reluctantly stepped away from the table and began doing pushups.

Ingrid smiled then said, "Seriously though, you're actually a pretty good guy, and if those meatheads think that those big dark eyes of yours belong to some kind of freak, well, they're mistaken. I think you're quite handsome."

Ezra smiled and went to defend himself, but she continued, "Listen Ezra, I'm afraid of what's going to happen when we get back home. With half our organization killed in the accident and no money to back it, I don't know what I'm going to do and well... I don't know how to say this, but I need a job and there's going to be a lot of people who want to study your new 'condition'. You might want someone you can trust."

"That's a very realistic possibility."

She laughed, but trusted Ezra and showed it with her eyes.

"Are you taking a flight home right away?" he asked.

"I don't think we have one. Military 'budget cuts' apparently. Your colonel regretted to inform me that we will have to hitch a ride on this boat all the way through Panama and up to the port of Houston."

"Fine with me. Sounds like a paid vacation," Ezra grinned.

"Well you're getting paid, not me," Ingrid smirked.

"We should get to work soon then," Ezra said. "But I think we should study my mind too, not just my body. This 'mutation' or whatever is changing me mentally, I can already tell."

"Sounds wonderful. We have to find some way to pass the time, don't we?"

"I can think of a lot of ways to pass the time," Ezra said raising his eyebrows.

"Fucking smart ass!" Ingrid said as she punched him in the arm while trying to fight back a smile.

"I'm talking about fishing. But anyways, I have some cool things I could show you," he spoke in lower volume, "I was clearing a bombed-out Mosque in Saudi Arabia a few years back and found some 12th century poetry. Would you like to indulge?"

She looked skeptical and said, "If you're hitting on me, it's *not* working," she said, "Besides, how would you read it?"

"الجميلة نجمة الناظر بلدي لأن" (*Because, my lovely star gazer*)," he said in Omani, "I can speak Arabic."

Ingrid bit her lip. "We'll see soldier, but I think for the time being you should think about some serious career changes!"

61

"Hey! Not so loud around the guys, they don't know I'm retiring yet. Exit-hazing knows no rank."

They both smiled then Ingrid suddenly grabbed Ezra's arm, drawing him in close and whispering into his ear, "None of these people know what we went through, and no one we ever meet will. That's why we need to help each other. I feel good about the future, and because of you, I still have one."

With that she walked away with a simple elegance, sending Ezra's heart fluttering. He shook it off though, as if love was intruding, and convened with his men.

"You can stop now Nerison before you sink the ship."

All the men laughed as the exhausted, beat-red rookie rose up panting from his push-ups to continue his meal. Ezra spent the rest of the evening with the young war fighters. They stayed up late into the night playing card games and telling wild stories. It all made Ezra sad that he would be leaving that brotherhood to start a new life, a life that was only just beginning. In retrospect it was all worth it to him, the pain, hallucinations, neurosis, the fear of death without redemption, the fear of life without love. All those years of suffering mirrored that one experience and thus he'd been vindicated. Ezra's loss of guilt made room for other emotions, and he felt a golden light in his chest whenever he looked at Ingrid.

Ezra entered the doctor's office the next day and found Dr. Parsons slouching in his desk chair and nodding out in the front of a busy float-screen. Multiple tabs on the screen were loading, some building simulations of cell reactions. Empty coffee cups were strewn over his desk. His eyes were droopy and dark. Ezra stepped inside. His feet made a crunching sound. The floor was a mosaic of shattered sample slates. The doctor noticed Ezra and scrambled to come meet him.

"Good morning, Ezra."

"You know that it's two in the afternoon, right?" Ezra said, double-checking his watch.

The doctor paid no attention to the question.

"Sit down, please," he began. He seemed fidgety and nervous.

"You've recognized your sixth sense, no?"

Ezra pondered for a moment then asked, "You mean like when I close my eyes and skim my hands close to the wall without looking at them or moving them away?"

The doctor looked at him, almost disappointed, and then said, "Well yes, your proprioception has likely increased, as to your ability to sense matter around you, but anyone who isn't too clumsy can do that. I'm talking more animalistic. You probably haven't gotten used to it, but like many organisms such as sharks, fungi, and bees, you have what is called magnetoception. This is when you have the ability to detect a magnetic field. Your case is advanced because you can literally open up that intelligence on a much higher level of input when direct sunlight contacts your skin. I'm sure if we went and sat on the black flight deck for a few hours you'd see just what I'm talking about, and I'm just warning you about this ahead of time."

"Warning me of what?" Ezra asked.

The doctor sighed then sputtered quickly, "I have highly underestimated your condition Ezra. There is no cure for what you have, and I'll tell you why that is not necessarily a good thing. Physically, you will become very strong, efficient, virile-

"Well yeah, did you see my-"

"BUT the mental aspects are more unpredictable. You may become full of compassion, belonging, and understanding, but you also have an equal chance of the evolving nerve cells in your brain becoming alarmingly predatory. Part of evolution is dominance, and you could be a liability if we humans decide you are a threat to our species."

"Come on Doc, you make it sound like I'm an alien."

He shrugged, not excluding the term.

"Come over here, I want you to have a look at something," he said, his hands still shaking anxiously.

He brought Ezra to the corner of the lab. There was a small globe-shaped contraption with three green holographic screens orbiting around its base.

"Using this instrument we can semi-accurately predict a mammal's natural life expanse within a few months. The reason I say semi-accurately is because it doesn't account for disease or other unnatural causes of death outside cell degeneration. This slide here is a male black bear I sampled in British Columbia. He will live a natural life of 28 years, 35 days." He picked up another sample and held it to Ezra's face.

"This one is yours. I couldn't find any evidence that dates your natural death before the end of the millennium."

"You mean the year 3000? What's my death date then?" Ezra asked, bewildered.

"I can't rightfully say because every time I test a different piece of you, be it a cheek cell, hair or blood cell, it's updating its molecular composition. Even after detaching itself from you, the cells give me different results, and the date gets pushed forward exponentially. Looking at your life by years is now impossible, because in that sense, you're getting younger all the time. This, remember, is your natural death date. You are still almost as vulnerable as anyone else to being killed, at least for now."

"Wow," Ezra said, astonished.

"It's a very complex biological transformation that's constantly in motion, you must understand. Even the most genius scientists of today will have the near impossible task of predicting your next phase. Think of it as photosynthesis, like plants use, but on the quantum level. That, in my professional opinion, is where most of your energy is now drawn from. In theory, you have no need to eat, nor sleep, nor drink water hardly at all."

Ezra nodded.

"There are people who have claimed such practices have existed for centuries. They could stare at the sun just as it was rising, when the light is less intense, and somehow feed from it, but I don't know if that's true," Ezra said skeptically.

"Sun-gazers, right. And there are mixed beliefs about that. But with you, Ezra, you don't have to use your eyes. Your skin will act as both your solar panel and your armor. And with that chiseled body your mind controls, those morphing cells could use your former human body as a template to create a killing machine. This is where my worries come from, Ezra. Your blood work could be 'in demand' by certain organizations, what with all the genetic testing you've been through it means you may have to completely remove yourself from society in order to contain its effects and escape from being a victim yourself. I'm marking everything in your file as confidential to ensure this new information stays between you and me until you decide differently. But just know that even though we can hide some of the specifics, most characteristics will be quite obvious."

"Thanks Doc, but I think I can manage just fine. By the way, you're off the case. I'm having Ingrid McAdam do the research from here on. Nothing personal, but like you said, I need to protect my ass."

He slumped, then said, "I understand. And I've erased every piece of you that I sampled. Curtis wanted a blood sample, but I won't do it. I'm more afraid of you than them."

"Because I'm not human?"

"Because you're an assassin."

"Fair enough."

"Listen though, you might have a real wave of craziness headed your way. Your issue in the States will be one of religious scrutiny and politics and hopefully not the harvesting of your cells for biological warfare. But you shouldn't trust anyone, regardless. Higher powers may want you, and if they want you, they may hunt you down."

"And then what? They'll take me and do experiments on me? You're making this sound like our country is run by Nazi chemists."

The doctor shrugged, again not excluding the idea.

Ezra went on, "You may know my body better than I do, but you don't know me. No one besides Ingrid and me knows the *full* truth of what happened. Neither of us will be treated as threats. We deserve to be heard and given a chance to live free. What are you afraid of? Look at me. *I'm the one in control.*"

The doctor started talking again, but Ezra began walking toward the exit. Ezra peaked out into the hall and saw Ingrid carrying some fresh towels to her room. He smiled and nodded, and she smiled back, her curling black hair bouncing in front of the most powerful green eyes he'd ever seen. At the end of his speech, Ezra gave the doctor only a sliver of his attention.

"...you'd better be careful Ezra, that's all I'm saying. Stay below the radar and don't underestimate your strengths and abilities, you may just end up hurting someone. Someone who doesn't deserve it. Someone close to you."

Three days passed. The ship was quiet. Besides a few on guard, the sailors were all tucked away into their bunks. Two hearts beat faster than the others, for they were awake and unable to part with the idea of staying in motion. The ship had a viewing room on its starboard side, purely for observation and relaxation. A mound of pillows and down blankets crowded Ingrid's resting body at the center of the room. A small knock at the door stirred her.

"Yes?"

"Hey, its Ezra."

"I know it's you. There's no one else who knocks around here."

Ezra walked in.

"I hope you have some way of protecting yourself from the hundreds of horny men running around here."

Ingrid reached under the blanket and pulled out a black handgun. Ezra examined it.

"An Israeli .45 Baby Eagle — not bad. Classy and businessman-like."

"Or business*woman*-like," Ingrid said as she stuck it back under the pillows.

"Where did you get it?"

"One of the seaman sold it to me."

"He must have been quite the gambling man," Ezra said.

67

"That and also very stupid and desperate," Ingrid said, laughing.

Ezra chuckled and sat down near the window.

"I had a strange dream last night."

"What about?"

"I dreamt I was a lone wolf."

There was a pause, as she waited for him to continue.

"I was deep in the woods. There were other creatures around me, but I stayed in the shadows as I felt the need to be hidden. I walked by a tree that rose above a mountain brook. The frogs croaked as I passed, which alarmed the other animals of my presence. I quickened my pace and felt them close in on me. Closer they came to me, making noise with rustling bushes and beating wings, until, cornered against a giant stump, I saw them get within only a few yards squaring up to attack me."

Ezra paused, contemplating.

"You awoke then, that's it?" she asked.

"Not quite," he replied.

"Why did the other creatures want to attack you?"

"Because I was a wolf."

"But you didn't hurt any of the animals, did you?"

"I didn't have to. I think it's because I had the *ability* to hurt them that made them fearful, so they took me as a threat that needed to be destroyed."

"What did you do?" she asked, a galaxy of curiosity floating in her eyes like a rogue star system.

Ezra looked out of the window to see a flash of bright lights flickering in the sky. He zoomed his vision to view a meteor shower evaporating in the atmosphere above. He thought about the question and watched still. He was waiting for something. He wanted to see a splash, an explosion, anything, but nothing

68

could get past the atmosphere's thick shield without dissolving. Ezra wanted to be like the Earth: he wanted to be *that resilient*.

"What did you do?" Ingrid asked impatiently.

"I ate them alive."

They both sat silently. Ingrid was intrigued by the dream, for she often interpreted her own. Ezra knew better than to practice reliving his nightmares. He felt this time, however, that his dream was some kind of premonition. He dared not speak more of it. He cleared his throat.

"Hey guess what?" he asked.

"What?"

"There's only one piece of cheesecake left in the cook's freezer and I'm eating it."

She squinted her eyes, not sure whether to believe him or not. Her stomach made the decision for her. Ezra ran away from her, laughing as he tried to escape the hungry woman chasing him. He led her up flights of stairs and down numerous corridors until they arrived on the admiral's deck. Ingrid ran in panting.

Over the admiral's table was a thin white tablecloth. Two glasses of red wine reflected the gentle candlelight flickering between them, and two silver platters covered a decadent dish, with matching silverware and copper mugs that held ice-cold lemon water.

Ingrid was speechless, but let Ezra take her hand and walk her slowly over to the table. The flight deck wasn't as large as the observation room, but it had an awesome ceiling view of the night sky. The Milky Way galaxy stretched across the skylight, that wide window to the cerulean heavens, bluing the room and complimenting the turquoise and emerald monitor lights. They both sat down to the decorated table.

"Oh so this is what you've been up to. How did you manage reserving the admiral's deck?"

"The same way you managed to get that pistol. Minus the flirting."

"I wouldn't doubt there was some flirting involved."

They both laughed.

"Please, enjoy!"

Ingrid opened up her dish to see half a piece of cheesecake. She laughed.

"What?"

"Nothing, it's just funny. You weren't lying. There really was only one more piece, wasn't there?"

Ezra opened his platter, unveiling the rest of the cheesecake. Ingrid laughed until she snorted.

Ezra smiled, "I guess I'll share."

Ingrid calmed herself down then said, "These napkins are really soft."

She took a sip of the wine and laid the plush fabric on her lap.

"They were gifts from the President of Syria."

"He gave them to you?" she asked.

"Not exactly," he said with a slight grin on his face.

Ingrid laughed and held her mouth so she wouldn't spit any out.

"I shouldn't laugh at that."

"The rotten bastard had it coming anyways. I'm glad I got to take part in the felling of a dictatorship, even if ISIL came in and ran the place after we left, just like they do everywhere else."

"You've had some wild times, haven't you?"

70

"Yeah. But I admit that I'm ready to slow down. Let's just say the past is catching up with me."

"Oh yeah?" Ingrid asked, taking another drink of wine.

"Indeed. I was sitting on the flight deck today soaking up the sun's rays. Even though it was far away, I could feel the slightest flick of a solar flare as its aftermath warped around the Earth's magnetic field. The feeling was subtle, but it purified my body and mind. The doctor was right. Solar power energizes me. It fills me with life and vigor... and an uncanny sex drive."

Ingrid coughed, trying to hide her shyness. She found his condition fascinating, however, and listened, astounded. She fluttered her lashes with a dreamy look on her face.

"Can you look straight into the sun?" she asked.

"I can, but it's a bit overwhelming. It's like looking straight into someone's soul and seeing the strange beauty of their entire life unfold before you, and not being able to look away."

Ingrid bit her lip and felt the romanticism of the evening hit her. A long silence ensued, until she leaned close to Ezra. Ezra suddenly grasped her shoulders and started kissing her. In that heated moment of passionate release, they felt the rocking of the ship pull them together, as if creating their own gravity. Ingrid gripped Ezra's shoulders as well, almost to a pinch, and wildly started to kiss his face and neck. They fell to the floor, abandoning the table with the shattering of a wine glass. Ezra began unbuckling his pants. Ingrid ripped her shirt off and exposed her breasts, which Ezra was moments from grasping when suddenly a beeping sound sprang from the control panel.

The ship's computer projected warning lights on the panel beside Ezra.

"What's going on?" Ingrid asked.

"Let's just hope it's not a Russian submarine," he said quickly.

Ingrid laughed then got on top of Ezra, straddling him and barely touching her lips against his, teasing him. She continued grazing her skin against his, as Ezra whispered, "Are you still scared?"

"Not anymore," she answered.

They slowly took each other's clothes off piece-by-piece and proceeded to make love in the blue-lit room. Nothing could interrupt them. Nothing could stand between them, not death, or time. They were the lover and the beloved, forged by ancient suns and rejoined by the radical motions of heaven's temperament, their only constant witness. They knew not which way to act, other than the way given to them by the hand of fate. Every emotion came from spirit-wounds of a distant longing, a hyper-conscious place blaring indifference and purity. Their love was true, and as they wrapped around one another with their warm, naked bodies, the stars above swirled and mixed like nebulas; like oil in water. Like clouds that give shape to the sky, or rivers that join to find the ocean together. The connection between them was bound by devotion, and *limitless compassion*, a union made only by giving up on one's self up for the other.

As each small bite and subtle touch sent their nerves shaking, Ingrid looked deep into Ezra's eyes. The impossibly dark oceans that they were had held light after all, a reflection of the blinking universe around them. *Everything is a reflection*, Ingrid thought, as she felt Ezra's phallus gently slide between her wet thighs. With each thrust her pores tightened and sent shooting pulses of pleasure through her spine. Ezra gradually got faster and faster, until the timeless moment of their synchronized orgasms put them in a state of glowing ecstasy.

In those following minutes of slowed breathing and openness, Ezra combed Ingrid's body with his photon-charged fingertips and blanketed her sensitive skin with electronic pulses that brought her heartbeat to match his own. Ezra took the light from the stars and transferred it from his skin to Ingrid's body. She was trembling.

"What is it, Ingrid?"

"Should we not have done that?" she asked, breathing heavily, purring with pleasure like a cat.

"What does your heart tell you?"

She kissed him sincerely as an answer, and in that moment, their bestial affirmations clouded any forethought on the importance of that kiss.

While the bodies of the dead were sent home for an honorary ceremony, Ezra and Ingrid spent four long weeks on the carrier. A Navy officer joked they were being punished for living. In truth, Ingrid had declined the invitation to the ceremony and accepted Ezra's commission instead. In Ezra's case, his parent company and the Department of Defense used the long trip to bide their time and decide what to do with him. Despite their efforts to be reserved, Ezra and Ingrid held a deep admiration for one another as they found romantic tendencies hard to contain. This didn't go unnoticed. Just how taboo their relationship could become was a matter of discussion in higher departments. Ezra requested a plane home only once but caught the hint after Curtis spent two hours calling dispatch personnel trying to figure out why the pilot's mission contracts were being extended. It ultimately made little difference to Ezra, who was getting paid to meditate on a cruise with cannons.

Ezra's body continued to astound Ingrid, both in the lab during study sessions and at night when their love came unhinged. When Ezra wasn't with Ingrid, he spent much of his free time reading or training. He reconditioned his new body to become more powerful than he'd previously imagined. And with each charging routine under the sun, centuries were added to his life. Through solar saturation Ezra could levitate several inches above the flight deck, achieving something no man could without falling or machines: flight. One hour of charging meant four hours of levitation, the same amount of flight time a fighter jet burned over three thousand gallons of fuel. Ezra had implemented a regimen for Ingrid. Since they had requested access to the doctor's medical instruments and lab, they used the time to conduct an extensive study of Ezra so that they could better understand his constant evolution. By hacking into the doctor's mainframe, they had access to documentation of millions of species, as well as the latest scientific devices. What they learned over those months would eventually change their lives, and Earth, forever.

One morning in mid-December, Ezra and Ingrid stood on the hull of the ship rejoicing at the sight of the Texas coast. The ship passed through a blockade of oil rigs in its approach. Ingrid lunged half her body over the railing to spit on the towering drill.

"Fuck you, assholes!" she yelled.

"You realize you're riding on a nuclear reactor right now?" Ezra asked.

"I don't care, it's all wrong. FUCK YOU, YOU GULF-POLLUTING SHIT-RIGGERS!"

Up above them on the outside deck was the admiral's perch. Curtis and the admiral were enjoying some morning coffee and couldn't help but turn toward Ingrid's shouting over their morning radio.

"Feisty one, isn't she? So Beller was one of the best men you had under your command?" the admiral asked.

"As bohemian as he may be, Beller is one of the best operators I've seen in my forty odd years of service. Hell of a sniper. He's got eighty confirmed kills."

The admiral nodded.

"Twenty of them political figures and high-ranking foreign officers. I wish I could tell you half the missions I've entrusted him in executing. Shit, the FBI investigated me because they said I was using him for my own private campaigns. These campaigns were executed by well-informed covert operators, but time was working against us and what we were doing at the time was imperative to victory in the mid-east."

"Is the investigation ongoing?"

"No because independent contractors that also work with the CIA don't have to tell anyone shit except the operational officers, and the nature of Ezra's contract waives these allegations against me or him. It did get me temporarily suspended from my position in Joint Special Operations Command, but it was all just a misunderstanding and JSOC held nothing against me. Somebody standing tall under the columns of democracy forgot to tell the chief some details about what we were doing, and it made a stir. They made it look unofficial and reckless. But at the end of the day, what happened was my commander was being an opportunist and allowed me a range of options in terms of local resources. What started as standard operation in central Asia unraveled into a strange alliance with a foreign rebel force who ended up being far more than a bunch of sheep herders. It's all unclassified now, but at the time we had no idea the capability of those people."

The admiral nodded slowly.

"Those idiots trying to be heroes and whistle blowing about every military policy mishap don't always realize the ramifications of their actions, or sometimes, lack thereof."

The admiral laughed.

"Things aren't how they used to be. I can't even stand up without some twenty-something-year-old homeland security agent slapping his cock in my face asking why the hell I'm doing back door deals with the PMCs."

The admiral chuckled.

"You remind me of the old breed, Colonel."

"I was an Army ranger in Vietnam, 52nd Infantry. Detailed for a bit with a special forces group and was in the same company as Ezra's grandfather's father, Eugene. He was a hell of a soldier as well."

Curtis handed the admiral a small, near empty bottle of brown liquid.

"Whiskey?" he asked.

"I didn't have breakfast," the admiral admitted sheepishly.

"Admiral, this IS breakfast," he said, pouring the drink into his coffee.

"What's your plan for your time off?" the admiral asked, "Got a wife back home?"

"Shit... yeah, her name's Brandy. I'm gonna feed her to the boys for a week and call 'em in for PT when the bender ends."

"What about your boy?"

"He's only detailing with us, as you know. When he goes back to his home unit at P.A.I.N. I'm not sure what will happen. He's about to get a lot of bullshit thrown at him. He'll have to handle it on his own though. They didn't even like that we were on the same boat together."

"You two must have quite a history."

"Ezra is like a son to me. It's funny... they try to keep family from entering the same combat units in the military anymore, but the irony is that no matter who you're with, they become kin after just one deployment. And as long as that kinship between the old warriors and the younger ones stays intact, a millennia of culminating battlefield knowledge will only be refined. The art of war... it's vital to our way of life! There just needs to be a bit more transparency. All this politically correct bullshit coming from the top is really starting to piss me off because it's hindering our forces."

"This unwritten code of men you speak of... it's in our brain chemistry," the admiral agreed. "Young men will always crave war. It's in their nature to become protectors of their country or tribe to prove themselves. So long as there are men, it will be that way and no other way."

Curtis nodded. "It's in their blood. The Lord knows it's in mine."

Curtis tipped his cup to the admiral then slurped down the rest of his spiked coffee and stuck an American flag in the empty bottle and set it on the table.

"Good day Admiral. Thanks for the Joe."

"Always a pleasure, Colonel."

Hundreds of protestors rounded the port decks as the gigantic ship floated into the bay. Ezra looked down and could see soldiers in the distance pushing back radical fundamentalist Christians holding signs saying, 'God hates Mutants' and 'Keep Aliens out of America!'

"What do those signs say?" Ingrid asked, knowing Ezra's sight was keener than a falcon's.

Ezra leaned over.

"Let's just say it's not the warm welcome I was expecting. Seems the media is having a heyday with our exposure and the evangelicals are pissed about it. I bet if you hock a loogie you might be able to hit one of them."

Ingrid looked nervous, but he reassured her, "Ingrid, don't fret. You will be escorted from this ship by the most powerful organism in the known universe. You have little to worry about."

"I'm worried for you," she said.

"For me? Ha!"

"But what if they don't let you back-"

"I have a strategy for keeping us safe."

The ship came to full stop and Ingrid looked at him for the answer.

"Hiding?"

"In plain sight, lovely. In plain sight."

That morning, there were no champagne bottles to pop or red carpet to unfurl. When Ezra and Ingrid walked off the carrier, people of various ranks and agencies surrounded the crew with skeptical faces. The two were escorted toward a massive concrete building. No one clapped. Only heavy breathing and whispers could be heard save the rumbling of freighter engines in the harbor's shallow waters. A few photographers snapped shots of the couple, but their priority target was Ezra. With the slightest gesture from a security officer, Ezra and Ingrid were split up only minutes after their first steps on land. Not even the reporters got a word in.

"Ezra!" Ingrid yelled.

"Don't worry, I'll just be a few minutes," he reassured her.

Just before entering the building, the naked sun launched a ray of light into Ezra's skin and sent a shooting euphoric sensation up his spine. Ezra smiled as the officer stared grossly at Ezra's wide maroon-black eyes.

He entered the building where four security contractors escorted him down several corridors into a small room in the corner of the supply building, somewhere far away from the awkward gathering at their arrival. He was told to sit down at the desk until further notice. A quietness filled the air, punctuated by Ezra's crystalline nails rolling on the oak desk he sat at. Ezra turned the swivel chair 180 degrees to look at one of the men behind him.

"You a soldier?" Ezra asked.

"Negative."

"Were you ever?"

"I'm a Marine."

"You work for P.A.I.N.?"

"I'm not obligated to answer," the man replied.

"For how long? About two hours?"

Ezra chuckled to himself then said, "News came back that there was a Peruvian alien on board, so Carson assembled a rookie task force, right?"

"Close, but not exactly," said a voice entering the room. It was Leonard Carson, the president of P.A.I.N. Security. He was a tall bald man who after his time in the air force traded in his flight suit for a business tux. He was an egotist trying to balance a life of running a private military company, appeasing his oblivious wife and family, and pleasing his young secretary mistress.

He sat down across from Ezra who turned the chair to face him. Leonard stared at Ezra blankly for a few seconds.

"Mr. Beller. Good morning. Do you still drink coffee?"

"No coffee for me, Carson, and I still go by my alias," Ezra replied as his mood shifted in an angry direction.

"Are you Jewish, Marchosias?"

"My Christian parents gave me my first name. In Hebrew it means 'God helps'."

"So you have a Hebrew name, and your parents are Christian, and your file says your religious preference is… 'other'… whatever that means. So when it comes to your religious beliefs, you're fairly neutral I suppose. And you say your name means 'God helps?'"

"What are you getting at?" Ezra asked.

Carson became agitated and looked at Ezra with a probing stare.

"I'm trying to learn a bit more about who you are because I don't quite know *what* you are."

"You've known me for over three years."

"Or so I'd thought. The day the transmission came in about your survival story in Peru, I had every agency official with their head up my ass waiting to hear if one of my employees had an unwanted host."

"Sounds like you've got a lot to be worried about, Leonard," Ezra said smiling sarcastically.

"You bet your ass I do. You've got some fucked up mutation, almost the whole team I sent with you is dead, and there's a scandal brewing between Miss McAdam and yourself."

"That can't be the reason you're so bitchy," Ezra said.

Leonard looked at him with eyes wide, unable to process the insubordination.

"Well on top of all that, I can't afford to restock the munitions supply right now and that includes your unit,

Marchos," Carson responded with a callous tone. "Since you've been away, only an eighth of the west coast has been evacuated and it's not going so well."

"You didn't think getting tens of millions of people to move to places like North Dakota would be easy, did you?"

"We lost thirty-eight men from The Horus Battalion who were gunned down last week on an escort through Washington. The civil war is well underway, even if the media isn't calling it that. The Cascadian rebel forces are gaining strength and it's only getting worse."

"You saw this coming. We all did."

"You're right. But I didn't see *this* coming. You coming back not as a human isn't exactly something I can prepare for. I was going to have you lead the next available unit into Northern California. However, you won't be in any part of it, at least under my authority."

He handed Ezra a paper outlining a termination of contractual agreements.

"I read the reports. You don't have a pathogen, Marchosias. *You are the pathogen.* I won't have anyone as controversial as yourself working for this company," he said, standing up and pacing the windowless room.

Ezra read through the sheet and signed it with a quick flick of his wrist.

"So what now?" Ezra asked, clicking the button on his pen in and out.

Carson looked surprised, as if he'd expected Ezra to put up a fight.

"Your pay stub is attached to a departing letter from the company. It's all in this folder," he said holding up a manila envelope. "We deposited your earnings from your last four missions into your account yesterday."

Ezra looked at the pay stub. Below his travel-pay and tax deductions read the net amount he had earned: two million, four hundred eighty-nine thousand, seven hundred ninety-five dollars and sixty-six cents.

Ezra slapped the stub on the table.

"No per diem? Columbian prostitutes aren't as cheap as they used to be."

"Don't push your luck," Carson smirked.

"So I am free to go?"

"Yeah sure."

"Not yet," said a man in a dark blue suit entering the room with two security agents. He was a young man sweating bullets from the heat. His lack of training and experience was apparent to the veterans around him.

"Hey another suit! You guys having a picnic or something?" Ezra asked.

"Todd Walker, Homeland Security," he said, whipping out a shiny badge. "He's got to come do a blood test for us, as ordered by the defense council."

"Right, right. Go ahead," Leonard said as he began texting on his phone apathetically.

"I'm afraid I won't be doing that today, Mr. Walker," Ezra spoke loudly over the bustling of feet. Everything stopped. Not a breath could be heard.

"Do you know what the difference between authority and enforcement is?" Ezra asked him, smiling. "There is a fine distinction, see, between a king, and the warrior devoted to him. If the king betrays his warriors, he earns death from a hand that knows well his stature."

"Excuse me?" asked the agent.

"I'm sure you feel the need to obey orders but let us assess this unique and delicate situation. I am not a prisoner, nor have I been charged with any crime in this country or others. The legal repercussions and bad press of this day could be the least of your worries if you just start making rash decisions based on the government's, well, *failing* foreign policy."

Todd shook his head. "No, this pertains to domestic policy, which is meant to protect American citizens-"

"Property and revenue," Ezra interrupted. "Not citizens. Besides, isn't this a foreign affair? I am a legal alien, technically. So let us shift gears before I make my demands."

"Demands? That's funny. Last time I checked you were surrounded by eight armed men-"

"Walker. Let him speak," Leonard said to Todd, putting his phone back down. He knew that Ezra was not so foolish as to disobey a federal agent without sound reasoning. The agent sighed and motioned for him to go on.

"Under standard procedure, it would be necessary for you to take an unidentified organism, whose DNA is unknown, into a secured, quarantined zone, which is exactly what this 'blood test' really is, I can only assume. However, both of us know that the 'pathogen' you think I have has been disproved with a simple blood test already taken by Doctor Parsons. I'm sure you've had access to the doctor's files, so then you would know that I know that I don't need a blood test. I am more likely to cure a disease than to spread one. Therein lies the complexity of this pickle we are in. If I can cure a disease, I could hypothetically sell my blood to the right person and topple the healthcare industry overnight, achieving what those before me could not."

"Get to the point," the agent said impatiently.

"I'm talking about how the government raided the clinics of homeopathic doctors who privately cured cancer for over two decades using electro-magnetism and high frequency sound vibrations in the 90's. There's no money in someone who literally pisses cancer away is there? So the terminally ill are kept alive only to be milked like cows, pumping the pharmaceutical companies with cash and filling all your lobbyists' bank accounts. So this is where the deal gets fragile; I no longer trust that you will take me where you say you're going to take me. I could be of value to many of your clients just as I could be of value to *their enemies*. Yet I have no interest in exploiting my body for either party. That last sentence is crucial to my case, should this become a legal affair. Feel free to write it down."

One of the contractors slowly moved his hand down and wrapped his hand around his pistol grip. He flipped his safety off with a small click.

Tensions heightened as the agent said, "This isn't a hearing, Ezra, but you aren't allowed to leave without my approval."

"And herein lies my salvation: *your predicament*. My lover, Miss Ingrid McAdam, is waiting for me in the shipyard."

Todd scoffed.

"It's true. We are madly in love. And she will not leave this place without me."

"We've already detained Miss McAdam for collusion with the Chinese government," said Walker.

Ezra squinted at the man and studied him.

"No you haven't, Walker. Your interrogation training didn't go as smooth, did it? They squeezed you, didn't they?"

Mr. Walker clenched his teeth and remained silent.

Carson leaned back in his seat making eye contact with each of his contractors while making a face that said, 'Watch out'.

Ezra continued, "You both made a huge mistake by putting me in this room. It's a bit small, wouldn't you think? Now, had you put me in a hall or a conference room with guards in the corners, there wouldn't be much I could do, but-"

"Let's knock off the fuckery already. Take him with us!" Walker ordered.

One of the soldiers grabbed Ezra's arm. With the swing of his elbow, Ezra knocked the man's jaw upward. Before the others could respond fast enough Ezra was already holding the unconscious man's rifle barrel to Walker's throat, his finger pulling with the slightest pressure against the trigger. Every barrel in the room was directed at Ezra.

"Desist, Marchos! Desist!" one of the contractors yelled. Carson cut him quick with a sinister eye, stopping his man where he stood.

"What is this, a six-pound trigger pull? A bit heavy for my taste."

"Everyone just calm the fuck down for second!" Carson yelled.

The agent was sweaty and flushed as he looked away from Ezra.

"You are threatening a government officer-"

"I will skull fuck you right now, mother fucker! Look at me! Look at me!" he yelled. "I am threatening a fool. A fool who doesn't understand what he is. Look at me when I'm talking to you! Do you think I fear death? This is about control. It's about you and your administration favoring the economists and the plan they have to stifle needs of the people. You think you can boss me around? I belong to a community of men who destroy human beings. The seven of you versus me? I'm used to those kinds of odds. Do you think I will show mercy because we fly the same flag? I am the lion in this jungle. I created you. Fuck you."

Even Leonard's platinum desert eagle pistol was now aimed at the back of Ezra's head.

"Ezra! Calm the fuck down already! You're gonna give the man a heart attack," he said sternly.

Ezra then spoke in a whisper, "If you managed to take me into custody, you'd have an even larger problem. Ingrid is your leak. She has too strong of a social circle to terminate quietly. She will expose the deep state's backdoor deals to claim the watershed rights of the west if you take me into custody."

The rifles stayed directed at Ezra's face.

"You gave her classified information?" Walker asked, looking nervously at Leonard.

"Nope. She figured it out all on her own. She's an intelligent young ecologist with a knack for busting the government's balls. I only hinted to the truths of her discovery. Did you think this would stay quiet forever as our country falls into civil war?"

He didn't answer.

"So I will ask you again what I tried to earlier," Ezra went on. "Do you know what the difference between authority and enforcement is?"

The agent shook his head, scared white as Ezra grazed his neck with the gun barrel.

"You are attempting to enforce with only the *illusion* of authority. This power you think you have is merely a title, given to you by puppets that hired you to enforce their laws ratified for their interests. But everything is about to break wide open; like an infected wound pouring puss and blood. This wound will not coagulate. It will pour until permanent change has been done to our nation's naked flesh. And from its tragedy a scar tissue will form, reminding the coming generations of what evils were wrought here. You all have pushed me into a state of fight or flight as any cornered creature would feel. I don't want to fight. I want to reason with you and talk this out. But if I have to, I will kill every person in this fucking room before one of these amateurs even thinks about pulling a trigger. I am simply more powerful. *I am above you.* My physical capabilities are critical to you understanding what my mind is capable of. I *enforce* justice and adjust its principles to *what I need* from you. That, Mr. Walker, is true authority. And I have it. I control a body which, depending on my motive, could become dominant over all mankind. Could you imagine if I wanted my race to *flourish*? The least you can do is let me live in peace."

"What do you suggest?" asked Leonard, getting impatient and anxious himself.

"A contract between you and me, Leonard."

"Mr. Beller this is-" the agent began.

"Shut your fucking mouth!" Ezra yelled, "I'm talking to Carson. Here are the terms."

Everyone stood still. The fluorescent lights flickered above them, making Ezra blink and flash a cardinal radiant shimmer over his eyes.

"Calm down Ezra, please just calm down. No need to make this messy," Carson said.

Ezra continued, "I'm going to pay P.A.I.N. Security the entirety of my pension fund in exchange for six months of security."

"Security from?"

"Anyone and everyone. The U.S. government primarily, especially this talking suit here, and the rest of your men who don't work for me now. You can spy on me, you can track me, and you can make sure I'm not affiliating with local rebels. Just give me six months to prove myself a decent citizen. Think of it as a four-million-dollar green card with benefits."

"We are contracted through the government," Leonard began.

"This isn't another one of your shitty bargains, Carson, this is your only option. I want the 3rd platoon from the Hood Battalion. They will be loyal to me. And I want them to be supplied with two Comanche attack helicopters and company grade recon drones. None of that second-grade bullshit."

"A Comanche isn't the best extraction ship, I might need those," Leonard whined greedily.

"No, they're for assault," Ezra said as he stared into Agent Walker's eyes.

The agent, while looking from Leonard, to Ezra, then back at Leonard, said to him, "You aren't thinking... you can't do this!"

"I know I can't. And at the same time – I am. He's got a point, Walker. Don't take it personally, but I wouldn't trust you either. I will notify the department that they will have twenty-five less contractors on duty once he claims his choice of residence."

Leonard was the first to lower his weapon. The agent looked horrified and astounded. He breathed anxiously and stuttered, "We can't have another scandal. This violates so many laws.... We can't just..."

"We're at war, Walker!" Leonard yelled. "He doesn't want to be a part of the exodus conflicts any more than anyone else does. He's willing to give us four million dollars and all we have to do is sit back and let him live a decent life. I'm not too keen on creating a political shit storm where we both lose our fucking jobs! *We* must take this deal; however ridiculous it sounds. If we don't, things will get ugly in the press and we'll lose more than money."

"What about his... condition?" asked Walker.

"Well there isn't a full report on his mutation yet, and honestly, I don't care to know it. I can see with my own eyes that he is a mutated... thing. I can see that he is not our kind. This was one of the most dangerous men on the planet *before* his mutation. I wouldn't cross him now. Let's be reasonable, Walker. We can quiet this down. We can let him go. Give him this time to prove himself as a citizen. It's not ideal, but we live in a strange time when decisions like this must be made for the better of many peoples. Stand down men."

The agent motioned for the agents and contractors to lower their weapons. Everyone panted slightly from the excitement as Ezra sat back down.

"You'll have your boys Ezra," Leonard said.

Ezra threw the weapon on the table with a clack.

"Shit!" The agent whispered in disbelief, his hands resting on his hips as he bit his bottom lip.

"Where do you want them?" Carson asked, dipping his head slightly and veering his sight from Ezra's impenetrable stare.

"Stage them at the Georgia Base. And if they're not already on rotation, introduce them to your new close-quarter combat facilities. You don't want that bunch getting restless."

"How did it go?" Ingrid asked anxiously as Ezra walked into the bustling main lobby of the shipping center. Photographers and journalists were sprawled out among the sailors, but they started moving in when they spotted Ezra.

"It went great! The homeland security guy was actually quite cooperative," Ezra said calmly. He smiled and kissed her on her forehead. "Now, my darling, I could really use some fresh air. Shall we?"

"Where are we going first?" she asked.

"Not yet," he answered. "No one here needs to know."

They said their goodbyes and thank yous to the rest of the biology team members and contractors. One of the scientists gave Ezra a business card and strongly recommended contacting him if Ezra was interested in learning more about himself.

"I appreciate the offer, but the only person I'm willing to work with right now is Miss McAdam."

"No problem. I understand. Just one thing, is there any way I could possibly get an autograph?"

"Well yeah... sure," Ezra responded hesitantly. He'd never been asked that before.

As the doctor reached for a pen, Ezra took his thumb and pressed it gently against the man's folder. Light smoke rose from the paper as he charred his fingerprint onto the corner.

The doctor stood, flabbergasted.

"How the hell?" he said as Ingrid and Ezra held hands and started walking toward the exit doors.

"Good luck Ezra!" he yelled.

As they walked outside, protesters merged and attempted to block their way where the fence met the gated entrance.

"You two!" Ezra yelled at two security guards standing behind him by the buildings entrance doors. "Yeah, you! Will you escort us out of this shit show?"

"Under whose orders?" one of them asked.

"I'm not ordering you, I'm asking you, as a favor. All those people aren't too pleased at my return. Just walk us to my car then you can go back to being a statue."

They communicated to their superiors via radio and got approval for Ezra's escort. As the four of them walked up to the gates, people started rallying and screaming at them.

"You should have stayed where you were, you God forsaken creature!"

"God will smite you for your blasphemy!"

"You! Lady! Stay away from that vile thing!"

"Go back to Mexico where you belong!"

The last comment made Ezra laugh, which only infuriated the crowd more. Children scowled at Ezra and threw rotten vegetables, which Ezra caught and started eating just to spite them.

"Back away!" one of the soldiers yelled as a few people started closing in. A big guy in a greasy truck cap ran up and spit on Ezra before the soldiers could push him back into the crowd.

"There's a lot of pissed off folks here and this is turning into a hot situation," one of the soldiers told Ezra.

"Our definitions of 'hot situation' are a bit different," Ezra said, taking out a handkerchief and wiping the tobacco chew from his sleeve.

"Well Mr. Beller I'm just looking out for your best interests, as you asked. Let's get you to your car before this becomes a riot."

They ran inside a separate guarded compound from the parking lot. Finally out of the mess, the soldiers waved them goodbye and Ingrid and Ezra got into Ezra's luxury sedan.

"This is nice," Ingrid said, as the orange hologram dashboard lit up and automatic tinting windows dimmed.

"Saying the private military industry pays well these days is an understatement. But aside from my mode of transportation, I've been quite frugal and have a good portion saved up."

"Whom do you bank through?"

"Ha! You think I would put my money in a bank where anyone can take it?"

"You're weird," she said.

"No, just cautious," Ezra replied. He turned the ignition then took an old bottle he had used for a tobacco spitter and tossed it out the window.

"What the hell?" Ingrid snapped.

Ezra smiled, "This world is gonna kill itself long before that plastic bottle does."

She glared at him. Ezra reluctantly opened the door and put the bottle in the backseat to appease her.

"The Earth thanks you for your graciousness! Now… where to?" she asked excitedly.

"Austin."

"Why Austin?"

"Because that is where *our* army lies: the freaks, the artists, and nomads. The endangered liberal class is our ally. They will support us in our odd union, and we need that kind of cultural reinforcement against the bigotry coming our way."

"So that's what you meant by hiding in plain sight? Are we going to be celebrities?"

"Yes, unfortunately. Being open, honest, and civil in front of millions is our greatest chance of not being hunted down by those rat bastards in the government. But that doesn't mean we can't reap the benefits of the lifestyle for a minute," Ezra said smiling.

They stared hard into each other's eyes until Ezra roared the car's engine into gear and sped away from the docks, past the city, and off into the open desert air where their eyes could peer at the majestically aligned horizon. So pure and open was that break from land to sky, that the image of the hot road giving way to mirage spoke as a mirror juxtaposing their cleansed and freed minds. Fresh warm air poured in and out of their hair as the couple relaxed and welcomed the rising sun's rays. No more words were spoken as they raced toward the overpopulated metropolis of the New City of Angels; a city of ten million ravenous faces.

CHAPTER 6
MOTHER'S AMBASSADORS

Austin looked like Los Angeles in the late 20th Century, except dirtier and wilder. With its buzzing worker bees, helicopter drones, and culture queen, there was little that separated the town from imminent disaster other than its ability to perpetuate a misplaced sense of civil reform. Vagabonds were everywhere, but not necessarily the unkempt kind. Hipsters, rockers, ravers, junkies, skaters, starving artists, wannabe models, and dancers scoured the street level of the city while the skyscrapers held pencil-gnawing investors who fought sleeplessly to keep a drowning entertainment market afloat.

Ezra saw right through the mayor's attempt at bringing the epicenter of the entertainment business to Austin. Just as L.A. crumbled in 2020 by sucking half the country's water into its desert sinkhole and receding from the Union, Austin would follow suit, not by exploiting natural resources—though it did— but by caving in on itself from a staggering growth rate without enough jobs or occupancies to offer such an incredible influx of people.

The charade was working in the meantime, and Ezra's plan was to take total advantage of his condition by turning science into spectacle. World Records. Reality shows. Action Movies. Celebrity parties. Red carpet glamour. He would embrace these glorifications of pop culture and use his fame as a platform for change.

Poof!

Gold and red silken sheets wrapped Ingrid's unfolding body as she fell back first onto the king size bed of Ezra's penthouse suite. She kicked off her shoes and nestled her face into the soft lavender smelling pillows.

"I could get used to this," she said in a relaxed tone.

"Said every banker on Park Avenue," Ezra joked as he hung up his jacket.

"Can't a woman feel pampered for once?"

"Of course Ingrid, that's part of the reason why we're here," he answered, peering through the curtains twelve stories up in their extravagant hotel. In the corner of the room sat a record player. Ezra sat down next to it and carefully picked out a vinyl from the collection.

"They still make those things?" Ingrid asked, looking over at him with an inquisitive expression.

He took the black music disk from its worn paper sheath and gently set it on the player. The arm of the player reached over and dropped the needle, picking up small particles of dust and down feathers as it licked the patterned surface, waiting for music to replace the crackling white noise. A heart melting piano melody shimmered as Ezra dimmed the lights and brought a bottle of wine and two glasses to the bed.

Ingrid laughed then asked, "What is this?"

A guitar entered the ensemble as Ezra turned up the volume on the music player.

"This is 'Polka Dots and Moonbeams' by Wes Montgomery. I believe the song was written earlier than this rendition, but Wes was always one of my favorite jazz guitarists. I guess I'm just a sucker for this '40's and '50s stuff-"

"No, I mean, what is this? What is this room? How did you get this place?"

"Oh, well I've stayed here before. They know me. I can afford to stay here as long as we need to, which should only be a few weeks tops. After we gather ourselves for a couple days, I'm going to ask that you write up a list."

"A list for what?"

"Business stuff. We'll discuss that later. I don't want to be your boss right now. I want to be your lover."

She laughed and kissed him. He kissed her. The trickle of a harmonic trill on the guitar matched Ezra's touches as he cusped Ingrid's face with his hand. They let the music pull one another into a romantic wine induced evening of dancing, of love making, of story-telling and soft lies, of charming accusations and lip biting and ordering needless room service at ridiculous hours, of laughing endlessly, and drunkenly tangoing down the halls of the hotel as they were shushed by angry hotel guests. It was an evening filled with everything lovers crave and loners long for as the carpet became their playground, a sea of soft hands grazing their melting bodies.

The next morning, Ingrid awoke to an alarm at 10:00 AM. Ezra was up and making coffee for her when she grasped her alcohol infected head with sweaty palms. She rubbed her eyes and threw her beeping phone across the room.

"You're a lightweight," Ezra said, turning off the alarm and ripping open the curtains before giving her some coffee.

"Go to hell! I've been sober on a battleship for four weeks!" she said, shielding her eyes from the blinding white light. "Sorry I can't sift booze through my body with perfect filtration like you."

"Yeah I mostly just peed it out," Ezra admitted whimsically, as he looked at the three bottles of wine they had managed to drain.

"My point exactly," Ingrid complained while trying to fix her wild hair and smeared mascara.

"I'm running some errands today. Would you be a dear and watch the fort while I'm gone?"

"Where are you going?"

"Shopping," Ezra said as he put on a black suit jacket and loosened his shirt collar. "We'll be on television on Friday. Do you have anything to wear for that?"

Ingrid shook her head slowly.

"I'll put that on the list."

"What else is on your list?" Ingrid asked.

"A few things from the department store," Ezra said. He went on, "If you would please keep the door locked and if you haven't done it already, remove the battery from your phone and throw it away. Use the one I've set on the table. It's virtually untraceable and your calls will be private, at least for now."

"Ezra. Are we really safe? Be honest with me."

"Fairly, but there are precautions we must both take. It's not just the NSA we have to watch out for."

"Who else then?"

"I don't know. Radical religious cults who believe I'm the Anti-Christ. Vengeful Shia that managed to slip through our borders. Random crazies. The cartels. The best thing we can do is go by a specific order of security operations, which I'll brief you on later today. But honestly I think we'll be just fine."

"We won't be in the city too long, will we?" Ingrid said with a frightened look on her face.

"Just long enough to prove a point."

"And what point are we trying to prove?"

"That I am not a threat, but a messenger of truth," Ezra answered.

"What truth?"

"The only truth that matters; that the human race will not last if their destructive habits continue. That if their species is to survive, it must survive by its *coexistence* with all of Mother Nature's creatures, including themselves."

Ingrid then smiled and said, "I'm curious where this monumental transformation came from? Who influenced you to take on such a crusade?"

"Her messenger," Ezra replied.

"Her messenger?" Ingrid asked.

"You," he answered softly as he slipped out the door.

Ingrid thought for a moment about what he might have meant but was interrupted by her thumping migraine once again. She fell back into bed, into a pained sleep, and dreamt deeply. In the dream, she witnessed inside of her a seed growing. The seed broke open and sprouted a little boy. The little boy grew and grew and suddenly-

Whoosh!

Ingrid woke up with a sudden lurch.

"Oh shit! I'm pregnant!"

"I say we name him... Michael," Ezra proclaimed confidently at dinner later that evening. They sat at a table in the middle of the hotel's restaurant. Jazz musicians dipped and danced to a fast tempo swing in the background while Ingrid's face went red with anger.

"That's your response? I tell you I'm pregnant and you give me an idea for a fucking name?"

"Now we have more subjects to study!" Ezra said smiling.

"This isn't funny, Ezra!" Ingrid said in a loud whisper. She grabbed her fork and stuck it in front of his face. "Don't fuck with me right now!"

"I thought you would be happy! I am! Look, Ingrid. I know that you want children, and I know that you want a child with me. We talked about this-"

"We talked about this, yes, briefly, stupidly. Christ! We've only been together a month and it's a lot different than actually doing it than talking about it! I don't know if I'm ready to have a child. Even after our studies on the ship we still don't even know how safe copulation is between us. You're not a human remember? This is practically bestiality."

"Bestiality? I mean... really?" Ezra said, as he reached for his Scotch glass. "I feel like this is a good thing."

"But you don't suffer the consequences!" she said louder.

People started noticing the uproar of their conversation. Ezra tried to calm Ingrid, but she became angrier.

"Perhaps we aren't meant to time something like this according to our own will. It must be nature's will-"

"Nature's will?! I AM nature's will! The child is growing inside ME!" Ingrid yelled as she got up. She walked out crying, leaving Ezra with dozens of curious eyes staring at him from the surrounding tables.

"We're having a child. Exciting!" Ezra said, smiling awkwardly. No one shared his sense of humor. He looked back at his food and felt slightly regretful at how he'd come off. And yet he was confident with his and her subconscious decision to bring a new life into their lives. Maybe they had moved too fast, but they were falling for each other, and the world doesn't wait up for anyone, especially lovers. The sporadic tendencies of being as recklessly in love as Ezra and Ingrid were only preserved their unwavering commitment. For through the flame and plunder, their dire circumstance had fused their fates, and this flame would not only remain lit but spread. Ezra was the spark, but Ingrid was the forest.

Later that night, Ezra came into the room and found Ingrid asleep on the bed. He set a red envelope and a gladiolus flower next to her shoulder before sitting at the desk and writing some notes for her to look at in the morning. On the paper, he wrote down five locations she'd like to move to, and he asked her to circle one. Below that, he wrote a list of things she'd want to bring, as well as the things she'd have to leave behind. It was all overwhelming for Ingrid, Ezra had realized, especially after just finding out that she was pregnant, but that's why he wanted the time in Austin for them to relax and live easily before making the move. Ezra's only concerns about her changes physically came about when they had had unprotected sex, and that by ejaculating inside of her, she may or may not turn into whatever he was. But she didn't. The baby could therefore be either half human and half mutant, or full mutant, or something different all together. Either way, he relished the idea of building a family, of finally settling down and doing what Sergio had advised him to do. Ezra and Ingrid were the most important test subjects in the history of genetics. But since only Ingrid did the studying, she and Ezra knew more than anyone else about the potential predatory effects involved with his mutating condition. They realized that much of the results they'd discovered could never be spoken of so that no one else would know the *full truth* behind what made Ezra's DNA possible.

Ezra and Ingrid stood behind a large red curtain. In front of them, the Damien Mathers Talk Show audience roared into applause. They watched through slits in the curtain and waited patiently as the fusion swing band kicked into a blast of horns and drums.

Ezra had been pampered in the dressing room. The hairdresser gave him a smooth shave, then patted his face and shoulders with fine cologne and styled his hair, which gleamed with a natural sheen as the hairs had evolved into extensions of his spine; sensory retina for his smartest senses. His black Italian suit and black eel skin designer shoes felt odd to slip into, as he was used to being in either heavy combat gear, civilian kick-back clothes, or hot mock-burkas that smelled like wet dog and firecrackers. He'd occasionally worn suits at embassy meetings but that was before the horrors of the oil wars forced everyone to wear pants with built-in tourniquets.

Ezra touched his chest to double check the additions he made to the suit. He had hidden razors, lock picking utensils, and other instruments of tradecraft in his pant cuffs, waistband, and shirt collar and he had slipped a carbon fiber blade neatly under his sleeve by his wrist, ready to wield in a moment. He'd put a tracking device in his shoe connected to Ingrid's phone, and likewise hid one in hers. And he had both hundred and thousand-dollar bills in his breast pocket; merely tip money for the after party. Everything in his life at that moment was *near perfect*, but he wasn't going to let his guard down.

Against Ingrid's wishes, Ezra put brown contacts in his eyes to make himself look a bit more human. Ingrid had grown out of just thinking his eyes were interesting. She believed they were the most unique and beautiful aspect about his altered self; his cosmic identity and quintessential trait to his metamorphosis. Changing them was like putting on a clown costume then stepping into the spotlight.

After mentioning the tragedy and extending prayers to families who had lost those in the crash, Damien turned to the corner of the room and waved them in.

"Ladies and gentlemen, please welcome the devoted young couple, U.S. Army Veteran Ezra Beller and micro-biologist Ingrid McAdam!"

They walked in and everyone was on their feet. The crowd went crazy for them, clapping, whistling, and even some young girls in the back were yelling, 'We love you!' to Ezra. Luckily for him Ingrid was not the jealous type, and in any case, that kind of attention was all very good exposure for Ezra. Austin loved them just as Ezra had predicted.

Ezra shook hands with Damien. He was a short, stubby, wide-faced Australian with a huge smile.

"How are you two?! Great to have you on the show! My God you look fantastic Ingrid. How were you able to wash out the vegetable slush that rained on you Tuesday?"

"Well it wasn't easy, but luckily Ezra shielded most of the harder ones from me. He ate some of them," she said before laughing. The crowd laughed with her.

Ingrid looked dazzling. She wore a shiny two toned black and purple dress with broken mirror mosaic heels and large silver ouroboros serpent bracelets. Peacock feather earrings hung from her lobes. That was Ezra's favorite part of her outfit, because he knew that she liked the name 'Pavonis', the name he'd given her on their way out of the Peruvian cave. Ingrid used it as a catalyst to create a new image for herself. The new version of Ingrid, the strong and passionate survivalist and wolfwoman was the human Ezra would come to love.

"It's true. We haven't had to grocery shop yet because I kept all the good stuff," Ezra joked.

"Potato and carrot stew, yes my favorite," Damien laughed.

After the crowd quieted, the couple took their seats and Damien started the interview.

"So Ezra, you were in the United States military for many years and you also worked for a private security company, which you've just recently departed. I'm just curious - what made you finally want to leave that line of work?"

"I felt my time to leave was near. There are others being trained to do my job as we speak. It was a fulfilling line of service but I'm glad to be retired."

"Well thank you for your service," he said, the crowd cheering and hollering.

"I love this country very much, which is why it hurts me to see so many of us divided and engaged in conflict."

"Yes it's a very disturbing time indeed. So much going on! So Ezra, Ingrid... let's talk about this mission. What an incredible, horrific, life changing, and daunting experience you both had. Many crew members were killed, which could have been all of them if it hadn't been for your bravery that led Ingrid and yourself to safety."

The audience clapped loudly, though Ezra felt no commendation was in order.

"Ingrid did just as much to keep both of us sane and alive, but truly the whole mission was a large failure and I am very distraught at the thought of the crew members we lost."

"Surely yes, it is tragic. But now that you're here Ezra, are you able to tell us what it's like in a place wholly unexplored by modern humans?"

The audience leaned in closely, silently. Damien insinuated the specifics of Ezra's condition, but that was understandable. Everyone wanted to know what his deal was.

"The jungle is a place of constant change, a place of constant death and rebirth. Life there is diverse. It has systems, as we do. It has colonies and means of transportation, as we do, but all on a very small scale of microorganisms bustling about. Though tropical jungles throughout the world share these characteristics, there were strange creatures Ingrid concluded had never been recorded. The spores that attacked Ingrid's respiratory systems and mine during the nightfall following the incident were part of an undocumented species of fungus. The spores were relentless, dangerous, and would stop at nothing to extract all the necessary nutrients to decompose our still living bodies. Luckily, I devoured a more powerful, but possibly less common species during the illness. This substance, whatever it was, is what eradicated those invasive chemicals in me and brought me back to a state of awareness that allowed us to be rescued. Ingrid has a theory that it is both of the species – the fungus and the lichen – that causes a unique version of symbiosis insinuating my constantly evolving state, and that the two are reconstructing my DNA with a rare dynamic of genetic entwinement never seen by scientists before."

Damien was genuinely captivated. "Far out, man."

The audience laughed.

"So how did you know which plant was safe and which wasn't? What did it look like?" he asked.

"The species that poisoned us was a spore cloud that could actually navigate through the air and attack willingly. Each poisonous spore glowed in the dark and kept close by while we slept. The substance I ingested, however, was a bioluminescent golden lichen, with quite possibly a myriad of life forms living within it. It was pretty disgusting."

Damien laughed then asked, "So you didn't know what you were eating? You just... went for it?!"

"Yeah, I mean, I had run out of options. I felt it would hopefully at least suck the toxins out of my body. This goddess of the universe's creation next to me was there too. And I could not let Ingrid die like that. Not there. Not after all she had been through that day. I had to try something."

The crowd gave a big 'Ahhhhh,' and Ezra smiled.

"That is some gamble my friend! And you stopped feeling sick, just like that?"

"No, I did not. In a fit of rage I ate the strange lichen and before I felt better, I felt nothing. I literally felt what it was like to be a part of everything in the universe that doesn't feel. Once you know what that is like, it's hard to describe anything else you see or hear as something less than completely extraordinary. My body is changed from this. The substance I ate has made me something other than human."

"You're not human?" he asked in disbelief.

"No, I am not. I know that I am not because I remember what it is like to be human, and this is far better. But if you'd like to get technical, Ingrid has done some remarkable research, and she's found that I do not have enough characteristics to be classified as a human. My species name is Homo Sarara and I am a Sararan, named after the extinct black bird of the Amazon."

Ingrid took over, "See Damian, when a human's first cells are being shaped in the womb, they inherit every mutation from their parents, plus over two hundred new mutations develop from the model of each parent. There is no escaping that. Everyone is therefore a mutant. Some just have some very interesting features to show the rarer variations in our genetic landscape. Now imagine this is happening to Ezra every few hours. If he were to step into the sunlight for even just a few moments these mutations would align to the sophistication of a series of 'organizer' cells, which inhibits some radical changes. Based on the tests we've done, he has a unique set of HOX genes in his vertebrae, which hosts these organizers. They direct cells on where to build what and why. This is why his wounds can heal in just hours. I tested him on a treadmill to see how long he could run without stopping. He quit at seven hundred miles because he got bored. If you could see his eye color, you'd notice his unique irises. He can detect polarized light and UV rays. He can also focus on objects over vast distances and in almost pure darkness."

Ezra dropped his head for a moment and one by one, took out each of his contacts. Upon lifting his head, the crowd gasped.

"What kind of drugs did the hairdresser give you? I want some!" Damien said.

The crowd laughed and Ingrid smiled, "You see, his eyes appear to be large pupils, but they are actually irises with deep purple retina rods. This is all scientific fact, as he is the living, breathing proof of evolution in motion."

Ezra nodded. "It's an intense moment in the history of mankind. I am a Sararan; the next stage of intelligent life on planet Earth."

The crowd applauded and stood, some whistling. When they finally calmed Damien continued.

"I'm glad our show is your chosen place to expose yourself, Ezra! You're not at some university or the Smithsonian Museum. It's all right here!"

The crowd laughed and he lowered his voice.

"What were your first thoughts about Ezra. Did you have any idea that you would be so close to this person?" Damien asked.

"Well I thought he was a real tool at first," she said, laughing. "We got off on the wrong foot, but things changed after the crash. I managed to fall on a soft bed of moss, and when I found him, way up in those mountains, something changed. We were in a survival situation. The illness that came over me that night was terrible and full of indescribable pain, and I truly love this man with all my heart for what he did and who he is."

Another mushy crowd sound ensued, which was soon halted by Damien's more controversial questions.

"Ezra, not to darken the mood too much, but are you aware that some religious institutions would like to see you dead or extradited to another country, just for being a mutant?"

"Yes I am."

"Did you know that a large portion of the Christian and Muslim communities thinks you are actually the Anti-Christ or Anti-Messiah? How do you respond to that, or how will you respond to that?"

After a short moment of silence, Ezra responded, "The soul cannot be defined, for it is the element of our universe which defies definition. Soul is everything unseen that is apportioned to the material universe in ways we don't understand, flowing through the empty canals between the electrons and nuclei of our bodies' atomic collective. Religion came into existence long ago so humans could solve the mystery of the *sole soul creator* and to heed God's word that it should provide them heaven's ascent. But now religion exists for money and control for super elites and it's become an epidemic of ignorance around the world. Since no one owns the definition of God, people fight over his teachings, his path, his faith, for God can be described with only so many pseudonyms. God transcends language. Yet, since we rational folk know that all the atoms in our bodies were first formed in the hearts of stars over millions of years before gusting on solar winds to slowly converge and make an anatomically unmitigated human being, in that sense all living things are divine creatures. When someone asks if I believe in God, I look in a mirror and I say yes."

"That's quite an egotistical way of thinking isn't it?"

"On the contrary, I believe the ego is shattered when one considers every act as an explicit movement of divine will. Suddenly integrity matters. Suddenly you feel the need to give and suffer with. That is what being compassionate means."

"So people are Gods? Then why do people rape and murder every day? Every few minutes!?"

"There is an aspect that has pushed mankind toward greatness, but they are inherently wrathful and confused as a result. The philosopher Friedrich Nietzsche described man as 'the sick animal'. I would interpret this not as a paradox, but a threshold to achieve, that humans are conscious of their intangible torment of longing for an answer, and yet they refuse to change their mind, but I think they're evolving beyond that now. Most humans are destined to be a contradiction from birth; fighting their way through life and hiding from the reality that they are just a complex form of bacteria trying to survive inside a series of rickety steel cages they've built for themselves, on top of the remnants of a poisoned and pained world. The concept of duality has never been more contrasted, but if people are expecting this to stage some kind of 'second coming' it won't happen. To all those religious institutions threatening me: God does not want us all to work in factories. God does not want us to congregate in massive cathedrals while the poor suffer, or blindly kill in the name of their faith. You've led yourself astray from the true message of the prophets. I'm not going to deny my stance in the conflicts we face as a nation and as global citizens. I've fought several wars and though I've helped liberate citizens of warring nations, those nations would not have been in those situations to begin with if religion hadn't perpetuated the negative relations that have existed for so long. We are destroying our planet, ourselves, and mocking history's lessons on a day to day basis."

Damien nodded. Ezra went on.

"On our journey back from Peru, Ingrid used instruments that transmitted electromagnetic waves from the sun and the moon into audio files. I listened to these frequencies for six months. Their music tells a simple story. A story of sorrow. A story of how alone we are. We are merely here as observers to view the rare work of our cosmos brought to life. Our reuniting with the divine is irrelevant to our lives on Earth so long as we continue to pull up the soil for metropolitan scabs that pulse with systemic violence and pollution. But apocalyptic fears are subjective. The war refugee already lives in a post-apocalyptic world. *Death* is when the holy union repairs itself, so why should we fear going into it communally? It's not a practical obsession. The anxieties of the modern world are caused by this collective belief that we must *master our domain*. This comes from many viewpoints but mostly the stricter versions of theology. Being in accordance with your own nature, however, will put you in accordance with God."

Ezra looked into Ingrid's eyes and she smiled. The room fell silent.

She held his hand and continued where he left off. "We're the children of stars cast down to this paradise, Earth: angry, confused, and in love with something we can't see. What Ezra and I are focusing on is how to reconnect with our roots in nature and ultimately our celestial lineage so we can better understand his mutation and therefore humans too. Scientific research and practice will lead us to the proper conclusions. Now when we speak of these subjects, I know that the media will try to manipulate a simple statement this into an elaborate story about how we are involved in the occult or witchcraft and it's just preposterous. People get frightened when they don't understand something, and I don't think it's extreme to say that Ezra's face does look a bit demonic to someone who has been raised in an orthodox setting. I understand if this is all very sudden for the world to grasp, but our themes are not new, they are mythical and ancient. The timing is perfect, however, for there is a rebirthing of epic proportions approaching. Ezra's story, to me, is the beginning of a new mythology that will teach the world *about the world* for the next two thousand years. By applying modern scientific research, I believe there is a lot to learn from all of this. This man, who is not a man, sitting beside me may frighten you; but he is not some mutated beast. He is the sweetest being I've ever known, and I love him. Imagine the possibilities if we just learned to understand his condition."

She kissed Ezra's hand. Damien nodded quickly, trying to get another question in before the commercial.

"Ezra, Hezbollah has issued threats of terror if you are not detained by authorities. Is there a message you would like to address to them, in response to these accusations?"

Ezra took a deep breath. The camera guy signaled that he had one minute.

"I've already been threatened by Hezbollah before. Their claims do not frighten me. What frightens and angers me is the future of the unstable middle east after so much blood has already been spilled to revive it. The warring religious sects originating in the holy lands have been killing one another with every kind of violence imaginable for thousands of years, and the Western push to bring these turbulent regions up to the modern pace has failed for over forty years. I have a deep concern for the innocent civilians in these wars just trying to live normal lives. Many of these families are torn to pieces from all sides. They're threatened by insurgents and used as human shields sometimes. Then if they escape the violence they have nowhere to go, because no one in Europe or America wants refugees anymore, and you could see perhaps how resentment can build. As I'm sure many of you all know, in many Muslim countries, children, especially girls, are unable to receive proper education if not already abused and unlawfully condemned. And nearly all of them are denied basic medical needs. I would give my body up, if it meant just *one day* of peace and understanding. Utter peace. Not a momentary space for political agendas to be redetermined, or a gap in border security so munitions can be trafficked with impunity. I truly desire peace in the hearts of these victims. Peace in the heart of silence."

The crowd neither clapped nor moaned. In Ezra's last words, a calm spread through the audience and in the studio. *Peace in the heart of silence.* Everyone who watched Ezra on the television that night felt touched, whether they'd ever admit to it or not.

After a moment, an explosion of cheers erupted as Austin's crowd rose in a standing ovation. Ezra was starting a revolution. But just as he'd learned in the service, every great revolution has a counter-revolution.

The cork of a champagne bottle popped up into the sky, and thus began an evening of celebration and gilded extravagance. Damien, his band, his dancers, and a wide variety of other celebrities and guests attended an after party held on the roof of Ezra and Ingrid's hotel. When the newly famous couple walked up onto the sky bar, they were blown away at the amount of support they'd gained.

The sound of applause and whistling came first as a warped hurrah before blaring into a complete roar as the couple walked out of the door and onto the roof. They blinked to see through the camera flashes. People were shaking their hands and congratulating them, and the body-modification addicts smiled with their swine lips, curving only at the corners of their mouth where dimple implants pinned their cheekbones like a marionette awaiting its master's strings. The director of the show excitedly gave Ezra his thanks and welcomed him to their city.

"Are you interested in making a film, Ezra? We could reinvigorate the theater, you and I."

"As long as I get to do my own stunts."

"I'd prefer it, good sir."

Ezra thanked him and made plans to speak again, then walked up to one of the bouncers.

"This is far more guests than I had expected."

"Yes Mr. Beller, but they all meet the criteria you gave the hotel. Everyone has been thoroughly screened."

Ezra spoke up so the bouncer could hear him clearly,

"That's all good but let your manager know that I'm not taking any chances. I've got my own security on its way, so get two of your guys up here to keep the helipad clear when they arrive."

The bouncer nodded and got to work on Ezra's orders.

"There are just some things you can't give up, can you?" Ingrid asked, smiling.

"And I am your latest and greatest lab subject, so I'd say we're both a way from retiring," he said, smirking back at her. Ezra posed for the camera one last time before telling off the press.

"Okay, no more pictures tonight."

One cameraman kept shooting, shot after shot without stopping. Ezra walked up to him, took his camera, and threw it off the edge of the building.

"That was a five-thousand-dollar lens!" the man screamed.

"Is that how much your life is worth to you?"

The photographer winced and walked quickly to the stairs.

Ezra walked on, having intimidated the rest of the guests with his rash antics and sending other journalists home, thankful that they'd listened to what he had said when he'd said it.

"Couldn't you just snap your fingers and shut their cameras off? Did we not discover you can manipulate electro-magnetic fields after our last tests?" Ingrid asked.

"What kind of host would I be to deny them their dignity before they had a chance to show it? The fellow who chose his vocation over his etiquette was put in his place. His right to be here had already won him the satisfaction of a publishable story, but he kept on like a parasite. He's just that. A leech. My mind no longer sees the difference between parasites and certain humans."

"Did that thought change happen before or after your mutation?"

"Before."

"Ugh I wish I could have a drink or a cigarrete," Ingrid said as she held her stomach. They sat at the bar and Ezra held her hand in his.

"You're nervous?" he asked.

"A little," she admitted, looking around at the guests socializing.

"Ingrid, I'm sorry about the other night. I was out of line. I should have been more sensitive. I was just happy for us, and to be honest, I already knew."

"I realize that now. But how did you know the gender?"

"I have magical powers," Ezra said while fanning his fingers in front of her face. Ingrid giggled.

"Here take this," he said as he handed her a small silver case. She went to open it, but he held her hand to stop her.

"Don't make a habit of this, but a little is fine. Go near the helicopter pad where less people will see you. It's mostly CBD."

"You'd like me to be discreet?"

"Yes, I would actually," he said.

"Tell that to your brother," Ingrid said as she rolled her eyes and walked away with the case of edibles; a concoction of chocolate, cannabis oil and other herbs made to combat stress.

On the other side of the sky bar, a loud, boisterous young Marine was drinking shots and yelling into the ears of two blonde models. Ezra hastily walked over to them.

116

"So do you two go both ways, or are you just into dudes?" Will Beller asked.

"Ugh! No!" one of the busty women answered.

"I mean... I've done some things," the other admitted.

"Nice! See! There is potential here. I'll tell you what, if you want to come by later, my room number is 429," he said as the women walked away and laughed. Ezra approached his little brother.

"Well hello Mr. Smooth."

"He-Hey brother! Good to see you! It's been far too long!"

They hugged roughly for a moment before Ezra asked him, "Did you get discharged?"

"No! What are you, crazy? I'm on leave. Just finished pilot training! Aren't you stoked for me?"

"Will, you have blow on your face and God, you reek like a sailor."

"Hey E-Z, I'm just glad to see you, ya know? Had to celebrate for my big brother's gallant return!"

"Yeah, well if any word of this got to your commanding officer you would be out. You'd better get your shit together."

Will suddenly looked embarrassed in front of his big brother as he wiped his nose on his sleeve.

"I get it. I've been there. Just remember, right now you're reveling in your off time while the enemy is hardening. He hardens because he must. He's not getting a paycheck. He doesn't get any leave. Your enemy lives only to destroy you."

"You're right, Ezra. I don't know what's wrong with me. I just... I wanted to celebrate a bit you know? Four years of school. Studying during the week and getting drunk with friends on weekends until we puked. All the while you were fighting ISIS and the Iranian regimes in the oil wars. Then two years of

117

training and helicopter pilot school right after that. I just wanted to get college life out of my system one last time before being an on-duty Marine. One last send off, ya know?"

Ezra smiled and put his arm around Will's neck. "I know, brother. You're young, but you've got to grow up at some point. And with the way things are looking, you're going to get combat experience sooner than you think."

"You think so?!"

"Don't get too excited. The fight might be right here, in your home country."

"I mean, I've been keeping up with the exodus conflicts. The anarchists are buying weapons from Mexican cartels. It's just a matter of time before this becomes national."

Ezra continued, "Don't tell a soul, but the private industry might break off from the government soon."

"But that would mean-"

"Full on civil war," Ezra told him. "Military against mercenaries with civilians in the exodus caught in between. And let me tell you from experience, contractors have better equipment and training. All of them are veterans themselves, many of them with years of special operations and advanced infantry experience. Just stay on your toes and have your phone on you always. If things play out like I think they might, I'll need someone I can trust on the inside when Sergio retires."

"What about Curtis? He'll never retire."

"Trust me, they'd put up a recon drone if we went to the same restaurant."

"Ah. I see. What about your own contractors then?"

"The Hoods will be staying with me for the next several months. They'll be loyal and true to protecting me and my loved ones. "

118

"When you say having 'someone on the inside', that makes me nervous. I didn't join up to become a double agent."

"And I didn't join up to become a mutant. And look at what happened. Sometimes our destiny chooses us. Sometimes we have to make sacrifices for the greater good and accept the outcome. That might mean *treason*, to them. But in your heart, you know what is best and I have faith you'll lead your men righteously, William. Fight for your home and the values you know to be true."

Will nodded and the bartender put two shots of tequila in front of them.

"Courtesy of the lady in blue at the end of the bar," she said.

Will looked over and gawked at the gorgeous Hispanic woman winking at him with her deep brown eyes.

They held their glasses up to her and she held hers up to them.

Will smiled and turned to Ezra.

"To your new family."

"And the family I've always had," Ezra replied.

They drank the shots and Ezra reached into his pocket and set his grandfather's knife on the table.

"I want you to have this. It's the final act of my retirement. It's time for you to carry the warrior's creed, William."

"Grandpa's knife. Holy shit. Thank you, Ezra!"

Ezra patted Will on the back before walking away. Any other day Will would have run to the beautiful woman buying drinks for him. But he sat by himself, staring into his empty shot glass with empty eyes. He and Ezra had been close as kids, but over time Will was just trying to catch up to his older brother. He suddenly realized there wasn't anywhere to follow him anymore. He walked over to Ingrid by the helicopter pad, pondering his life path.

"Mind if I join you?" Will asked Ingrid as he sat down next to her.

"Not at all," Ingrid said, smiling at him with squinty red eyes. She handed an edible to Will, who was reluctant.

"No thanks. I can't," he said.

"But then why were you doing coke?"

"I don't know, I just got carried away, I guess. I was excited to see Ezra; it was the first time I'd seen him in years. And what does he do? He lectures me like Dad used to. Except Dad's talks would either start or end with a beating," he said, chuckling.

"You're kidding," Ingrid said, never knowing of Ezra's abusive past.

"Nah, I ain't. He's dead now though. Rotten son of a bitch died of cancer 'bout the time Ezra joined up. He wasn't all bad. Did what he could without Mom around."

Will's slight southern drawl began coming out as the liquor shots loosened him.

"Where's your mother?" Ingrid asked.

"Mom died when we were kids. Ezra really hasn't told you about our family much, has he?"

"No. I didn't know there was so much complexity to it."

"Where are your folks?"

"Also deceased. In a car crash several years ago."

"I'm sorry to hear that."

"I'm sorry to hear about your parents too."

"I think it affected Ezra more so, but he found his true family after he joined up. Some of his closest friends followed him into the private industry. Couple of them are blood brothers for life."

120

"I wonder what that would mean now," Ingrid said, thinking about the concept of Ezra's blood mixing with the blood of his mates.

"Well, you can ask them. They're here," Will said as he stood up. A thunderous Blackhawk helicopter flew in from behind a skyscraper. It hovered above the helipad next to them and lowered slowly as the high beams blinded the frightened guests. The wind from the mighty steal bird had all of the women holding their hair and pushing down their billowing dresses. Ezra smiled and leaned back against the bar as twenty armed, men from the infamous 'Hood' battalion of P.A.I.N. Ordinance jumped off the deathly, numberless, jolly roger stamped ship. The brutes walked through the crowd toward Ezra like a priesthood of tactical hooded assassins. A tall black man with an eye patch led the group through the party as the guests parted in fear like sheep. The contractors were dressed in all black, with menacing weapons and light kits and black and grey shemaghs covering their faces.

The gigantic dark leader approached Ezra face to face.

"We got demobilized from Nigeria over a hundred days into deployment to watch you drink cocktails?"

He and Ezra stared coldly at each other.

"If those were your orders, you'd better stick to them," Ezra said, squinting but not blinking from his locked stare.

The whole party was silent. The two men suddenly began laughing.

"Come here, Gadreel!" Ezra said as he wrapped his arms around the man. The hug was returned with full force, and everyone in the party began to gossip in the ears of those beside them.

"Good to see you, old friend," he said in a deep voice to Ezra.

"Gadreel?" Ingrid whispered to Will, as they had walked over to the bar to be a part of the commotion.

"Yeah all the guys from the Hoods are named after Christian or Hebrew demons. The psych-ops guys came up with the idea for scaring enemy Muslim fighters. While you're in P.A.I.N. you don't go by anything else."

"That's pretty ironic considering Ezra is a Hebrew name."

"Right?" Will said, chuckling. "It's like he's an angel and a demon."

"So what was Ezra's alias?" Ingrid asked.

"Marchosias. The winged wolf demon who wishes to return to heaven but is deceived in that hope. Solomon promised Marchosias he could return to heaven 1,200 years after the fall. But what then, I suppose? What then?"

From across the sky bar, Ezra's deep, dark eyes looked off for a moment, as if a wave of sublime nostalgia washed over him. For the first time, Ingrid saw his thousand-yard stare in full. His dark past had been unearthed by his comrades' arrival. She thought she knew Ezra, but she was just beginning to understand why he had become the intense being that he was, long before his epic transformation.

Ezra left early the next morning to Zilker Botanical Gardens near downtown Austin for a proper solar recharging and meditation. He left Ingrid ten thousand dollars cash and a note on the table that told her to roll down to the shopping district with a paparazzi entourage. That kind of security was more practical for their current situation than armed men, since no one would be keen to attack her on film five minutes from the police station.

He walked by a news stand where a headline on a paper read, 'Survivors of Peruvian plane crash hold roof party: invite heavily armed guests'. Another said, 'Alien Invasion: Is Ezra Beller a political threat or a medicinal cure?'. He chuckled when he saw them, and walked on, shaking his head as he went.

Ezra entered the park through a white arch where a red Dharma wheel had been carved into its keystone. He moved along the cobblestone walk and into a ring of flowers, kneeling next to the soft sweet-scented petals where he watched a lone honeybee zip around from orchid, to iris, to daffodil, to blossoming cacti, daintily pollinating as it went. It flew around his head and body as he took in the smells, soaked up the radiant sun, and acquired saturating rejuvenation with each breath. As he dug his hands into the dark soil of the garden, a very strange thing occurred. Small plant buds poked up through the ground and grew between his fingers. The harder he pushed, the larger they grew. One of them sprouted several inches with one push. The bee buzzed down and walked around on Ezra's skin for a while before flying off into the garden's colorful inner circles. Then someone spoke behind him.

"Wonderful creatures, aren't they? It's unfortunate they're endangered. They're just so... necessary."

Ezra knew who the person was by the tone in his voice. He turned around slowly to see if his senses were being deceived.

A handsome, dark skinned Nepalese man in plush white robes stood several feet behind Ezra. He held his arms behind his back and stood as still as a statue while butterflies landed on his shoulders and flew in and out of his straight black silken hair.

123

"Vishnu," Ezra spoke in a soft voice. The image of a great grey bird flashed in his mind, wet ash slinging from its flapping wings.

"Tis I," the man said in a calm voice. He looked no older than Ezra, but Vishnu's true age was unknown. The reason the butterflies flew around him had less to do with his calming, sweet scent, and more to do with the fact that he could manipulate and attract life forms almost as well as Ezra could, but without the Sararan powers Ezra possessed. It was a strange coincidence to the Immortal, how he had just discovered his creative abilities in the garden's soil not a moment before Vishnu approached him.

"What are you doing here?" Ezra asked.

"I came here to ask you that very question, old friend."

Vishnu looked at him with a visceral gaze, as if he knew the answer to every secret, as if he were a playwright coming to watch his words pirouette on the world stage.

"I am here to set the record straight about my condition. Then I'm running away."

"Who or what are you running from, Ezra?"

"Everything and everyone."

There was a long silence between them, as Vishnu took in a deep breath and looked upward. Small birds chirped and flew from limb to limb in the tree above him, as if carrying ribbons to complete an invisible canopy of geometric perfection. Vishnu's third eye was open to these observances, wider than Ezra's even. He was more powerful, both in his mind and body, than any human Ezra had ever met.

"Listen, if you are here to kill me-"

"I would have done it already," Vishnu assured him.

"So what do you want?"

"Your undivided attention, for the remainder of the afternoon."

"I don't understand."

"You will. Come. Walk with me."

The mysterious man took Ezra's hand in his for a few seconds and examined every inch of it. He felt the contours of Ezra's palm, and the hardness of his crystalline nails. He was intrigued, but only smiled and gave no verbal clue to his curiosity. They walked the circumference of a large pond slowly for a while in silence. Vishnu let the shock of his presence subside in Ezra, enough time for them to speak openly with one another. Vishnu picked up a lotus from the ponds edge. He spun it in his fingers above his head and smiled, twirling the pink pedals before the sun like a shutter, and he began his strange tale.

"Midway through his long life, my master Zou Cheng was living in the mountains of what is now northern China. One evening, a military commander came to the steps of his temple to seek his cooperation in letting his army pass, and Zou was compliant, but under the strict condition that they walk single file to reduce damage to the foliage that surrounded the copious beauty of his carefully tended temple gardens. The commander agreed and made sure that every soldier knew of this order. So the army passed, and every one of the ten thousand soldiers obeyed. On that day, not a leaf nor twig had been broken outside the narrow trail that their weary feet had dug in. Zou spent many weeks rehabilitating the trail, replanting his trees and flowers, and erasing the evidence of the thousands of footsteps. One year later, the men returned, but they had been cut down by enemy forces to less than one hundred men, a mere company. The commander once again went up to Zou's temple and asked him, ever so respectfully, for safe passage through his gardens. Zou was reluctant and asked that they go around his land all together. The commander knew that Zou's garden extended well beyond the horizon, ridge after ridge after ridge. He begged that he be allowed to go through the land with his small group, so long as they walked single file, just as before. He pleaded desperately and told Zou that his men had suffered greatly and only wished to be home with their families. Zou, in an act of great generosity, allowed them one last time to walk through his garden, under his conditions. So the army marched through, many of them stumbling and beaten from battle wounds. One of the mortally wounded men collapsed beside the trail, not more than fifty feet from the temple. Zou saw this and shouted at everyone to halt. The soldiers held fast, and stood silent, fearful of the master's imminent wrath. The fallen soldier lay exhausted, but he was still breathing. Zou approached the soldier, and as he did so, two others went to help up the wounded man to his feet. Zou motioned for them to stay away.

"He said, 'You will not retrieve this man. Like the flower stems he has fractured, so is the stem of his spine. Yet, like the petals of the flower that still glow with color, his mind persists to recognize what is around him. He will stay with the flowers. See as they see, and they, him.'

"The commander nodded to the soldiers, who gazed at their leader with questioning eyes. As the army marched on, leaving behind their fallen brother, each looked at the broken man atop the broken flowers. When the last man had passed by and the company had marched away from his sanctuary, Zou gave the man pain medicine and herbs and guided him gently to deaths door with a redemptive blessing. And the man who fell never returned to the Emperor's domain, nor to his wife and children who anxiously awaited his return.

"Months later, the Emperor sent a messenger to Zou's temple, since Master Cheng was the last person who had seen the wounded man. The messenger approached the temple and asked if the warrior had survived, and Zou took him to the location of his fall.

"'Here,' Master Cheng pointed to the ground.

"The messenger looked all around saw nothing but flowers and vines and trees.

"'He, a life form of one, is survived by many,' Zou responded.

"The messenger asked, 'I don't understand. He is buried here?'

"'He has dissolved and merged with nature. He was severed by humanity, and now he is one with the universe.'

"The messenger looked at a white and purple flower dancing in the breeze, held up by a rigid stem.

"'Ahhh. I see now. He is there.'

"Master Cheng nodded, 'He is there. He is everywhere. He is free from form. He is with *the friend*.'"

Vishnu paused and looked at Ezra.

"For much of his life, Master Cheng was a Zoroastrian, those who believed the bodies of the dead should not rot in the ground but rather be placed aloft in a tower of silence, where only the fires of heaven and the raptors and scavengers of the sky were permitted to devour the body. But after centuries of praising fire and light exclusively, Zou began to understand the power of fermentation and the natural cycle of decay as a mode of reincarnation and spiritual cleansing, for Earth's pestilence, he found, is itself a means of percolating lost spirits as we die and sink into the carbon crust beneath us, our misguided souls wallowing in that ghostly void like crippled whales, returning at birth to our binary platform to face the stark coercion of the elements once again. The Earth is an ovum and there are infinite ways to usher in and recalibrate her energies. This knowledge Zou has bestowed to me is something I take seriously, and I've fought for my whole life to fulfill his wishes. Thus you must heed my words and accept what is inevitable."

"And what is inevitable, Vishnu?"

"The rebirth of planet Earth, a consequence ten thousand years in the making. *The extinction of humans*. The end of this aeon and the beginning of something greater."

"So what do you want from me? I just want a home, and a family, and to live peacefully with a garden and a small farm to pass on to my children and my grandchildren."

Vishnu laughed and then said, "If only you could remember your past lives as I can. You're not a farmer, Ezra. You're a killer. You just don't know whose side to be on anymore, as right you should question your agency."

"I'm not on anyone's side."

"So what is the nature of your destiny? What does your *blood* tell you?"

"Do you really want to know?"

"More than anything," Vishnu said sadistically, stroking the leather lacing on his katana.

"My Sararan blood tells me to extinguish them. To put an end to fiat currency and global control by the super-elite. To quell over population with a deadly act of purification, killing off weak minded humans until a new society can form, far more cohesive with all Earth's life forms than any before."

"You already know then," Vishnu said, bowing his head with respect.

"But I will not give in to those thoughts. They're irrational," Ezra said.

"It is a choice that transcends rationality. How can you deny what is to come?" Vishnu asked, looking him dead in the darkness of his eyes. "Your emotions give you away."

"A wise man once told me, 'Anger tastes sweet, but it is deadly'. What happened to that man?"

"I'm not asking you to act on your emotions, I'm asking you to act on your destiny. I have lived by the sword and I shall die by it, as any right man would have it. Do you know why I told you that story?"

"Let me guess... you're Master Cheng and you're allowing me to pass through your garden," Ezra said, knowing his ex-comrade spoke in metaphors.

"No. YOU are said Master, and you're allowing these sheep to pass before you and mock you and all you have to do is gently coax their wounded souls to their self-designed fates. You are the dragon in the mountain. The universe chose you and you won't accept this privilege?"

"No Vishnu, I will not cross my oath to never kill again. Even in the face of death, I must have hope."

"You sound weak, naïve... like a frightened child unable to accept the devastation coming your way."

"I am not naive. My life could end in no other way than devastation. That I am certain of."

"Then join my cause, that which is primed for the longevity of a Sararan takeover, so you can live infinitely and prosperous with your family, creating the world in your image, *your sanctum*. Do not give in to sympathy. There is nothing left for the human race. They will die out eventually, and by that point, leave all the planet's ecosystems in utter ruin. What could you possibly owe these people, other than the collapse they've been craving?"

"I owe them my compassion. I was once one of them."

"But you're not one of them."

"It doesn't matter."

"It does for the rest of us."

Ezra and Vishnu stood next to the pond, staring into each other's eyes as they never had.

"What are you?" Ezra asked, disgusted by the twisted mind of his former comrade.

"The vastly more important question is of course, what are you?"

The conversation quickly turned into one they had had long before that day. Ezra began to remember the fateful night he'd met Vishnu, and suddenly he felt the air turn to negative temperatures as a painful memory played out, a memory locked away in a corner of his mind, awaiting a trigger like Vishnu to unearth his forbidden secret.

Eight years earlier, Ezra walked the snow drifted streets of Katmandu, Nepal. The cobblestone roads wrapped around poorly insulated buildings and stone temples that protected isolated Buddhist monks in hiding. Fear blanketed the town and no other lights could be seen glowing besides the ones hanging high from bent wooden poles as he walked against the harsh gale. Tides of arctic drift rapped the locked doors with a clamor and whistle.

Ezra was on a special assignment, so secret he didn't even know his objective yet. Curtis gave him the folder personally, and all Ezra knew was that he was supposed to find an old white and red tavern where the man he would be looking for frequented, a man that Curtis had done joint training with years before in Northern India.

He knocked on the large door of the rickety tavern, the icy wind blowing furiously under the swinging streetlight's dim glow. A one-armed man with long wispy gray hair and a left eye cataract answered the knock.

"What do you want? Bar's closed! Don't you know there's a curfew in this city?"

"I'm looking for someone. Maybe you could help me find him."

"What makes you think I'll help you?"

Ezra flashed a few thousand-dollar bills in front of the man's face, and he gave a warm chuckle. The man made a wheezing sound and looked like a crypt keeper.

"You Americans think you can buy anything with money! Well that's just splendid, but how do I know it's not counterfeit, or that I won't be killed for helping you?"

"The bills are real, and you may be more upset at the outcome if you don't help me."

His smile lit up as if he was looking into the eyes of a lost child.

"Ahhhh, I see. Ho ho ho. Step inside Ezra, I've been wondering when you would show up!"

The old man sat Ezra down at one of his tables and poured him some raksi. The wood that held up the place upright was several centuries old. One could smell its peculiar essence, as if the fluctuation of stable and hard times gave it a strange aura of mixed energy. No sooner had Ezra sensed this feng shui that he noticed a dark man in bright white clothing sit at the end of the bar. The man sat alone, sipping raksi and smoking casually behind a mask of straight black hair. Ezra, dressed in all black, chuckled for a moment to himself as he noticed their contrasted uniforms. Which of them was yin, and which was yang, Ezra would not know for some time.

Ezra got up and walked over, and in a very simple way asked, "Good evening sir, could you spare a cigarette?"

Only his eyes turned toward Ezra for a moment. His head remained still, and he said nothing. He sipped his warm rice drink casually, ignoring him.

"I thought just about everyone could speak English these days. Oh well," Ezra muttered as he walked away.

Ezra sat down again, and the old man came right up next to him.

"Let me give you some advice my friend. It is not wise to insult a *Zurvan Elite*."

"I insulted him? How so? What does that mean anyway, 'Zurvan'?"

"We will come back to that," he said.

"What do I call you?"

"My name is unimportant. I know you because Curtis gave me a head's up a few days ago. Said you'd be banging on the door any minute looking for him."

"So let's get right to it, shall we?" Ezra asked.

"Rightly so. You'll pay me $6,000 up front for coordinating this meeting, and you'll pay him $30,000 for helping you."

"Why such a high price for the tongue-less Sherpa?" Ezra asked in a low voice.

"Speaking this way... is it honorable where you come from?"

"I'm just curious to know what I'm paying for, that's all."

The old man leaned in. "He's an expert in both ancient and modern warfare practices. Know that your arrogance will not be tolerated. You are one of the greatest warriors known today; I know your kind. But you are still no match for his fatally swift methods and ghost-like abilities. Never cross him. The man that trained him was the greatest martial arts master in the world, Master Zou Cheng. He lived to be almost eight hundred years old and over his long lifetime he trained in places that personified the four elements: in the fire pit of Derweze in Turkmenistan, beside the crystal clear waters of Matano Lake in Indonesia, against the brisk winds of Siyeh Pass in the Glacier territories of North America, and on the ancient spruce colony of Fulu mountain in Sweden. Imagine conversing with a 4,000-year-old tree. Would you speak or would you listen?"

He didn't let Ezra answer. "Having established an intimate relationship with each of the elements - fire, water, air, and earth - he was able to harness an incredible amount of power that unlocked the key to immortality. These practices were passed down to the man that denied you a cigarette a few moments ago. You should consider yourself fortunate for being in one piece."

"Right, I'll keep that in mind. So why is he called a 'Zurvan'?"

"There was an ancient religious sect called the Zurvan's who were a group that worshiped the primordial creation deity of Zoroastrianism; the largest religion in the world at one time, long before the Lamb of God was crucified. Zurvan was the parent God to good and evil, according to their beliefs. Since they've died out, a new group combined the ancient practices with Taoism and naturalist ideals and they've collectively risen to a higher status through generations. But they have no ranks. They have no hierarchy. They have given themselves to seeking a constantly daunting spiritual gauntlet. Most are hard to find, as they are always in steady motion. And they've got a specialty skill each of them does."

"So what's his specialty?" Ezra asked, nodding toward the man in white.

"You could say he's a *disruptor* of sorts."

The old man looked toward the end of the bar and introduced them.

"Vishnu, come. I want you to meet Lieutenant Ezra Beller."

Ezra reached his hand out, but Vishnu ignored him, knocked back the rest of his drink and casually walked toward the door. Without modulating the tone of his voice, he said, "I hope you brought a token for the Gods. *We're going to hell again.*"

This was either a reference to the region they were headed, or some dark metaphor. Either way, Ezra found his words chilling. He left the bar and followed Vishnu onto the snowy sidewalk outside. Vishnu was walking faster all the time and was difficult to keep up with. Ezra managed to pick up the pace and get to the building Vishnu had entered, several blocks north from where the bar was. Inside the door was an empty concrete room with bright fluorescent lights beaming into his eyes. In the middle of the room was a large, knee high chest. Vishnu locked a massive dead lock behind them, then took a key from his necklace to unlock the chest.

"Here's a gift," he said as he threw Ezra the chest's padlock.

"What for?" Ezra asked.

He turned to Ezra with a blank face.

"Because I'm a nice fucking guy," he said, using some western sarcasm to mock Ezra.

"I mean, what do I need the lock for?"

"Its application depends on your needs. An Iraqi company produces them. It takes a tank round to dismantle one."

Ezra grasped the heavy chunk of metal and asked, "Don't you think this will just be extra weight for our mission?"

"We're not going into the mountains to hunt insurgents... were you not told?" he asked as he kicked the chest open.

He immediately started unloading supplies, which included suits that had non-reflective micro-screens, which could be programmed to desert, forest, arctic, and even motion-oriented camouflage. He pulled out face paint, various officer uniforms from around the globe, medical supplies, a variety of detonators (in locked plastic boxes labeled armed/unarmed along with location descriptions), flash bang grenades, tear gas, military grade digital radios, and a GPS system with a kit holding marble-sized capsules containing nano-drones.

"Aren't those reconnaissance drones only issued to specific U.S. Navy and Air Force personnel?" Ezra asked.

"Yes they are. Why, jealous?" Vishnu asked.

He then pulled out more gear: topographic maps, urban street maps, ocean maps, trade route maps, underground city maps, stolen infra-red satellite camera interfaces, compasses, gas masks, helmets, gloves, raincoats, tactical clothing, boots, kneepads, MREs, trauma kits, survival supplies and everything else one would need for modern combat missions aside from weapons.

"And what do you mean we aren't going into the mountains?" Ezra asked, watching him sort out everything.

135

He kept assembling the supplies on the floor and held a few items of clothing up to Ezra's chest for sizing.

"From the West Bank to Tehran is where the Earth will depress and hell will emerge, thanks to the side of my family whom we call the 'betrayers'. We're going after them now so that won't happen."

His words were haunting. Ezra knew as Vishnu did this poetry had two sides.

"Your family?" Ezra asked.

"Yes. My two younger brothers are high ranking political figures of the Arab world."

"This must be seamless then."

"Yes, it must."

"But why wouldn't they send a strike team with me and just use you as a contact? No offense," Ezra asked him, puzzled.

"Because this is a two-man operation and you and I are the best for the job. Curtis and I have similar goals, at least in this case, and no one else wants anything to do with a mission as fragile as this one – not even your own government, which is why Curtis sent you and didn't even tell you where he was sending you. I know that you are not the kind of man who is partial to being held back, Ezra. However, I can assure you that my assistance will only heighten your strengths and cut down on the mission's complications. When you fight with me, you fight ten steps ahead of your enemy. But just because I flood myself with assets doesn't mean it always plays out like symphony. Come take a look at something."

He led Ezra to the wall behind the trunk of supplies he had just un-stowed. It looked plain. Only sheets of drywall were in place. Then on a small blank area on the wall next to him he began typing an excessively long code where there was neither a visible keypad nor monitor. Yet the boards rose up to show a vast array of beautiful modern weapon systems behind glass casing. Several blue fluorescent lights illuminated his arsenal; an ultra-mag bolt action sniper rifle, automatic pistols, various improvised explosives, bullet belts, grenades, sub-machine guns, assault rifles, and at the center of the case, the crème de la crème: a glistening titanium alloy AR-15 battle rifle chambered at .300 magnum with an upper and lower receiver strong enough to be optimized as a shield.

"Please tell me I get to use that," Ezra said, looking at his reflection on the rifle's shiny metallic body.

"If everything goes to plan, you will," Vishnu remarked as a screen dropped down in front of the weapons.

Onscreen were pictures with profiles of various militant leaders and politicians, all with a similar visage.

"You've done some homework," Ezra said, fairly impressed with Vishnu's intelligence.

"In order to identify your targets, you'll need to know their cohorts too."

Ezra looked at each picture carefully.

"These men," Vishnu pointed at one of the pictures, "this is the vermin we've been ordered to exterminate. Hasam Abu Bakr, the economic advisor for the United Arab Emirates. He'll be meeting this man," Vishnu pointed to another picture, "Ibraham ibn Muhammad, chief of the Iranian defense council. Hasam plans to sell Ibraham the Israeli defense codes needed to nuke Israel off the map. We need to kill both of them to stop the deal."

"So how are we going to do this?" Ezra asked.

"Hasam and Ibraham will be attending a business summit in two days in southern Lebanon. The summit will take place in the remote city of Aita Ech Chaab, Lebanon for the meeting. We'll be waiting for them in Shtula, Israel about one and a half kilometers away, hidden at an elevated location. You'll be firing your rifle across the border so that by the time their struggling security team goes through customs and elbows their way into Israel, you'll already be on a flight back to your base in Germany."

"Won't that make tensions between Israel and Iran worse?"

"That's always a risk, but there's a bigger picture you're not seeing here, beyond what's happening between you and me. The question is, can you confirm a kill from that distance?"

With full confidence Ezra answered, "I can kill both of them with one round if they're holding hands."

"Good," Vishnu said with a small smirk. "Your target will be Hasam. Mine will be Ibraham. We will perform command fire, killing both targets simultaneously."

Vishnu made the screen snap back up to the ceiling and he typed in another code. As the plexi-glass wall lifted, Vishnu handed Ezra the supplies they'd need and gave him a gesture to begin assembling his kit.

"I'm not used to going to such lengths to take the life of one man. It's added pressure, and in a way it's also frustrating and underwhelming. There are so many fuckers out there that need to be killed along with our targets."

With that Vishnu smiled and put his hand on the top of Ezra's shoulder.

"Anger tastes sweet Ezra, but it is deadly. Use your logic. In the scope's view you'll see his chest explode and the other informants and secretaries panic in confusion. They'll disperse like frightened antelope. You'll watch my brother's dynasty of malice fall before your eyes. Is that not enough?"

After Vishnu reassured him, they gathered the supplies they needed in silence and left the bunker. As they started trotting down the icy streets to Vishnu's private airport, a heavy feeling suddenly bore down on Ezra. A feeling he felt before most combat engagements. That feeling when you don't know if you're coming back or not.

Upon their arrival in Israel, Ezra stepped off the humming jet and proceeded on all fours with a tumultuous puking session.

"What base is this? Who's checking us in?" Ezra asked between gags.

"We don't have to worry about such things," Vishnu chuckled as they stepped out into the hot desert, having gone slightly back in time and into the desert, as if they'd entered a different world. Heat waves rose from the distant dunes and elegant olive trees. Vishnu put his arms up to show Ezra the vast desert surroundings. The base was abandoned, with grass growing between the cracks in the aged asphalt.

"But don't we have to report to our... superiors?" Ezra asked, his eyes red with tears as the acids from his stomach burned his throat.

"Have you become so accustomed to a leash that you cannot act of your own will?" Vishnu asked. He handed Ezra some water, who took a huge gulp, spilling the cool liquid on his flak vest.

Ezra panted for a moment then said, "I don't get it. You employ logistics but you're not a part of any military. You have integrity but no morality. What the hell are you?"

"I am the greatest martial arts master alive whose conscience is the supreme law of his destiny. What are you?"

Ezra didn't answer. He wasn't used to such an open-ended mission, without formal protocol or any legitimate resources for back up or extraction. They were totally on their own. This sort of warfare made Ezra fearful and nervous. However, clandestine assassinations were Vishnu's specialty, and a secret obsession waiting to be let loose on the world.

The next day, Vishnu and Ezra drove a small pickup hastily along the bouncy gravel roads of northern Israel, where there was nothing but poor communal huts supported by sticks and dried mud. These people chose to live in exile away from the warring districts by the West Bank. They were a simple folk, with neither money nor devices. Jews, Muslims, and Christians of all sects living together in collective privation, devoting their life only to God and each other's companionship. The sign above the village entrance read, in Hebrew, Arabic, Turkish and English, '*God is good*'.

Vishnu stopped the vehicle at the edge of town. Both he and Ezra got out, looking in all directions to evaluate their surroundings. They grabbed their gear and walked down the street slowly.

"So this is Shtula," Ezra whispered.

Vishnu and Ezra wore black full-face Burkas to blend in with the Muslim women walking the streets. Vishnu carried a duffle bag in one hand, and a rice sack with a submachine gun tucked inside in the other. Ezra held the titanium rifle under his robe, careful to hide the large weapon from any onlookers.

They blended in with the strange primal community where everyone knew each other but could not ascribe the two figures an identity unless spoken to. The villagers went about their day and looked at them with blank expressions. A group of women with white burkas passed them, and Ezra locked eyes with one, as he could see the sunlight reflecting off of her bright green iris's traveling back through the light mesh cloth. Ezra could feel her stare unmoved. He could feel everything around them pulsing, along with his steady heart rate and the relentless beating rays of the sun.

They marched into an alleyway to evade any unwanted sightings of them entering the building where they'd make their sniper nest. Once the area was clear, they went into a church and began their sweep. It was a mostly vacant bell tower in which only a single priest resided. The priest was alarmed at first, but Vishnu took the man's hand in his own and talked softly to him. Vishnu told Ezra to join them in prayer before the priest left. It was the first time he had taken part in prayer since church as a child. He followed Vishnu's lead, impartial to the ceremony. Once he left, Vishnu slid the door closed and Ezra slipped the gigantic lock pin through the hatch, closing it with a loud click.

'They'd waste half their ammo just trying to get in,' Ezra had thought,

"Don't forget to take that when you leave. It's not evidence remember, it's just a lock," Vishnu said, smiling. Vishnu became excited when he was about to kill people. He ran up the stairs as Ezra followed close behind.

They threw off the burkas to reveal their second disguise: grey robes and dark red turbans. Vishnu took out the collapsed sniper rifle from the duffle bag and started to assemble the pieces together. Ezra quickly re-assembled the metallic AR-15 with a larger caliber barrel and unfolded and aligned his range finding spotting scope. After glassing the landscape, he opened his field book and began scribbling information as Vishnu loaded rounds into his rifle's magazine. Then, silence.

For the next few minutes, Ezra and Vishnu spent their time looking over a mile away into Lebanon, as they nestled onto the center stone table in the arched church tower. Vishnu checked his rifle. He then began feeding Ezra information on distance references, wind variations, the elevation difference, temperature, humidity, social climate, natural choke points, and estimated placement of their target's entry.

Vishnu gave Ezra a two-minute estimated time of arrival after spotting a car from a distance. The butterflies were alive in Ezra's innards. He started caressing the rifle, feeling its body and snuggling up next to it comfortably. His breathing slowed and his heartbeat steadied. Ezra focused his entire being on the moment.

"T-minus one minute thirty seconds until target's arrival. Upon a mutual target confirmation I will count down from five and we will perform command fire on one. Rhythm is crucial to our shots being in sync. Our escape route is parallel to where we came into the town. We'll be just three blocks east of where we entered. There will be a helicopter waiting on the outskirts to take us to Jerusalem in less than 15 minutes after enemy engagement. And by the way, if you miss the shot, I am going my own way."

"Why?" Ezra asked, feeling uneasy about the sudden alteration of their plans.

"To finish the mission."

"But I won't miss-"

"I know you won't," Vishnu said quieter, looking through his scope and loading a fresh round into his rifle. They both held as steady as the stone they propped themselves against.

They sat in silence for a moment. Only a lone raven's caw echoed in the distance above the whisper of a slight breeze.

"A scavenger's cry. That is a good omen," Vishnu said, looking at the black bird on the roof next to them.

Ezra then watched the stream of black Mercedes roll into his sights. His field of view was enlarged, but they were so far away that the heat waves bent his image this way and that. Still, his crosshairs had to be solid, even if the image was not. The first men to step out were Ibraham's security, soon to be unemployed. The next were lesser diplomats that were equally unimportant. Hasam was a few cars behind them. Ezra focused on Hasam. He calmed and steadied his aim. It was I the longest shot he'd ever attempted in a combat setting, and also the most important one.

Vishnu used soft words: "White tunic exiting third sedan east from the stairwell. Officer Class; it's Hasam. Then to the left – a brown military uniform exiting black SUV. Ibrahim. Both targets confirmed."

"Target confirmed," Ezra copied.

"Are you ready?"

"Affirmative," Ezra said.

Hasam was speaking with the other politicians coming to greet him. He walked up the stairs, waving, and smiling under his thick mustache. As he stopped to turn and greet someone,

Ezra took in a deep breath and let half of it out, holding his aim like a statue.

Vishnu began the countdown.

"Five… Four… Three… Two…"

POOOOM!

The bullets left their rifles. A woman screamed. A dog barked. An empty casing sprang from Ezra's gun and bounced off of the church bell above them with a resounding 'ting'.

Ezra looked through his scope as he reloaded.

"Fucking shit! I missed."

The commotion in the distance could only be seen, not heard, but there was definitely a sense of panic, as people either ran into the building or back into their vehicles. Ibraham's blown apart body was pulled into the suburban.

"You have a few seconds, so calm yourself. We will perform another command fire-,"

Before Vishnu could instruct Ezra, a shot rang out followed by another casing made a 'ting' on the church bell. Ezra started panting.

"Shhhhhit! I miscalculated."

"He's gone. The target is compromised," Vishnu said in a frustrated tone. Vishnu had killed his target with one shot, where Ezra had failed with two.

"Goddamn it!" Ezra yelled at himself.

To Ezra, it was a huge mistake, but they'd still confirmed Ibrahim's death. They packed up the gear and left the tower immediately, making haste and zigzagging diagonally over the cracked sidewalks and through the sandy alley ways. Suddenly Vishnu went to depart in the opposite direction, and he stopped to hand Ezra the duffle bag.

"Take the satchel and the battle rifle with you. My sister is piloting the craft. She'll know what to do with everything."

"I'm sorry Vishnu," Ezra said.

"I will admit that it's too soon to guess the broader implications of today. By God's will, we will have changed history for the better. Is that not the ultimate goal of the assassin, to liberate a nation's peoples from tyranny and restore justice? Regardless of what becomes of this day, however, you owe me an immense favor for your failure, Ezra. If your mistake does in fact break up the Zurvan order, your life will be mine until death. We are no longer devoted solely to spiritual healing, as we once were. We are channeling our powers into a violent motif unstoppable by western conquest. We are everywhere, and we are nowhere. We are more dangerous with knives than your high-tech missile systems are from the air, and we will be watching you, Ezra. Don't you *ever* forget that," he said sternly.

Vishnu's words sank into Ezra's chest uncomfortably, though there was nothing he could do at that time besides stand there.

Vishnu took off his grey robes and tossed them aside, unveiling some dirty, brown tattered cloth draped over his body. He tossed aside the scarlet cotton on his head donned a black turban with tightly rolled marijuana joints woven into its creases. To Ezra's astonishment, he then walked over and sat down curbside with some local tribesman. After taking a deep breath and settling into the more enlightened version of himself, Vishnu then joined in on the men's mystical conversation, laughing, smoking, and speaking Arabian whimsically as if he'd been living with them for years. For all Ezra knew, perhaps he had been.

"What are you doing, I thought you were-"

"This place is about to be swarming with you-know-what. For now I'm a simple Dervish. Tomorrow I'll take care of the rest of the mission. Goodbye Ezra."

Ezra walked the other way. He was astonished and angry at himself for his mistakes, but at least the mission was over. When he approached the outskirts of town, the chopper was already humming on the ground waiting for him. It was an old Russian ship from the cold war era, and likely wouldn't have passed most safety inspections. A lovely Japanese woman in a bright green and gold dress and a white shawl smiled and waved him in from the pilot seat. Her motions were deliberate and mathematically beautiful, with every finger contracting and moving in circular precise motions.

Ezra yelled to her as he jumped into the co-pilot seat, "You must be-"

"Shakti! Pleasure to meet you, Ezra. Where is my brother?"

"He's staying behind. Hasam lives."

She nodded and then said, "Stow your bag behind the seat there. We'll arrive at the airport in about forty-five minutes. Oh, and Merry Christmas!" she said smiling.

After all his jet lag, Ezra had completely forgotten that it was Christmas day. It was no wonder the Christian tribesmen were rejoicing with Vishnu. The helicopter lifted off and a huge feeling of relief hit Ezra. The evidence was out of his hands and he was on his way home from being on an illegal mission in Asia for a week.

Ezra threw off his turban and put a chaw under his lip. He sighed and looked out across the motionless empty desert scape. The helicopter sped quickly over the ground, but Ezra felt he was stuck in time somehow. Shakti noticed this but didn't interrupt him. She knew enough to not prod. She said nothing but Ezra could sense her curiosity.

"Are all your siblings named after deities?" Ezra asked, spitting into an empty water bottle.

"Some are named after prophets, some philosophers. Ezra is mentioned in the Hebrew bible," she said.

"Ezra the Scribe. He lived thousands of years ago, not far from here, actually. I believe the name means, 'God helps'."

"Does God help you?" she asked.

"He's not helping me now," he said.

"Well I am helping you. Maybe God sent me," she said, toying with him.

Ezra smiled then laughed before saying, "Maybe, but I believe humans only act to benefit themselves, even when they're doing nice things for others. Humans, for whatever reason, seem separate from the rest of nature."

She nodded in agreement, then said, "Someday they will pay dearly for it. We are here to remind them, beings like you and I and my brother, that their actions will not go without consequence. My brother may seem as cold as a stone sometimes, but his allegiance to keeping the Earth balanced is his only concern. Know that you have my loyalty Ezra, so that a proper connection between my family and yours may be concrete," she added.

"You're not one of the betrayers then?" Ezra joked.

She laughed heartily then said, "No. They're busy figuring out what to do at the moment. With the buyer of the deal dead but the seller alive, who knows if the codes will still be purchased. All we can do is pray that it doesn't happen."

"They might, and it will be all my fault if they do," Ezra said somberly.

"Don't feel such guilt. We have to wait to see what happens. Still, it's unsettling to know what they're capable of. Men, *you just can't trust them*."

They cruised over the barren landscape. Small huts popped up every few minutes, but it was far from any developed civilization. As they neared Jerusalem, Ezra imagined Ezra the Scribe, The Torah in hand, walking back to his broken city from being in exile in Babylon. In ancient texts, it was said that God revealed to him—in a vision—the face of the Anti-Christ. Ezra began to wonder if the scribe's vision was of the future, and in that sea of eternal limbo that blanketed the desolate land he gazed upward into the sky to see a great metal dragon with a man's face peering down through its menacing, singular eye.

Ezra opened his eyes and released himself from the memory. Vishnu was standing there, still by the pond, patient but still expecting an answer.

"I don't want to be your enemy," Ezra said, trying to remain neutral.

"You preach peace to the world, and yet no one knows your dark secret and that Hasam, the man you were meant to kill, did in fact sell those secrets to Iran. Iran dropped their bombs on Israel, obliterating everything except for Gaza just four weeks after our mission. Luckily, the French sponsored coupe in Tehran was successful or else the entire world might have been destroyed by thermo-nuclear war."

"And I feel it every day," Ezra said, dropping to his knees with weakness, "Every waking moment, the screams of millions of citizens crying out. The thought of so many lives lost by my hands causes me suffering on an incomprehensible level."

"Don't beat yourself up too much, Ezra. They would have found a way regardless. But that doesn't change the fact you owe the Zurvan Order a favor. So when the waves of change hit you, make a choice. *Make the right choice,*" Vishnu whispered.

He walked off, the blue and orange butterflies following him every step of the way as he whistled an ancient melody.

"One last thing," Ezra said, "What of Hasam? Did you ever kill him?"

Vishnu stopped.

"If you don't know the answer to that it means you've been fighting for the wrong reasons."

The man of many lives walked away. Ezra stayed there for a minute trying to process everything. Over the years he had tried to block out that mission and his indebtedness to Vishnu. In the time being, there wasn't anything he could do for the wanted terrorist, except keep living the secret.

Ingrid was sitting on the bed in the hotel room when Ezra returned early that evening. She quickly muted the television and smiled at Ezra.

"Hey love. How was your day?" Ezra asked.

"It went well. I bought a lot of stuff, but I didn't spend all the money you gave me."

"You didn't? What the hell kind of shopper are you?"

She laughed and said, "Not a very good one, I guess. How was your day?"

Ezra sat down with Ingrid and told her about how Vishnu had found him, sparing her the details of their past. He told her of how they now had someone else to watch out for.

"You don't think he would hunt us down, would you?" Ingrid asked.

"No. He wants something from me, but I don't know what. Regardless, it makes me uneasy. He's a murderer and a wanted man. We should leave this place soon."

"I agree, but there is one more little experiment I have for you while we have the resources of the city at our disposal."

"What's that?" Ezra asked.

"Don't take this the wrong way, but would you be willing to see a shrink?"

"I've already seen one. Explain," Ezra said skeptically.

"I'm thinking if someone was to hypnotize you, now after your mutation, your brain function would allow you to be able to tell the history of Earth and maybe the universe," Ingrid said with a twinkle in her eye. Ingrid's imagination was fascinating to Ezra, and he kissed her on the forehead before agreeing.

"Yes I will do that. Call your psychiatrist tomorrow, and let's just hope there's no long-term side effects."

CHAPTER 8
SCAR ATLAS

The next day, there was a knock at Ezra's door at around 2:30 PM. He stood up and walked over with a gun behind his back. After looking through the peep hole, he put the pistol back in his pants and opened the door.

"Good afternoon, please come in, Doctor."

A skinny man, bent low with age, entered the room and introduced himself.

"Hello Ezra. I am Doctor Haden Walner. Ingrid called and told me to make room in my schedule today, seeing how you will be leaving town soon."

"That is correct. Thank you for coming on such short notice."

"You're welcome, it's my pleasure. Alright then, well let's sit down and begin."

Ingrid brought out some coffee and tea as the doctor and Ezra sat on the couch.

"So Ezra, let's start with your childhood," Dr. Walner said, putting on his glasses.

"Let's not," Ezra responded, looking at him coldly.

"Ezra, I can understand how past experiences may be hard to face, but it's better that I get to know you a bit more so we can move past them together."

"Pass," Ezra reiterated before sipping some tea loudly.

"Sorry he's being difficult, Doctor. But we aren't necessarily looking to help with his PTSD or talk about his childhood. We know there are many other doctors and methods for these things. For now, there's a very specific deed he needs from you. Something you specialize in."

Dr. Walner looked at both of them, confused.

"I want you to hypnotize me and ask me how the universe began," Ezra said bluntly.

"I'm not quite sure I follow-"

"Ezra has DNA that has been assimilated to a fungal life form that we believe is one of the oldest and purest organisms on Earth, and quite possibly alien. Purest in the sense it has a very simple but powerfully adaptive genetic code."

"Yes, I've been watching the news," he remarked.

"We think that if you put him under hypnosis and ask him how it all began, that he will be able to tell us, with specificity, the answers to questions that people have been asking since the dawn of humankind," Ingrid said.

Dr. Walner sat for a moment, thinking.

"Well, this is truly an unusual case. The process would be highly unorthodox-"

"We know," Ingrid and Ezra said simultaneously.

"There are so many risks though. In most cases I wouldn't worry about experimental hypnosis methods, but there's a chance he would have trouble coming out of it by being trapped in his subconscious, or worse..." The doctor paused. "Have you considered the possibility he may not return, mentally?"

"It's a risk I'm willing to take, Doctor," Ezra said.

"Well hold on a minute, you don't actually think this could be dangerous or something, do you?" Ingrid asked.

"You're asking me to use a humanoid hybrid as a quantum antenna to navigate the atlas of time and space. Anything could happen, Ingrid," Dr. Walner said before sighing, "Maybe nothing."

There was an uneasiness in the air for a minute. Ezra nodded and shrugged.

"I'll be fine. Let's do this."

"I don't know about this," Ingrid moaned.

"This was your idea," Ezra told her. "Don't worry. I'll be fine."

Ezra laid on the bed as Doctor Walner moved some pillows around to make him more comfortable. Ingrid closed the shades and the doctor began his instructions.

"Ezra, close your eyes and let me take you to a soothing place. I want you to feel calm and relaxed. Imagine you're floating in space. Just floating, not caring about anyone or anything. Just floating. Floating by stars and planets peacefully. Keep floating Ezra, you're feeling more relaxed. You are on a silver cloud of warm and peaceful thoughts. Shhhhh. Be calm now. Shhhhh."

"Is it working?" Ingrid whispered.

The doctor nodded.

"Ezra, how are you feeling."

"I'm feeling... good," Ezra responded sleepily.

"Okay Ezra, I want you to go all the way back to the beginning. Before the stars, before the big bang. Tell me how this universe came to be. Travel quickly and be explicit."

There was a long pause. Ezra's eyelids twitched for a moment then he took a deep breath.

"Why isn't he talking?" Ingrid whispered.

The doctor pondered for a moment but said nothing. Ezra lay calmly and did not speak. He breathed slowly. His eyelids twitched once in a while. They waited patiently.

After almost fifteen minutes, the doctor stood up and whispered in Ingrid's ear.

"Perhaps he won't speak because there was no language in the beginning. But it's all... dreams within a trance-like state... I doubt there is a way he's experiencing something truly astral, you know? Television, war, the epidemic of partial psychosis in his generation... his imagination may project images he's already seen or felt... it's very difficult to distinguish what he will tell me is true and what was just projected."

Ingrid nodded. They waited patiently and after another few minutes, Ezra began moving his arms a bit, and opening his mouth as if to say something.

"Ezra?" asked the doctor.

Ezra looked as if he was in pain. He started making strange faces and then, to Ingrid's horror, large lacerations began forming on his body as if he were being whipped and beaten by some invisible scourge. Dark tears of blood streamed from his still closed eyes.

As he began convulsing, Ingrid grasped the doctor's arm, who sat in shock and helplessness.

Ezra's red tears streamed down his sliced-up body, drenching the bed with his pouring flesh. He lurched and moaned.

"OH MY GOD! STOP THIS!! STOP THIS!!" Ingrid screamed.

"Ezra, I'm going to wake you up now-" the doctor said frantically, snapping out of his shock.

"Father, why have you forsaken me? *Why have you forsaken me?!*" Ezra shrieked.

Small bloody holes started forming in Ezra's head as the doctor held him down in his violent stigmata. The trickles raked his face just like the suffering Messiahs crown of thorns. Holes in his hands and feet formed and he splattered the walls red with his flailing.

"Ezra... five... four... three...two... one. *Wake up!*"

Ezra awoke from his hypnotherapy completely exhausted and weak to the bone. He was deathly pale. His muscles were barely functional. His breathing, broken and weary.

"Ezra?! Oh my God!" Ingrid said hysterically as she cusped his bruised, wet face.

"Just... water. I am *thirsty*," he said.

The small, Christ-like Ezra managed to sit up and calm down, but the image of the crucifixion was hard for him to take in, especially because he claimed to have experienced every development of the cosmos up until that fateful day on Golgotha's mount. Why time slowed to that moment, he didn't know. What he did know, was never to try such an experiment again. It took some time for his Sararan cells to regenerate his body and heal the wounds, the same wounds of Yeshua, right down to the last nail hole.

Ingrid brought tea to Ezra's tired and beaten body.

"I will tell you what I experienced," Ezra said weakly.

"Shh, not now. You should rest," Ingrid said, wiping the blood from his face with a wet towel.

"We needn't keep the doctor here much longer, and he should hear this because he is a necessary player in this experiment."

"Okay. If you can compress fourteen billion years into ten minutes, I will allow it," Ingrid said. Her motherly instincts were already kicking in as she walked over and rinsed the towel.

"Go ahead Ezra. Tell me what you saw," the doctor said.

Ezra wheezed as he began the tale in a raspy, tired voice.

"There was just this small blinking sun in total blackness for a while. Then a wave of photons wrapped around themselves, causing static, a shimmer of red, orange, then yellow. Then a flash of light piercing the emptiness ten times faster than the light following behind it, for it wasn't visible light. It was ultraviolet perhaps, something humans are incapable of seeing. But it sped outward like a dome for all existence. Then...BOOM!" Ezra's shout startled Ingrid and Dr. Walner, but he continued, "A milky white glow spread vast. So large, it imploded before moving outward. The explosion was so vast. Rivers of matter and energy shot across the universe a trillion miles long. This boom created the colors, the sounds, the smells, and eventually the life made organically from the birth of time and gravity."

"Wow. That's an incredible image. What other life did you see?" the doctor said.

"None. None at all. As if Earth truly was the only paradise meant for life."

"Why is that, do you think?"

"I don't know. I saw small organisms thrive in the oceans all over the blue planet. They worked their ways to larger areas. They evolved onto land and conquered it. Life grew and become extinct, and many times over the Earth recycled its life forms. Then an early human stood up and stuck his spear into the Earth, claiming it. And from that day on, they could not be killed off as past species had. It's as if humans are... non-recyclable. And they won't stop until..." Ezra paused.

"Yes Ezra?" The doctor asked.

Ezra's thousand-yard stare returned, and Ingrid knew they were finished.

"I'm sorry but think it is time for Ezra to rest, Dr. Walner."

"Not a problem, Ingrid. I hope the best for you Ezra, and for a speedy recovery."

Ezra looked up at him but said nothing. Not even goodbye.

Ingrid paced down the hall of the hotel with the doctor, talking with him and trying to understand what had happened.

"Ingrid, I did try to warn you of the potential outcomes."

"I know, doctor, don't take any blame for what happened. You did everything we asked. We never should have tried this."

"Well, if what you say is true about his regeneration abilities, there shouldn't be any long-term damage. In fact, I don't think it was a futile experiment."

"What are your thoughts?"

"Well you know, the crucifixion of Christ was so long ago, many people, from atheists to other religious peoples, don't believe that Christ was the son of God, or even a prophet for that matter."

"But this doesn't prove anything biblically. Ezra could have experienced this from memories or passages, not actually going through what Christ had as if there was some kind of... astral integration of bodies. Do you think?"

"Did you notice that he quoted Christ several times at the end of his hypnosis? 'Father, why have you forsaken me?' and 'Water, I am thirsty'?"

"Are you a Christian?"

"No, but I believe, especially after seeing Ezra's version of our history, that Christ was a vessel for God, subjectively. That is why he was a healer and could perform so-called miracles. Maybe he just knew how to tap into the atomic plane of our universe, perhaps a dimension we don't understand. Of course you and I know for a fact that Christ didn't actually ascend to any 'heaven' physically. Even if he were to travel at the speed of light, he would still not have left our galaxy. Nietzsche once said, 'the kingdom of heaven is the condition of the heart, not something that comes upon the earth or after death'. Christ's ascension was an ascension into himself; enlightenment."

"So you think Ezra's reaction helps support the idea that anyone can achieve nirvana?" Ingrid asked.

"Or more accurately put, most everyone has the ability to open themselves up and absorb the energy that circulates around everyone and everything. I'm tempted to call it nirvana but it's up to the subject, of course, to relieve themselves of those trivial labels. Regardless of what it is happening here, it is very rare and very powerful."

"Especially Ezra because of his mutation?"

"Yes, especially Ezra. A being with his abilities certainly has a much greater chance to become a voice in the trans-humanism movement. Perhaps if Ezra exercised an acute form of spiritual practice, he might discover some amazing traits within himself."

"The only thing left I am curious about, is why he cried tears of blood?" Ingrid asked.

Just then, a dark figure leaning against the wall answered, "Crimson tears. A symptom of all fallen angels. If he were to attempt the ascension to heaven, he'd be denied, for the sky marks the boundary of his contempt. Thus his kingdom is here

158

in the wake of mankind's waste. For the Earth will be split, like the skulls of his and my enemies. Town after town, state after state, until one day a real flood will come. And all the waters of Earth turn to blood."

"Excuse me? Who are you?" Ingrid asked.

"I am the lash of nature's wrath, and I am not alone."

"Vishnu?" Ingrid whispered.

"Indeed," said the voice. "I'm impressed by your work, Ingrid McAdam. You've an expeditionary approach to your sciences. The articles from Sumatra and Bali were my favorite. But I noticed you mislead the reader by mixing up the frog genus's Microhyla and Occidozyga. You may want to contact your editor, lest your reputation be fouled by mere dyslexia."

Ingrid just looked at him, afraid to say or do anything in the face of the world's top ranked terrorist. The doctor did not recognize him but studied his affection.

"Take good care of yourself and your man. You may find raising a child will be difficult in a cold, harsh world," Vishnu said.

The assassin went down the hallway toward the open elevator. He walked in, turned around, and tilted his head goodbye as the doors closed. He disappeared and Ingrid shuddered.

"That was strange," Dr. Walner said, "You've obviously got a lot more on your hands than I wish to know. Give Ezra plenty of rest and then you two should get far away from here. There are lots of religious nuts down here in the south. I will keep the events of today confidential, of course."

"Thank you, Doctor," Ingrid said with a worried face. The doctor tipped his hat and walked away.

"Oh Doctor... what about your payment?"

"Don't worry about it," he said without turning. "Let's just say I was never here."

Ingrid returned to the room where Ezra lay in bed, still healing from his episode from earlier. Beside the bed sat his old comrade Gadreel, as he had come quickly with some medical supplies at Ingrid's request.

"Hello dear," Ezra said as Ingrid walked into the room.

"Hey, how are you feeling?" Ingrid asked while waving at Gadreel, who smiled and nodded in return.

"I'm doing much better," he said, wheezing still. His lungs sounded terrible with each inhale, but they could draw breath deeper and clearer than after he had initially woken up.

"Gadreel was just reminding me about some of the wild times we've had."

"You know your man is very brave, don't you?" Gadreel said, smiling.

"It was our first deployment in Saudi Arabia. Well back then, when he was green still, he had all these expensive trinkets and shit on his gun and a tactical belt full of shit that was totally useless, especially in the sand."

Ezra laughed but it hurt his chest, so he stopped abruptly.

"Anyways, by the time we were in Syria a few deployments later, he was a far sharper warrior. I remember one morning our outpost was attacked and this crazy mothafucka had only his underwear and boots and helmet on as he rushed out to the sandbags."

The comrades chuckled and Ingrid smiled. She was glad an old friend came to visit him in his weakened state. She could see it was visibly helping him heal faster. Just then the hotel phone rang. Ingrid looked at Ezra with an inquisitive look. Ingrid answered.

"Hello?"

A young teenage girl could be heard on the other end of the line.

"Hello Miss McAdam. I'm sorry to disturb you but there is an angry mob downstairs and they seem... pretty mad."

Ingrid walked over to the window to see if what she was saying was true. Hundreds of protesters with signs could be seen on the sidewalk and street.

"Well call the police, you numbskull!"

"We have, Miss McAdam. They are monitoring the crowd, but the protesters are across the street, so we can't kick them out. They have the right to peacefully assemble. I just wanted to let you know. Please let us know if there's anything else we can-"

"Shit!" Ingrid said as she hung up the phone.

"Unwanted guests?" asked Gadreel as he stood up.

"Yeah, hundreds of them. Those fucking bigots again," Ingrid steamed. "How ironic, considering the circumstances."

Gadreel walked up to the window and looked out with his one eye.

"They're no ordinary Christians either. Those are the psychos from the Westboro Baptist church," he said.

"It's almost time, Ingrid," Ezra said weakly.

"We can't go now!" she exclaimed.

"No, but we can go soon. I had Gadreel and Malthus put all of our stuff into a van this morning while you went to get breakfast."

Just then a short, young man with a blonde buzz cut dressed in black and blue camouflage came into the room holding about thirty muffins.

"This hotel kicks ass, Ezra," said the man with chocolate crumbs falling out of his mouth.

"What's going on?" he asked as every eye in the room fell on him.

"Ingrid, meet Malthus. He's the medic. Malthus, this is Ingrid," Ezra said, smiling wide.

"Hi Ingrid. Damn, Ezra. How did you land a girl like that?"

Ingrid shook her head but couldn't help but smile and blush.

"Like I said, everything is where it needs to be, we just need to get into the van and go by 9 AM tomorrow," Ezra said.

"What about the people who would follow us? Won't they know?"

"If there are, they're going to follow us," Gadreel said as he started walking toward the door, "Ezra has a decoy van ready, so we'll go first to distract them. I'll see you in a few days Ezra. By the way, where do you want us to stage?"

"Ask Ingrid, she's the one that picked our location," Ezra said, searching for the piece of paper.

"I hadn't picked one yet," she admitted.

"Just pick one. They're all good spots."

"Fine. Um... Montana sounds nice?"

"Montana it is then! The cabin life will suit us both," Ezra said. "Meet us at the air strip north of Polebridge two days from now."

"We'll see you there," Gadreel said.

Malthus looked at Ezra and Ingrid then smiled with chocolate lips.

"Have a good time, love birds!" he yelled as Gadreel pushed Malthus out the door, the muffins still in his arms.

"Hey can we go downstairs and do some crowd control?" Malthus asked.

"No," answered Gadreel in his deep voice.

"When am I ever gonna use this tear gas I've been carrying everywhere?!"

"Shut the fuck up already," Gadreel said as their voices dissipated down the hallway.

Ezra stood up. He was still sore, but his wounds were scarred over and he was no longer bleeding.

"Ezra, I'm scared. Vishnu was here earlier, and he was really creepy and spoke cryptically and I... I don't trust him at all."

"I know he was here. He's been speaking to me telepathically. I didn't even know that was possible until now. I have learned a great deal about the metaphysical realm today. We'll be fine though, love. We're about to go off the grid. *Way* off the grid."

Ezra awoke to the flicker of passing pine trees through the van window. He was in the woods and could feel the serene qualities of the solitude. He looked at his hands, which showed no scarring. He looked at his arms, and there weren't any laceration marks either. He was completely healed due to his ever-evolving cells.

Sitting upright, he felt the calmness of a long-needed rest hit him, and he smiled, having finally made it away from the cluster of the city and away from the hatred of the bigots that wanted them ousted. He looked over at Ingrid in the drivers' seat, whose green irises appeared as circular windows to the needle laden background that flashed like a picture show behind her. The woods were her element and Ezra could sense it in her.

"How long have I been out for?"

"Morning sunshine! Oh I'd say about 22 hours now," Ingrid said, relieved he was finally awake.

Ezra looked out the window. Peering East, he could see into the uninhabited and widely still preserved territories of Glacier National Park. It was a beautifully dark and mysterious land that bled into Canada's wild. The way the clouds culminated at the pointy peaks and poured wind into the lower elevations made Ezra long to be up in that icy, secluded world. He imagined himself atop one of the spiny summits, where no life, nor means for living presided, besides the aging lichens in which his body could relate. It was a cold atmosphere held up by white snow that blanketed billion-year old rocks eroded by the harshest weather on the planet, where ocean waves once crashed and receded back to a land reptiles once ruled.

Ezra rolled down the window and breathed in the freezing air. A large cloud began to block out the sun as a blizzard was fast moving towards them like a herd of ten thousand white warhorses.

"Yes," Ezra said. "I don't see us leaving here anytime soon."

Ingrid smiled and wrapped her hand around his.

"How have you been driving this whole time, by the way?" Ezra asked.

"Coffee. Tons of coffee. Like four pots of coffee."

"You could have stopped and rested for a while, you know?"

"I didn't want to compromise the secrecy of our escape," she said.

"Well thank you for that. That's highly professional of you. Do you want me to take over?"

"No, we're almost there anyways. Where is this place exactly? Polebridge is coming up soon," Ingrid asked.

"It's about 15 miles past that."

"But that would put us-"

"Right on the edge of the United States and Canada," Ezra said.

They drove for another half hour or so, bouncing along the snowy backwoods road as houses and cabins became less frequent and more rustic and were replaced by age old lodge pole pine stands; the kind of thick where the branches are high but the trunks are thin and naked and numerous, and you can see for a mile into the wood with the right eyes. The snowdrifts pushed up by the plows were as high as the van itself, since the road had to be clear year around for the border patrol, despite the closed port. After they'd entered a sort of clearing, Ezra motioned to park the vehicle, because the driveway to the cabin was completely snowed in. After strapping into some snowshoes and putting the rest of their supplies on sleds, Ingrid and Ezra walked the quarter mile to their new home. The blizzard's edge neared them, and they felt the snowy flakes dissolve their fears and worries, and cloak them in their placid wintry wonderland. When they turned the corner to see the cabin, Ingrid gasped.

A large, old two-story cabin sat comfortably next to the southeast bound river, whose snaking path of ice blue water held tree logs at its curves to form carefully structured beaver lodges. Beyond that, the sky-scraping peaks of the park loomed in the distance and appeared as white titans retaining their monolithic dimensions through the ages. A few hundred feet away from the main cabin, four small but cozy cabins, also part of the estate, spread south with the fourth at the edge of a sprawling airstrip. Across the landing, massive pines and aspen trees lined the edge of the forest. A single road connecting to their driveway wound its way beside the field and into the dark wood, where deer could be seen finding shelter from the oncoming storm. To the south, white cranes walked idly between mounds of cat tails punctuating a small frozen marsh.

Ezra and Ingrid stood there, listening only to the gentle psithurism of the breeze weave through the branches. They hugged one another, free at last, ready to not only begin a new life for themselves, but also *give* life in the form of a child. A true son of the stars. An angel amidst men. Michael, or, *he who is closest to God.*

CHAPTER 9
LOVES LAST ORCHID

Ingrid and Ezra loved their new home. The quiet life at the cabin was soothing compared to the hectic lives they'd both once lived. Far from any town or city, they kept to themselves mostly; chopping wood, knitting quilts, gathering food, cooking home-made recipes on a wood fired stove and stoking a cozy fire in the evenings that they'd snuggle up to. On perfect blue-sky afternoons of mid-winter, when the sun sank low and all day appeared as morning, they'd put on their snowshoes and hike along the river to look for animal tracks while letting the birds pluck berries from their outstretched palms. A bull moose regularly visited the beaver ponds in the mornings and Ingrid studied the large ungulate with great admiration. She had a myriad of simple side projects, the nearby field and river being her plot for scientific discoveries.

As Ingrid's belly grew, so did her appetite, and Ezra made trips into the Flathead Valley for fresh food they would have difficulty harvesting in wintertime. The Hoods offered to fly in supplies for them, but Ezra insisted they stay at the cabins to protect Ingrid. For the first few weeks, he and Gadreel would drive the narrow corridor of pines, their connection to nature deepening in the ocean of trees. They'd bring their rifles sometimes and skip the trip to town to hunt elk instead, following the tracks deep in the mountains, sometimes hiking for several days to procure their game. They both agreed this was preferable to contributing to the increasingly murderous agriculture industry. And as time went on, Ezra's Sararan abilities made town trips obsolete as he began using his 'seed sprouting' technique. Ingrid began injecting mitochondria and plant zygotes into Ezra's blood to add to his index of species stored in his DNA. Soon, they didn't need a garden, no matter the season. Ezra's hand had all the means for self-assembling permaculture. Only water was needed to complete the equation, which he could suction from the air into his pores.

Gadreel and the other contractors took up the other four cabins of the estate, which not only gave the couple relief by way of security, but also wholesome company during the isolated chapter in their lives. Every so often, the men would have their families there and the whole group would have large bonfires that were fed well into the night. Children went sledding down a small hill nearby while the adults drank mead and told stories, laughing beneath the abstract glow of the northern auroras and a starry sky diluted not by street light pollution, where the teeth-like mountain ranges gnashed at the ever-swirling night sky. As they felt safer every passing month, Ingrid and Ezra grew happier. They were at peace and able to explore a world all their own as if the planet's violent climate was too far to reach them.

One morning in May, Ingrid awoke to the pitter-patter of raindrops falling on the cabin's metal roofing. She sat up and rubbed her eyes. Outside the window, a grey fog spread over the river and field. The pines at the field's edge held in a peaceful darkness as the spring rains penetrated the thick forest behind them. The river ran high. Massive logs tumbled downstream and could be heard scraping the bottom as they churned the water into a muddy gauntlet. A strong current of splashing rapids and deep whirlpools made it a devastating elemental not to be forged.

"Ezra?" she asked, after gazing for some time.

She walked downstairs to the cabin main floor and looked into the kitchen. There she saw Ezra wearing her apron, as he danced to some Columbian music and flipped huckleberry pancakes on the griddle.

"Good morning, darling," he said. He was completely covered in flour, hinting at his lack of baking experience. The pancakes looked edible enough.

"How wonderful!" she exclaimed.

"I was going to bring you breakfast in bed, but apparently I'm too late. I had to throw out the first batch," Ezra said.

"Wasting perfectly good huckleberries no doubt!" Ingrid said, sitting down at the counter.

Ezra put up his finger. "Well we don't need to steal Lily's anymore at least."

"And when is our lovely mid-wife stopping by?" Ingrid asked.

"Lillian should've been here around ten, so any minute I'm guessing."

"I really love her," Ingrid said, rubbing her rounded tummy. "She has such a welcoming and joyous aura about her. We're lucky to have someone so close by that can help us with the birth."

"Yeah, Polebridge is a lot closer than the valley. Plus we don't have to be disguised or anything here," Ezra said.

Just then, there was knock on the back door.

"Come in!" Ezra said.

A petite brunette woman in her 40's walked in. She wore a funky purple shirt, flower overalls, and she had large, round, red glasses that made her eyes look enormous.

"Hello, my beauties!" she exclaimed with her arms held wide and a smile that stretched from ear to ear.

"Hey Lily, it's so good to see you!" Ingrid said as they kissed each other on the cheek and hugged.

"You might not want to hug me, I have flour all over me," Ezra said, laughing.

"Oh shush and come here, ya big lug."

She hugged Ezra then turned back to Ingrid.

"So how are you feeling today, hun?"

"I'm well, thanks. I slept well, too. I'm pretty hungry though."

"Well no kidding, you're feeding two people! Let's take a look-see at how big you're getting," Lily said, pulling out a measuring tape. She wrapped it around Ingrid's belly and took a good look.

"How's it looking?"

"Perfect, Ingrid."

"I've been feeling him kicking a lot lately,"

"Oh have you?" Lily said, giggling.

"Yeah, Michael is a pretty rambunctious little one."

"Breakfast is served, ladies," Ezra said as he put the steaming pile of purple spotted pancakes in the center of the table. The cake's spongy texture soaked up the slow melting pads of butter. Thick maple syrup dripped from the edges of the pile as the three dug in.

"There's bacon too if you'd like some, Lily," Ezra said, passing the plate around.

"No thank you, dear," she replied.

To Ezra's surprise, Ingrid grasped the plate and topped her pancakes with several pieces of bacon before adding a layer of whipped cream and more syrup.

"My, my, look who's eating meat so voraciously," Ezra said, looking at her with his wide dark eyes.

"A pregnant woman's got to eat what she's craving," Ingrid said, stuffing a large mound of breakfast food into her mouth.

"It's totally normal Ingrid," Lily said, "so don't feel ashamed for temporarily giving up your vegan ways."

"Nope. I'm sold. Bacon is too delicious," Ingrid said smiling.

They all laughed and continued with their meals. The smell of freshly cooked breakfast, coffee, and firewood filled the cabin. It was warm and homelike inside. Outside smelled of raw Earth, the air was cool, and the ground was soaking wet to the point of saturation. A day like that meant getting on raincoats and boots, for dinner was equally important to Ingrid's appetite and a very special delicacy awaited them in the forest.

After Lily was finished with breakfast, she told Ingrid she'd check on her in another week. She kissed them goodbye before speeding off in her rusty old pickup truck.

Ezra stepped out onto the porch to get some fresh air and to stretch for a minute. He looked toward the other four cabins and saw smoke rising from the chimneys. Behind them, two fully armed attack helicopters and a double rotor transport ship were parked in the field, a strange backdrop for the pastoral scene. The mercenaries had made their cabins home, and even after going on routine hikes and doing circuit training programs, they were getting soft. But for once, Ezra knew they didn't mind the prolonged R&R. All of those men had had such non-stop combat experience in the last few years that a paid vacation was just what they needed, for they had been too strong for too long. Ezra found that being close to nature helped with many of the men's experiences, becoming more apparent over the months as silence permeated their surroundings and gave them a chance for introspection. Ezra was there to talk to them since he was a seasoned veteran himself, and because of his Sararan qualities he could connect with the men through a thin but alluring telepathic level of understanding. For some of them, sometimes this meant breaking down in Ezra's arms while he reassured them that their purpose in life remained, even if they couldn't sense it right then. He taught them the value of darkness, and the value of light, and how you need both to combat what they were dealing with. Some of the things Ezra said during these visits came from a place of inner knowing, as the information was a surprise to even himself. He didn't feel he had prophetic capabilities, but rather he was just compelled to heal the wounded, something augmented since educating himself in the fields of medicine, science, math, and philosophy. It had become apparent in his words, in his thoughts, and in his actions that he like all creatures are capable of more than their instincts allow. And even though he'd become smarter and stronger, he was modest, even with himself, and vastly underestimated his abilities. He didn't care to test his powers on a large scale. But like all who have rode gallantly on the fringe, it is impossible to escape the vortex of destiny. Ezra knew this truth but kept himself in a quiet denial. He wanted to enjoy his family and his peace as long as he could before the tides of war ultimately turned against him once again. As the eye of a hurricane of violence sighted in on Ezra's complacent state, the soft winds of eternity lied their terrible lie, and for a short while, the very notion of death evaded him. Just the same, Ezra was not unconscious to his mortality, or worse, his immortality. Yet something blinded his third eye.

As he stood there on the porch, lost in thought, Ezra muttered to himself, "What buried curse hath been unearthed inside of me?"

Ingrid walked out and looked at Ezra. She suddenly felt something wasn't right.

Ezra felt woozy and stared at the ground. He then said slowly, "If I am guilty, then so is all life, as are enemies of the sky, as are thieves of Gods work, and betrayers of God's love. Yet I am not one who casts down shadows from the mirror of the morning star. I am Lucifer *who hath been cast*."

"Ezra?" Ingrid asked.

Ezra snapped out of his daze, forgetting what he'd said.

"It was him, wasn't it? Is he... possessing you?" Ingrid asked quietly, her breath short.

"Vishnu broadcasted a spell," Ezra said, realizing what had happened.

"How?"

"The magnetism of the Earth," he said nodding in confidence and looking toward the cloudy sky. There was a short silence.

"So you were-"

"Possessed, yeah," Ezra said, spitting. He walked over and kissed Ingrid on the cheek.

"I'm fine. Trust me. You ready?"

They walked by the river, watching its crashing waters tear at the bank while roaring with ten million voices. Once at the field's edge, they cut into the wood, the river's commotion fading into the gentle sound of rainfall on the leaves until only a murmur of the North Fork could be heard above the forest's subtle song.

"It's like the Peruvian jungle," Ingrid said, noticing the fungus on the logs, and dark rotting appearance of the wood. She shuddered for a moment, but let the thought escape her just as quick as it came. Ezra walked over to her and put his hand in hers.

"It's nothing like that forest, my love. This is our home. This is our sanctuary."

They walked around, looking intently at the leafy forest floor for the oddly spongy brown mushrooms. Suddenly, Ingrid yelled, "Found one! No, two! No, four!"

She pulled out her small satchel and put the mushrooms inside, eager to find more.

"Fantastic!" Ezra yelled.

"Hey wait! Couldn't you just hold one of these, put your other hand on the ground, and grow it yourself?" Ingrid asked, puzzled and amused.

"I could, but what's the fun in that? We have to leave some things wild, if not at least for our own amusement."

She smiled and continued the hunt, finding small patches near the marshes edge, and close to puddles or tree roots.

After a while, Ezra motioned for Ingrid to come to where he was.

"What is it?" she asked.

"Look here," he said.

Ingrid looked where Ezra was looking but couldn't see anything right away. It was just a small grassy patch. Then suddenly the patch moved.

A small turtle had gotten flipped over on its back and was having a hard time getting back over.

"Oh poor guy. I'll save you Mr. Turtle!" she said in a cute voice.

She flipped him over, and to her astonishment, there was an engagement ring tied with golden twine to the top of the turtle's shell.

Ezra slowly dropped to one knee.

"Ingrid Eleanor McAdam. Will you marry me?"

Ingrid's eyes flooded. Even though she knew Ezra would eventually ask her, there had been no ceremonial act of going forward until that moment.

"Yes Ezra James Beller. I will marry you. I love you," she said with tears streaming. She reached down and untied the twine. She put the ring on and hugged Ezra closely.

"Well don't make me cry!" Ezra said as a single bloody tear fell down his cheek.

"Sorry. I know. It's scary when you cry," she said before giggling a bit. "I love that you used a turtle to ask me. You're so adorable."

"It seemed most fitting, seeing how it's your favorite specimen."

"No Ezra, you're my favorite specimen."

As the little turtle continued slowly on his way, the young, happy couple walked around the woods for a while longer, their satchels full of tasty fungi, their hearts full of love. Ezra noticed a large cedar tree next to a clearing that had a bald face where there was no bark. He took Ingrid's hand and walked over to it, looking at it for some time.

"It's a cedar tree," Ingrid said, laughing.

"Yes I know," Ezra replied.

"So what about it?" she asked.

Ezra pulled out a pocketknife and walked closer to it. Ingrid stayed a few feet away, curious at her fiancé's actions. Ezra began scratching something into the wood with his knife, but then he stopped.

"What?" Ingrid asked.

Ezra smiled and closed his eyes. He put the knife away and extended his finger to the wood with his sharp crystalline nail and focused his energy on that point. A small stream of smoke began lifting from his sketches as he wrote in cursive. The smell of burning wood rose into the wet afternoon air.

"There. All done," Ezra said, stepping back to look.

Ingrid walked up and touched it. The etchings were still warm, and read 'Ezra and Ingrid, forever'.

"You're so corny!" she said, laughing.

"So?" Ezra yelled as he picked her up and started carrying her around the clearing. They laughed and played, like children, like beings free from form, like two butterflies dancing in a light breeze. They were becoming true lovers; they were *becoming one*.

On a sunny afternoon in mid-June, Ingrid found herself walking slowly over the grass and sticks of the forest floor, which were cool and moist beneath her bare feet. A warm breeze threw her long curly black hair this way and that, shuttering her green eyes, which opened widely to drink in the greatest day of her life. She was adorned in a white and tan gown made of hemp and fine Italian silk. Small Yogo sapphires were sewn into the cuffs of the sleeves and reflected the sun's light into hundreds of tiny fractal ultra-marine dots, spotting her woven dress like blue suns orbiting her large belly.

Twenty steps ahead of her stood Ezra below a small but quaint altar he had built for their ceremony; an archway made of birch tree, vines and flowers, a symbol of their devotion to nature and a mythical portal into a world of everlasting union with the beloved. Larks and hummingbirds swirled around Ingrid as she approached the shrine. They were attracted to all the colorful flowers, which had been cultivated—with the help from Ezra's charms—into a large rainbow garden in place of an audience. Through its center, a corridor had been left clear for Ingrid to walk through to him. She walked past the half circle of pink orchids, purple lilacs, blue hydrangeas, green gladiolus, yellow daffodils, saffron Indian paintbrushes, and finally, brilliant scarlet poppies. As Ingrid passed each row she smiled as her hands grazed the plethora of flowers that stood tall on the forest flat. She combed the petals with her gown as each step brought her closer to her lover and gave her the redolence of their blossoming. The smell in the air was heavenly beyond all description.

Ezra had his dark shoulder-length hair combed back and wore a black long-sleeved shirt with a viridian silk cape. He smiled at his bride and reached for her hand. She stepped closer and then stood opposite of him, giggling a bit before loosely holding his hands in hers.

As they stood, eyes locked, an elderly man walked from behind the archway, as if coming from a different dimension to officiate the ceremony. His white hair and beard were long, and his bright white robe seemed to glow. Though his eyes had seen much, they were not weary. He had a calm demeanor about him. For he was neither happy nor sad, troubled, nor carefree. He was a mysterious old man who had offered to be a part of the ceremony of his own accord. Though his origins were unknown, he was a local to Polebridge for as long as the people had known him.

The old man began the ritual by binding their hands with a green and gold silk ribbon. His hands were soft, with many creases, and Ezra could sense as the old man's fingers grazed his own, that they were no ordinary hands. The touch gave him a humble feeling of remembrance of a time passed, not of the old man's own life, but of a time *outside of time* when the winds and river whisper a secret to the thirsty ears of seekers and those who sought hard enough could obtain the ability to interpret that unremitting word, which rendered a transcendence that absolved all others into what many humans would call enlightenment. Ezra had felt this through the old man, as he longed for the singularity of his soul to dissolve into that kind of majesty. Electricity ran through the old man's nerves. Pure blood circulated in his veins. A soundness permeated the three of them on a level of nirvana that before that day had remained unknown in the tangible world Ingrid and Ezra thought they knew but had so much yet to learn. The man took a deep breath in and looked upward toward the sky before he spoke.

"Lion Ezra. Lioness Ingrid. We are here, in this beautiful orchard, to discuss what need not be said, for both of you have already made your commitment to one another in everlasting love. However, for the sake of sacred matrimony, and to have the stars, sun, sky, river and Earth bear witness, I shall marry thee in the bosom of mother creation so that thy souls will be forever engrained in this existence. I shall commence this heavenly engagement with an Om mantra. Please, children of the eternal cloth, join me in the mantra."

They began the Om, and as they did, a calmness permeated them. Once the mantra faded, he continued.

"The Earth is like a furnace, and yet we do not always notice its constant burning. But even when the forest is alive and well, the hearts of lovers are burning because the furnace is also *in us*. Like the sun, so many million miles away, we feel its heat. Close your eyes. A cloud moves in front of it, and then it reappears, and we know that feeling, and strive for it with great wanting. So is the distance of the lover. The lover can be halfway across the planet, but the fire is there, within both the lover and the beloved, for all time.

"This furnace is also a furnace of suffering. Rumi said, 'The door there is devastation', and he meant that in the most literal way conceivable. To love is to enter a gauntlet. It is worse than death, to lose the beloved. It is the worst torture. And yet you take that risk willingly when you bind your hands in marriage as yours are now. This promise is a holy one. This union is a cause for joy and celebration. Yet it is also a serious commitment in taking the heart of the other and placing it with yours. You take her eyes, Ezra, and Ingrid, take his, and show each other that this is exactly what you desire, to let go of yourself and become the other; for Ezra to take on the feminine, and for Ingrid to take on the masculine. Let yourselves reach toward the unknown and feel the duality in the cosmos. It will bring you great wisdom, but I cannot speak of it anymore. You will have to learn this on your own. You will have to reach until the balance is met and your spirit knows what it means to be shapeless and free.

"Lioness Ingrid, do you have your vows?"

"Yes, I do," she said.

"You may read them now," the old man said smiling.

"Ezra, since I started falling for you, I forgot what it means to be afraid. When we got back to safety from the evils of that fateful day in the Andes, your touch was all that was needed to calm me and reassure me that I was safe. I realize now that it was not your protection that made me fearless, but my love for you that in turn made me want to protect you. Maybe I don't know martial arts, or how to shoot a rifle yet, but I will protect you and our family just the same and I'll take this honor to the grave with me. I love you, Ezra James Beller. I would do anything for you, and I know that you would do the same for me. It warms my heart every waking moment I am with you, and to feel my child growing in me and knowing that he is yours, that he is *ours*. I could not be happier than in this moment, becoming your wife. We will have a beautiful family, and I promise to be the best wife a man could have. I promise to be yours for all time. I promise to be there *until the end*."

There was a long pause after she finished. Ezra and Ingrid chuckled for a moment. Ezra's eyes lined with crimson, but he held back his tears.

"Thank you, my love. That sincerely... blows my vows out of the water."

"She seems like a keeper," the old man muttered comically. They all laughed, then Ezra began.

"It was as if my guardian angel swooped down to save me from my torment. The history books will tell the story of how Ezra Beller saved Ingrid McAdam in the Peruvian tragedy. But I know the truth. Ingrid saved Ezra. You brought me back from the dead. I was in a state of wrath and disgust. I was depressed and would never admit it to anyone. You saved me, Ingrid. I will always be thankful and love you for that. But it didn't stop there. You continue to save me. You teach me about the organisms of Earth, how they're important to the biosphere, and therefore all humans. It gives me purpose, learning these lessons. You teach me about love, about the importance of loving life, so fragile yet binding. You save me by reminding me I am loved, and that your love for me is growing all the time. I know that it will, as my love for you grows as well. Every time I watch you wake up, it is like watching a flower open, or the sun rising up over the peaks on a clear morning. You save me by yielding a boy whom I'll be survived by. He and you are my only ambitions in life. My family will come before anything else, and this home will let us live the lives we deserve to live. I will forever continue to do anything and everything for you, Ingrid. I will forever cherish your existence as one higher than mine. I love you Ingrid Eleanor McAdam. Marry me, and we shall continue to bloom as one."

Ezra pulled up their tied hands and kissed hers. Ingrid cried joyously.

"Thank you, both of you. Your devotion is apparent, and I need not brief you any further on the journey you are about to partake. By the powers vested not in myself, but in the natural world you see, hear, feel, and smell around you, I pronounce you wife and husband. You may kiss one another."

Ezra and Ingrid kissed deeply and sincerely. The kind of kiss that lasts minutes, and yet knows not its own length. It was a kiss that made the entire world go in such slow motion that even the hummingbirds could be seen flapping their wings like a great eagles above the billowing sanguineous poppy pedals.

As the old man untied their wrists, Ezra brought his hand up to Ingrid's face, and wiped her tears away with his thumb.

They smiled and began laughing. The old man laughed with them. Music began playing all around them in the form of large dew drops rolling into puddles, fluttering leaves in the soft breeze, and bobbing flowers that choreographed themselves to a familiar drama.

The married couple walked out of the woods and onto the road that cut through the field towards home. The setting sun's sarcoline glow raked their faces with subtle warmth. Ezra felt the tall grasses on his fingertips as he held Ingrid's hand with the other. Every touch was a gift. Every sense in him was alive, as were Ingrid's, for she was experiencing this heightened sensitivity vicariously through him. To Ezra, his mutation was neither a gift nor curse. He no longer cared what vessel his soul found fit to be home, so long as he was with her. Ezra only wanted peace, and though peace slowed his evolution, it did so only slightly. His love for Ingrid kept him from wanting to engage his powers and yet his powers became stronger still with every kiss, every slight, sensual touch, and every heartbeat spent close to Ingrid and their unborn son. This love perpetuated his ascension, as he was climbing to Nirvana like an air bubble shooting up through the oceans deep. Only when he was about to surface would he reconcile his destiny. Though these thoughts were far from Ezra's mind as he and Ingrid walked in silence, breathing in the sweet summer mountain air and listening to nature's symphony. Gophers chirped, the lazy summer river babbled, and overhead, the wings of nighthawks whistled like war cries of Salish ghosts as they dove through the air.

In the distance by the cabins, a large bonfire had been started in preparation for the reception. Lily and a few local Polebridge folks were attending, as well as Gadreel and the rest of the mercenaries and their families. As Ingrid and Ezra got closer, Malthus' fiddle could be heard playing a Celtic tune as the festivities of the celebration commenced.

Flower petals were thrown into the air as they entered the gathering. People whistled, yelled, and clapped, joyous in the waning of the day. Children with white roses in their hair ran about, chasing Lily's Saint Bernard puppy whose ears were so big they flopped in front of her scrunched face while she clumsily pranced through the grass. The guests cracked open champagne and whiskey bottles. Laughter filled the air with the smoke they puffed. There was a splendid feast of Turkey, scalloped potatoes, wild peas, yams, cranberry pecan salad, and homemade apple pie. Their cake was made with huckleberry cream cheese and vanilla frosting, disappearing in minutes after Ingrid reluctantly cut into its beautiful texture.

As the night went on, Ingrid's Irish came out in full. Though she hadn't had a sip of alcohol, the drunken energy of the party had her lifting her dress up and tap dancing on the picnic table by the fire. Malthus' fiddle playing was accompanied by a drum and flute from a few of the other mercenaries and the dance picked up. Ezra had forgotten about the sweet music his comrades could play, and he was amazed how well they did, especially after a couple drinks. His brother William made a surprise visit and the party was officially in full swing.

Ezra was calm and happy. He took part in the celebratory cheers and such, but unlike his bride, he remained somewhat reserved. An hour before midnight, when the stars of night stretched over to the west until they met only a crescent of that painted horizon, Ezra sat on the porch of the main cabin, away from the celebrations. The children were asleep upstairs and the Saint Bernard pup was snoring on Lily's lap in a hammock by the river.

The old man, who had been mysteriously missing during most of the reception, came up to Ezra, seemingly from nowhere.

"Hello Ezra," the old man said, puffing on a tobacco pipe.

"Oh hey, I thought you had gone home already," Ezra said, a bit surprised.

"Home I'll never be. But this place," he paused, holding his pipe up to the heavens and closing his eyes as if making a quick prayer, "this place is the closest I've ever felt to being home."

"I know just what you mean," Ezra said, "but home is also a state of mind."

"This is true, young bear. Our true home is inside of energy; *in music.*"

Ezra looked over at his friends playing their instruments around the fire like a dancing trio of demons. Malthus was singing some old Appalachian mountain song between fiddle verses.

"Do you play? You should join them!" Ezra said whimsically, half joking.

The old man laughed. "I used to be a musician of sorts, but that was a very long time ago. I used to write poetry. Now I live in those words."

"Did you ever record? Is there a way for me to listen to your work?" Ezra asked. The old man set down his pipe and tobacco on the porches edge. He smiled and shut his eyes, as if remembering a warm memory, long forgotten until now.

"Oh how it felt to be alive in those days."

"Jim?" Ezra asked, wondering what he was thinking.

"Music is the language of the cosmos. It is God's word personified. It mustn't go silent. The song of life must play on."

He looked over at Ezra.

"I know what troubles you. I have foreseen this future of yours, Ezra. Your final battle awaits, and you will have to make the greatest choice on Earth since man created sin. You know in your heart what must be done. Whatever happens, remember that you cannot let them take the music away."

Jim got up slowly.

"The night is upon us. I must not be late for my next journey. Goodnight, Ezra. You're a fine fellow. Let every storm pass through you like a soft breeze but let the moth's wing-beating keep you up at night. I will be with you and Ingrid along your journey in one form or another. Take care."

With that Ezra blinked and smiled widely in bewilderment, unable to speak. Realizing who'd officiated his wedding, Ezra watched carefully as the frail man walked slowly next to the river under the rising moonlights glow. He walked on until finally disappearing into the woods, leaving neither a footprint nor strand of white hair in his absence. Ezra went inside to the cabins living room and placed a vinyl on the record player. As the remaining partiers filtered into the room and tilted onto the furniture sleepily, Ezra just laid on a couch in the corner, with Ingrid fast asleep in his arms, smiling and listening to The Doors as he never had before.

CHAPTER 10
FIGHT OR FLIGHT

It was a hot morning in August when Ezra awoke sweating, screaming, and bleeding from his eyes like a strangled vampire. One aspect Ingrid and Ezra learned about the Sararan condition is that although Ezra didn't need to sleep, he did need to dream. Ezra had to learn this the hard way. It had been quite some time since his last full night's rest. As he went into rapid eye movement, a rush of both past experiences and ominous premonitions entered his mind at an alarming rate and an inescapable nightmare played over and over. Vishnu's consciousness slithered into his mind and echoed the haunting words, 'A curse can be a gift, but this gift can't be free'.

Ezra wiped his eyes with his shirt and got up to look out the window. Down by the smaller cabins, Ingrid was getting water from the well and talking with a few of the mercenaries who were in the process of loading cargo onto the ship. A wind from the east combed the dry grasses as the men hauled their gear across the field.

Ezra shook off his night terrors and wiped his eyes, careful to put anything containing his blood into the biohazard waste bin. He walked down the creaking steps of the cabin to the porch. He gazed down the river to see a very peculiar sight. A light smoke hovered above the water and filled the air all around him. Far to the east, he could see a mighty plume rising from the base of Kintla peak. The smoke column blotted out the rising sun like a mazarine hemorrhage protruding from the mountain's spinal cavity.

"Some forest fire, huh?" Gadreel said, walking up to him.

"Yeah that's a big one all right. It's about fifteen miles away though. I'm not too worried," Ezra said, using his hawk-eye vision to view it more closely.

"You'd be surprised at how fast they can move," Gadreel said. "But at least you have the airfield for sanctuary."

"The field is on this side of the embankment. It's not like it could jump over the North Fork River. I mean... Could it?"

"Are you serious? That beast could burn a quarter of the state if this wind gets poppin'," Gadreel said cautiously.

"I'm surprised no one's used forest fires as a weapon on the front yet."

"They will. In July, when it's warmer."

"Who will?"

"Everyone."

Suddenly they heard the pop of a rifle and looked over at the men loading gear. Ezra's pores tightened as his eyes darted to the source of the shot.

"Just a misfire!" someone yelled from the field.

Gadreel sighed angrily.

"These boys are gettin' soft out here. It's not good for their nerves."

They stood in silence for a moment, watching the tremendous force of nature burn in the distance. A light wind wafted against his skin and Ezra felt a strange energy from Gadreel.

"You're leaving soon, aren't you?" asked Ezra.

"Unfortunately, yeah. Tomorrow we demobilize. I'm surprised Carson even let us stay an extra few days. Our next assignment is here in the states it sounds like."

"The exodus?" Ezra guessed.

"Yep. You know it's funny, he and the rest of the agencies thought the east coast population would be harder to move into the nation's center, seeing how there's more people, but nobody on that side of the country gave a fuck. It's all the same to them. They took the incentive check and packed up. It seems people in the west would rather try to gun us down than move five feet from their porch."

"Well, luckily I'm within the boundary," Ezra smirked.

"Just barely," Gadreel laughed. "Another eighty miles west and you'd be in some hairy shit."

"Man what is going to happen to this country?" Ezra asked, baffled.

"Shit, I don't know. All I know is that no matter what happens, this shit is just gonna get worse and worse. Remember how close we thought we were to nuclear war after the Israel bombings? But the real threat to us is America herself. The country is caving in like every other empire in history. And when it finally does, I'm bugging the fuck out and renting one of these cabins from you."

"You can stay anytime, friend. No rent required. Come back whenever you please. We might even move further north, if you know what I mean."

"I hear that... shit.... Northwest territory guerilla escape-plan, my nigga. I'm disappearing when my contract is up. Until then, Carson's gonna continue being the government's bottom bitch until he can get the contract to end all contracts."

"Which is?"

"The prospect of drone and unmanned amphibious tank craft. A general can mow down a whole continent without ever stepping foot in it, and unlike nukes you can still breath, no fallout. Grounds troops would be obsolete... a few operators here and there would coordinate the attacks and prevent blowback, but that's about it."

"Even in a world of mechanical men, there will always be assassins who know the bitter taste of their own flesh," Ezra said.

Gadreel shook his head and spit on the ground.

"I would fuckin' hope so."

"How long until your contract ends?" Ezra asked.

"This is my last year. The contract's conditions are fulfilled as of December 18th. I'll be free as a bird," Gadreel said while looking up at a hawk circling the river with large outstretched wings.

Gadreel pulled out his tobacco, snapped the can and threw a dip under his lip with his robotic thumb and forefinger where an enemy sniper had shot off his trigger finger.

"Well Gadreel, I just want to say thank you, for everything. I know it was your assignment, but your protection really means a lot to me."

"No problemo, E-Z-B. Hey I needed this. We all did. I will be back too, I promise. By the way, what are you going to do without us? Aren't you worried about someone infiltratin' your shit?"

"I plan to customize my own security system with some toys I bought."

Gadreel smiled "You got wasps, didn't you? The nano-machines that plant poison under your skin?"

Ezra nodded "Poison or sedatives. I chose the latter. Any cloaked killer in the night with so much as a sliver of entry space between his clothing fibers will drop within seconds."

"How many are there per capsule?"

"About seventy thousand," Ezra said.

"I'll make sure to call you before I head up."

"Unless you plan to go to sleep right when you get here, I would suggest calling first."

They laughed and hugged.

"I'm going to go see what this 'misfire' situation is about but in all likelihood we'll be leaving sooner rather than later because of the wild fire. At least you won't have three helicopters and a line of guards around the field ruining your view anymore."

"I'm going to miss them too, actually. It warms my heart to know that I have some of the greatest warriors in the world to protect me from some of the greatest assassins in the world."

"Ain't no thing, brotha. Gotta say even though I envy your life here, I kinda wish you were coming with us... like old times. Keep it real, Ezra. Can't wait to see the little man next time I come up."

They hugged and Gadreel wiped his forehead from under his black beret and walked off. As he did, Ezra's stomach lurched, and his hands got hot and sweaty. Something wasn't right. His right hand started to tremble, which hadn't happened since the mission in Peru. He looked down and saw a purple hue on his fingertips. When he brought his hand to his face and focused closely on the substance, he could see small dark purple stingers with red tips rooted in the combing lines of his fingerprint.

"What is it?" Ingrid asked as she walked out onto the porch, bringing Ezra lemonade and setting the perspiring glass onto the aged wood.

"Look," Ezra said.

Ingrid took his hand and analyzed it.

"Weird right?"

"It looks like you ate the rest of the huckleberries I was saving for pie."

"No seriously. This is weird. It... it can't be good," Ezra said, feeling anxious.

Ingrid scraped off the substance with her nail and put some on a plate sitting close to Ezra.

"I'll look at it later."

"Yeah, thanks."

"You okay?" Ingrid asked, suddenly showing concern.

"Yeah. Sorry. If you're not doing anything, can we look at this now?"

They walked into the cabin and went upstairs where Ingrid's instruments were set up in the corner of the loft. Upon walking over to her workbench, she wiggled the plate to get the dust onto a sample plate before inserting the sample into her video microscope. After some switch flipping, knob rotating, and screen focusing, a close up and highly advanced image of the powder could be seen on the monitor.

"Whoa," Ingrid said.

"What is it?" Ezra asked.

"The lens is zoomed in almost as close as it can get on this setting without losing image quality. They're stingers. Extremely small. It appears there are hundreds of thousands. Actually, these look a lot like a version of the Io moth caterpillar's barbules. Try not to touch me if this happens. They're small stingers containing a powerful venom."

"What do you think this means?"

Ingrid stood for a minute thinking and staring blankly at the monitor.

"You're going into 'fight or flight'. I can't imagine this happening out of the blue unless you were facing some kind of threat. Your body is reacting to this by setting up a defense. Are you worried about something, love?"

Ezra thought for a moment. He didn't want to give away his weakness, but it was staring right back at him from the monitor's screen.

"The Hoods are leaving. We will be all alone, Ingrid," Ezra said softly.

"No, we won't be," Ingrid said rubbing her tummy and smiling. "Besides, we have each other, always. Come here Ezra."

Ingrid put her arm around Ezra's chest and embraced him. Ezra knew, deep down, what would eventually happen to him. But how long he could go and whom he could save before it was too late remained a mystery. Ezra's role as a Sararan ambassador for peace quickly deteriorated that day, as he was becoming more like Marchosias, the demon his comrades had nicknamed him, denied sanctity or forgiveness. This name was bestowed on him long before the genetic transformation freed his heart and mind, in a time when Ezra changed constantly due to his environment of chaos and horror. There was never anywhere to go but through. Fighting wasn't Ezra's only option, he was just excruciatingly good at it and would never allow himself or his loved ones to be threatened. And as much as Ezra knew about his abilities, he was still underestimating himself. He knew he could do impossible things. He realized he could be as hard as diamond, as fluid as water, as hot as fire, or as cold as a glacier. *Through*: Ezra's subconscious motto and the reason his cells assimilated so ferociously to evolve into the ultimate organic weapon system. What he'd seen and felt so far was only the prototype of his Sararan self and it became clear to him he was already shedding his abstractions to make room for higher cravings.

A few nights after the Hoods had left, Ingrid awoke to Ezra leaning over her wearing a deathly serious face. He shook his head slowly.

"Shh. Do not move or make a sound. Breath lightly and slowly," he whispered in a voice quieter still than the gentle moan of the low rivers trickling.

Although still only half asleep and confused, Ingrid suddenly felt horrified. The waning crescent moon shone through the large upstairs room as Ezra walked slowly in front of it. He seemed to move like a floating smoke as he stepped gently through the suspended dust particles held motionless in the loft's air.

Ingrid tried to limit her breaths, but her heart was beating so hard that she swore it was all she could hear besides the light harmony of crickets outside. She could see a thunderstorm coming in the distance outside the window. Far away, lightning bolts soared above the relentless firestorm still gnawing its way westward, creating static with the coagulating clouds that cast themselves over the lurid crest.

Ezra nestled behind the pillar next to the stairway, disappearing into the crevice like a bat. As Ingrid watched out the window—her only source of light—a head suddenly came up from the stairwell, silhouetting the moon. It was a masked man. Quieter than snow falling on snow, darker than the walls of the deepest caves, it was perhaps not a man, but *a shade of a man*.

Ingrid tried desperately not to panic as the shade began to turn toward her. She pulled the blanket over her large belly and began to cry. And just as her whimpers became audible, she watched in slow motion as her husband broke his promise.

Ezra turned from his dark nook and touched the shades wrist – behind the glove, under his sleeve. Ezra inserted the stingers from his fingertips, sending paralyzing toxins into his nervous system. Making no sound, the shade fell into Ezra's arms. Another sting on the back of the shade's neck and it was over. Ezra disbanded his oath to never kill. The dead agent meant nothing to him, and yet Ingrid knew it meant everything to them. Ezra's hopes of not being hunted, of seeking a peaceful life, of raising a family who loved him and could grow with him; it was every hope they'd ever had poured into a mosaic, disintegrating into oblivion piece by piece.

Ezra looked at the device the man was holding. It was a Taser gun.

"They want us alive," Ezra whispered, standing up without any desire to be sneaky anymore. As he shifted from calm and collected to full of rage, Ingrid witnessed something she wished she hadn't.

Two more shades came up behind him from the stairway and shot their electric wires into Ezra.

Ingrid shrieked, as she stood up out of bed and ran to the corner of the room.

Ezra stood tall, hindered not by the volts as the electricity charged his cells and only enhanced his body's rapidly producing adrenaline. A rapid double kick to each their necks and the shades were dead before they hit the ground.

"Let's GO!" Ezra yelled.

In a tunnel-like blur of horror, Ingrid ran with him to the stairwell and down to the kitchen. She puked on the floor, unable to fathom what was happening as she watched Ezra rip a drawer out from the floor level cabinetry with a loud clatter. He slipped on a vest with twenty loaded magazines and then pulled out his titanium rifle, glinting in the azure moonlight. Just as Ezra threw the sling over his neck and put the weapon to his shoulder, another shade burst through the back door. The shade lifted his weapon, but Ezra was already pulling the trigger. Two bursts from the rifle lit up the kitchen bright with muzzle blast and the nameless assassin slunk under the kitchen table, motionless, his brains spewing onto the floor. Ingrid screamed and dropped to the ground as Ezra ran outside. Her face fell into her hands as she heard more shots barking like a hellhound through the night. The enemy began to shoot back as the fire fight blazed around the cabin. Mirrors shattered. Wood splintered and pieces of the old cabinets rained all around.

Ingrid stayed nestled near the stairs amidst the chaos. More shots ensued as Ezra reloaded. A few more shots rang out and after that there was no return fire. Only Ezra's blazing weapon could be heard spewing lead into the woods as the remaining assassins retreated.

After a few seconds of quiet Ingrid heard steps race toward her. She screamed.

"I'm here, Ingrid!" Ezra yelled.

He pulled her to her feet, and they walked out of the back door. Ingrid stumbled, that glass falling out of her hair. She was shaking and nauseous. Ezra picked her up with one arm and carried her.

"No please! Don't do this!" one of the masked assassins groaned, his mangled body leaning against the firewood pile outside. Ezra promptly grabbed him by the shirt collar on his way to the van and drugged the man as he choked.

He opened the back doors to the van and set Ingrid down.

"What are you going to do with him?" Ingrid asked, hysterical.

"Whatever I want. He's my prisoner," Ezra said, pulling off the shades mask, making him just a man. The bearded assassin looked terrified.

"Please, don't kill me. I have a wife," he looked at Ingrid. "And children on the way, like you! Please!"

Ezra used the man's own gun and pistol-whipped him with a loud 'fwap', knocking him out instantly. Blood trickled from his head as Ezra bound the man and shoved him in the van. Ezra looked around. The crickets fell quiet. The storm belched behind the mountains. A pack of wolves howled somewhere in the distance, as if feeding off the madness of it all. Large, scattered raindrops fell on their heads as the golden storm approached. A fearful static filled the smoky summer air.

"Get in the passenger's seat and reload this," Ezra said with a calm but serious tone. He handed his rifle to Ingrid and slipped the belt off of his neck.

They raced from their home, speeding down the dirt road and leaving behind the scene of a massacre at the isolated northern cabins. The only surviving member of the nameless order lay unconscious in the van, bleeding and traumatized. Ezra made the turn south and looked at Ingrid, who sat in shock, unable to load the weapon or move.

"Ingrid, dear? I need you to reload my gun," Ezra said looking into his review mirrors, still paranoid.

Light blue electrical sparks crawled along random parts of Ezra's face and body. The Tasers had charged his cells. The energy in him was as the coming storm cell; like a conductor of charged particles ready to engage in the molecular universe around him.

"Honey, we are safe. Look at us. We're safe. But I don't know what their back up situation is and I-"

"Ezra?" Ingrid asked, breathing heavily.

"What?"

"I'm going into labor."

CHAPTER 11
SERENITY IN SIN

Ingrid's first phase of childbirth had begun at the worst possible time. As she pulled on Ezra's sleeve, Ezra tore up the road even faster.

"Don't worry, Lily's is the next turn!" he yelled.

Ingrid cried and leaned against the car window.

They sped through the forest as the clouds loomed toward them, the dry summer storm dropping thick hail from above. Lily's house came into view just as the winds became strong enough to throw branches across the road's narrow corridor. Lily's seashell chimes swung in front of the single porch light on her front patio. Ezra roared the van into the driveway. Lily stepped out of the door to see who'd come so late and in such dire conditions. She stood squinting in the gale holding her frightened pup close against her bosom.

"Is everything alright?" she yelled.

"It's time!" Ezra shouted back as he walked around the van to help Ingrid out. They went inside the house and Ingrid sat in a big cushy chair.

"When did you begin labor?" Lily asked frantically as she set down the pup and reached for Ingrid's hand to check her pulse.

"Not fifteen minutes ago," Ezra said. He wiped the rainwater from his face and made his way to the kitchen. Drawer after drawer, he opened all of them.

"Ingrid, how are you holding up, dear?" Lily asked.

"I'm scared," she said frowning, her eyebrows turned upward.

"I know honey, it's scary stuff but everything's going to be ok. Here, let's get you to the birthing room and put on some relaxing music."

"Where are your mushrooms, Lily?" Ezra asked.

"There should be some in the bin in the fridge."

"No, where are your *magic* mushrooms?"

"Oh, in the greenhouse. Why, dear?"

Ezra marched out of the door and through the storm to the greenhouse at the edge of the yard. Lightning bolts shot across the sky and the clouds grumbled like the belly of a hungry God. Ezra stepped into the greenhouse, shuffling through more drawers in his search of the fungi.

Inside, Ingrid lay quiet. She was not yet in extreme pain, but the process was well underway.

"I need your energy right now, Lily," Ingrid said, walking over to the birthing room.

"Of course, dear, I'm here for you."

"We don't have a lot of time," Ingrid sobbed.

"What do you mean? What's going on? You two look like you saw a ghost!"

"We were attacked. There were men sent to take us away. Ezra killed them. We came here and my water broke on the way. I'm so scared, Lily."

"Oh dear, that's dreadful! But it's going to be okay now. You know you are safe here," she said, combing Ingrid's hair with her fingers.

"Are you ready, Michael? Your mom needs you to come out, sweetie pie!" Lily was sending positive waves into Ingrid. She laid Ingrid out onto a soft bed and checked her dilation. Ingrid breathed deeply and calmed, putting out of her mind the midnight attack and welcoming the spirit of Michael who had become restless in the womb at the onset of battle.

As Lily prepared Ingrid for Michael's arrival, Ezra crashed around in the greenhouse looking for his specimen. Finally, he stopped and looked down at a small plot that harbored several red mushrooms with white dots.

"This should work just fine," Ezra said, lightly touching his fingers against the cap's soft texture.

He walked out and the storm was in full swing, though the hail had stopped in place of raking winds and more thunder. He stepped back into the house where Ingrid was being calmed by incense and reggae music.

"Did you find what you were looking for?" Lily asked.

"Yes I did. I'm sorry Lily, it's been a wild night-"

"Shh. Don't be sorry, just be here now for your family."

Ezra kissed Ingrid's forehead, sending some of his static energy into her being, and reinforcing the courage she so needed.

"I love you. Thank you for protecting us," Ingrid said softly as she wept.

"I love you too, Ingrid."

"What are you going to do with the man in the van?"

Lily looked frightened.

"What man in the van?!" she asked, her eyes wider than ever in her large glasses.

"I'm going to get some answers. That's what I needed the mushrooms for."

"Which ones did you take?" asked Lily.

Ezra held out his hand and showed her.

She shook her head, "That's too strong. The effects are unpredictable. You're going to torture that fellow!"

"That's the idea."

"Where?" Ingrid asked.

"Behind the greenhouse."

"That's rather awful, considering your son is coming into the world soon," Lily said angrily.

"Well I'll tell Michael one day that I did what I had to do to ensure his and his mother's safety. Whatever you do, don't come out there."

"Don't worry, we won't," Ingrid said, getting agitated.

"Yell if you need me," Ezra said before walking toward the door.

"We need you now!" Lily yelled.

Ingrid felt her first contractions and puked into a bucket as the screen door slammed behind Ezra.

The tired and beaten shade awoke that morning to an umber sun hitting his face. His eyes were weary, and he could hardly see at first. His hands and wrists were bound, along with his torso, which had been tied tightly to a tree stump next to Lily's garden. Ezra paced with his hands behind his back and clicked a pair of needle nose pliers, walking slowly between the ends of the yard.

"Good day to be alive, isn't it?" Ezra asked, breathing in the smoky air deeply with his nose. The glint of morning sun cut through the dew on the leaves, refracting like gems.

"What do you want?" the man stuttered.

"I want you to feel something."

Ezra walked up to the man and put his hand in front of his face.

"Do you know what this is?"

He held the small red mushroom in his hand. The man shook his head.

"This is the Amanita Muscaria, or the Fly Agaric. A nasty little mushroom that causes hallucinations, nausea, spinal depression, and in rare cases, death. Ancient Siberians would eat these. They said it let them see into the future. Through cell synthesis, with my hand, I've given you just under the lethal dose, but with these things you never really know, so this will be a good experiment for both of us."

"No. You wouldn't!" the man shrieked.

Ezra looked at the man inquisitively.

"You have a very weak backbone for an assassin."

"I am not an assassin."

"I can see that," Ezra said, turning slowly toward the horizon and looking at him with the corner of his right eye; his dark retina reflecting the burnt morning glow. The forest fire approached in the distance, faster all the time, for the storm's rains had done nothing to suppress it, while strong winds had fueled its torching through the night.

"I work for a pharmaceutical company-" the man began.

"Hold on... Do you feel the poison yet?" Ezra asked.

The man did not answer.

"Ezra!" Lily yelled from the porch. "Ingrid is dilated three inches!"

"I'll be there soon!" Ezra said.

The slam of the screen door was all he heard.

"What are those for?" the man asked, nodding toward the pliers.

Ezra clicked the pliers together and stared at the man blankly. He knelt down close to him so he could whisper and be heard.

"Right now, my wife is in a very extreme amount of pain. It's no coincidence that you will also be in a very extreme amount of pain today."

"What if I talk?" the man whimpered, looking down at his already severely broken leg.

"You can talk all you want but words are fleeting. I need a reaction from you."

Suddenly the man's eyes began to roll around, as if he was no longer sure where he was.

"You're going to tell me everything I need to know, you got that?"

"I will do that and more!" the man said looking ominously at the sky.

"I know you will, because I'm going to give you a preview of what will happen, each time I hear a lie."

"No please! Please don't!" the man screamed.

Ezra suddenly stood up and struck the man's temple with his knee, pushing him back against the stump and holding him there. The man shrieked wildly as Ezra forced the pliers into his mouth and ripped out a front tooth from its bloody socket.

As he cried, blood and tears collected into the man's beard. His pupils grew and he became an opaque green like some deranged idiot.

"Are you with me still?" Ezra asked, smiling.

The man sat there, his head swaying like an old tree about to crack. Blood gushed from his chin as he licked the inside of his mouth.

"So you work for a pharmaceutical company," Ezra said. "Go on."

"I was hired onto... a strike team."

"What's your security or combat experience?" Ezra asked.

"I have some. Just a small-town cop."

"Then how did you get hired for this job?"

"They wanted nobodies."

"Inexperienced nobodies?"

"Yes."

"Why?" Ezra asked sternly, tapping the pliers on the man's forehead. He looked up at Ezra with dreaming eyes and nearly passed out again from the pain in his trance-like state.

"Ezra!" Lily yelled from the porch. "Get in here!"

"I'll be right there!" he yelled.

"Are you going to miss your child's birth for this?" the man asked.

"Shut up. Why did the people who hired you hire you, and who are they."

"We weren't meant to win. We weren't meant to complete... the extraction."

"Who hired you?" Ezra asked.

"Cassandra Larson," the man spoke slowly.

"You mean former Vice President of the United states Cassandra Larson? You're lying."

"No. I wouldn't lie to a man such as yourself. It was her," the man said as his eyes beckoned insanity and fell into the rising sun's rays.

"Why did she hire all of you just to fail?"

"So you could snap. To lure you out of hiding. She wants your blood. A lot of companies do."

"Why did you agree to the assignment?"

"Because I owe a debt to a law firm owned by the same company that Larson has shares in. We all did. If I hadn't done the job they would have taken away everything from me and my family," he said, watching a pine beetle land on his nose.

"So they think I'm going to want to find her and kill her, do they?"

"Yes."

"But that's an obvious ambush," Ezra shook his head, getting impatient.

"You could stay and get consumed by the fire we started, or run and be found by authorities, because well, they're going to want an explanation for all those bodies you left back there. So you and your family will run from country to country seeking asylum and it will never end. You will never be safe. Your only choice is all out war. I think Cassandra knows your predicament well."

Ezra clenched his jaw.

"She presides in St. Louis, correct?"

"Yes. She is there... as corrupt as ever," the man said, blood dripping from his bottom lip. He began staring at the light, becoming entranced by it.

"Then St. Louis is where I'm going if that is how this must end," Ezra said, dropping the pliers and walking to the door of the cabin.

"What a beautiful sentiment... to be so close to annihilation, and without hope for absolution... he spreads his wings and flies. Like a butterfly... like a butterfly," the man said, staring straight into the sun as it rose above the amber smoke, his pupils large and fixated, his red mouth opened wide with a demented smile, his face resembling the colors of a smeared Munch or a dead man risen from a shallow grave. He was gone, never to return.

Ezra ran inside where Ingrid was splashing about in her birth tub and screaming in agony.

"You motherfucker! You'd rather torture someone than be here for your son's birth! You're a terrible father! I fucking hate you! You fucking asshole!" Ingrid yelled.

"It's natural for her to be angry, Ezra," Lily reassured him, totally calm.

"Come here, my love," Ezra said as he wrapped his arm around Ingrid's sweaty forehead. She panted and pushed, feeling a horrendous anguish no man could know. As Ingrid transferred into her third phase of labor, the three of them connected on a plane of support and healing. There wasn't any talk of assassins, St. Louis, or tortures. Ingrid's screaming fell in between some very large breaths and the gentle upstrokes of reggae guitar playing in the background. There wasn't anything Ezra could do besides sit there like a good husband and let Ingrid try and tear holes into his arm with her nails. The commotion heightened, the screaming got more intense, and Ingrid's face lit redder than ever, until at 3:01 PM that day, Ingrid gave three massive pushes and Michael Ian Beller emerged. He was a healthy little baby, perfect in size and color. He neither screamed nor choked on the smoke-filled air as Lily handed him over to his parents.

Ingrid came to, as if she'd just returned to her body. She smiled at Michael, then at Ezra, then Michael again. Tears of joy started streaming from her as Michael put his arms up to stretch his fresh little fingers. His face held an ancient wisdom. His hands were so pure it seemed they could conduct the stars and weave worlds.

"He's lovely," Ezra said, stroking Michael's face with his thumb.

"He looks like you," Ingrid said, tearing up; euphoric from it all, and simultaneously exhausted.

They sat there for a few minutes, as Lily cut the umbilical cord and performed the afterbirth procedures.

"I'll get him washed up if you guys want to do the same," Lily said, picking up Michael and taking him to the sink.

"We can't take our son with us," Ezra said, regretfully breaking this awful truth to Ingrid.

"I was thinking about that. We will just stay here," Ingrid said, still in a state of awe.

"We can't stay here, Ingrid."

"I don't care. I'm not leaving my child."

Lily looked at Ingrid for a moment.

"I will look after the child, Ingrid. But you cannot stay in this valley. They will find you," Lily said. "I will take Michael to my sister's in the valley. There he will be safe from the forest fire and your enemies alike."

Ezra chimed in, "I know this is the hardest thing you or I could ever possibly do, but he will be here waiting for you once we aren't being hunted-"

"And when is that, Ezra? When will we finally be safe? Is that ever going to happen?"

"I'll go alone then. The person who hired those men is in Neon City. It's a dangerous place regardless," he said.

Ingrid began crying again.

"You can't go alone. They'll find me and take me away anyways," Ingrid admitted.

"Then what shall we do?" Ezra asked.

Ingrid looked over at Michael's clean naked body lying on a soft towel next to the sink. She looked into the baby's eyes, which were human. She looked at his hands, his mouth, his hair, his golden and green eyes; all of his features were human. The child was no scientific anomaly.

"They won't want him. They want you, Ezra," she said looking at her husband.

"You'll come with me?"

"With the greatest reluctance imaginable. With such sincere regret that it hurts me just to say these words. Our little boy is our life. We must come back."

"We will come back, Ingrid. Michael needs his mother. He needs his father. We will come back and be the best parents ever."

Ingrid laid her head down and began crying relentlessly. She stopped functioning. She couldn't handle leaving her child so soon. So became the first tragedy of Ezra and Ingrid's unfolding nightmare: the abandonment of their newborn son.

CHAPTER 12
CHAOS IN THE NEON CASTLE

Ezra stowed the dead man in the van and took it to the edge of an old logging road. He parked it and left it with a passage under the windshield wiper saying, 'Father forgive them for they know not what they do'. He expected some fire fighters to find it within a day's time. Ezra jogged back to Lily's, enraged at the idea of a politician attacking his family only days after security forces left his estate. With so much he held dear at stake, Ezra would be set loose into the fray of war again, unable to suppress his battles any longer.

The new parents spent another few hours with their first born, watching his squinty eyes try to see, listening to the strange, small sounds he made. They were elated the birth had gone well; all things considered. When Ezra explained they had to leave for the safety of their son, Ingrid would not go. She kept close to Michael and said she'd rather stay and face the consequences. But as she grazed her son's forehead, she did remember her vows and knew too it would be safest for Michael that they go and finish the deed together. They kissed their son and hugged Lily goodbye before riding south in Lily's truck. The couple passed a convoy of fire engines, dozers, and buses containing hand crews on their way to fight the massive forest fire. Helicopters with water buckets and large military ships were flying to and from the column's front, where no force of man could spur leverage against its ceaseless fury. Every now and then a civilian vehicle would pass them, which Ezra could only hope was Lily's and Michaels ride to the valley's safety.

Between the terrible acts of violence and the love Ezra felt around his wife and their newborn son, Ezra could begin to see a pattern of violence moving as if a Richter scale of energy was erupting in his mind over the last day, the needle clawing at one end of his mind and scraping along to the other. But who his true enemies were, he did not yet know for certain. Ezra was nervous but he knew that if he made maximum use of his resources in defeating those who were after them, they could return. This was his last job. His *one last kill*. Then they could finally return home to their nook in the mountains, where their newborn son lay peacefully in his crib, longing aimlessly with small cries that beckoned his parents to return.

When they had arrived at the Flathead Valley, Ezra pulled into a gas station just outside of town. Ingrid had risen from a sleep and her grief and pain were all too present.

"My love? Do you want me to go in and get some stuff? Anything we will need for the drive before we hit the road again?"

"I'll go."

"You really shouldn't, sweetheart."

She slowly got out of the truck and walked almost drunkenly into the store. As Ezra put the fuel nozzle in the tank, he looked back north as the smoke rose high into the sky. The aggressive fire had spread west on the tails of an ominous wind. Ezra shook his head, cursing as he did so. He'd transferred some weapons and supplies from the van into the bed of the truck, which he covered up with a tarp before topping off the tank. Ingrid came out.

"They didn't have the juice I wanted."

"Can it wait a few hundred miles?" Ezra asked.

"Sure," Ingrid said.

She got in the truck and Ezra roared the vehicle forward and skidded from a cloud of dust. He grazed her leg with his hand, sending small doses of medicines into her blood stream. The sun dipped down behind them like a receding red giant as they glided onto the roadway headed east, eager to break free from the fading saffron light that illuminated them, so that darkness could once again serve as their guiding force into the unknown.

The night was quiet. There was a still emptiness beyond what the vast prairie voided with its endless rolling coulees separated by hidden fractures of wind erosion. Every so often there would be strange buttes mounted in the distance, ancient volcanoes with their tops crumbled to nothing like a Martian landscape of plateaus and inverted craters. Behind them the visible stars hung low and cast a silver streak as the Milky Way turned like a great clock calculating milliseconds and millennia alike. Ezra thought hard about everything that had happened. The attack. The escape. The assassin. The fire. The birth. Their son had certainly come into the world during a most trying time. It had also become clear to Ezra why his son was not a Sararan, but he wouldn't know for sure unless he had the chance to raise him.

Ingrid slept sideways against the seat as the wind gusted through the window, whipping her hair over her pale face like ripped black flags. Ezra felt her pain. She had been through so much. But with his anger and destiny guiding him, Ezra could do nothing but press on and seek guidance from the celestial map above him. He looked into his rearview mirror. The mountain peaks poked above the rising horizon behind them, getting smaller with every minute.

Awhile earlier they had driven through Browning, in the Blackfeet Indian Reservation. Trash woven barbed wire fences mocked the raging winds, three-legged dogs wandered the streets, and a lonely drunk walked toward the casino below a billboard warning youths of the dangers of methamphetamine. The reservation land had been doomed since its inception, and this further complicated Ezra's emotions. How white settlers had treated the natives of that land made him sick. Ezra would use this anger against the politician who tried to take him, knowing still that every motion toward vengeance was exactly what Vishnu was craving from him.

The next evening, the bright spotlights of Neon City circled the skies in the distance as Ezra sped down the highway. Ingrid lay asleep still. Her hands curled up into a ball in her lap as she rested her head on Ezra's shoulder. Ezra's new mind was beginning to take shape. But he felt cursed with a strange madness, a masterfully crafted hatred molded over decades, breaking only for the greatest months of his life, then reinforced again by the defensive fatherly nature he'd been bestowed. Ezra felt his cells charge as the setting sun bled out, giving way to the rising gibbous moon whose mirror light did yearn to quench his insatiable thirst for violence.

A calmness had taken precedence on their drive through the plains but was about to be disrupted by the immensity of the largest city in America; St. Louis: the never sleeping, always vibrant metropolis of fifty million and counting. It was the means to an end for the inward moving exodus, as it was freedom's final gasp. Like a graveyard for the American dream, it appeared from the outside as a shining beacon of life and abundance, but its activities halted all variations of order and civility, rendering a pre-apocalyptic mecca of debauchery and spectacle for a socially antiquated nation.

"I heard his cries in my dreams," Ingrid said, awake at last to her nightmare of reality.

"Michael," Ezra said, saddened.

"He needs us," she said, unable to sob, for her tears had been spent. Only exhaustion and dread filled her red glazed eyes.

"He will be in the best hands for now, my love," Ezra tried to reassure her. "You can check in with Lily at any time. I got a text from her a few hours ago. They're safe in Kalispell at a friend's. He has milk, a doctor, and Lily will be watching him the whole time. And unlike us, there's no way to trace him."

Ingrid did not respond. As she leaned back into her slump, her eyes slowly stared at the incredible beam of lights coming toward them as their car crested a hill. The metropolis was a pompous brilliant imperium, bleeding the scent of gasoline, human mass and its movement. Hundreds of skyscrapers emanating ianthine lights separated the winding, coagulated streets. Music could already be heard bumping downtown as hundreds of speakers shared a satellite network of earsplitting electronic dub throughout, syncing the entire city to the same party. Neon City was the American youth in motion. It was their mark, amplified to the point of hosting the largest, never-ending rave on the planet. It was a place of futuristic vanity, multi-million-dollar music managers, producers as rock stars, drug gangs as jurisdictional authority, and when the night came stoplights became black lights. It was a place so full of party culture and lost dreams that specific sanitation agencies were assigned to mop up behind the flowing mass. The endless carnival was like jumping through the television screen, dosed with every scent, psychedelic swing and sting one would need to forget about what they thought they knew about the world.

The couple entered the city with their burping pick-up as people stared from their luxury sports cars and balconies with amusement. As they entered the inner-city district, traffic slowed, and a young painted woman jumped on the hood of their truck and began hula-hooping. She wore only a silver and white bikini and she dipped and glowed under the black streetlights. Some of the loudest, strangest music they'd ever heard blared from every street corner. People in high fashion dress, acclimated to the uproarious lifestyle, danced along with other rave cultists from all over the world. The streets and parking lots were packed with people in motion, with glitter and champagne foam falling from the buildings above them.

"What are you celebrating?" Ingrid yelled to the young girl, who just smiled and danced.

"Life!" she yelled.

She flipped the hoop up onto her fingertip and in a twirl gently hopped from the truck to the sidewalk, continuing her routine with fluidity and dazzling those who watched her. She turned around and smiled at the couple before holding her hoop still, only to back flip into a roll and disappearing under the dancing legs and thick weed smoke. A topless roller-skating beauty wearing a vinyl orange skirt and black and white checkered tights zipped between people holding a mirror chessboard dotted with pink powder piled on the squares. To Ezra, she seemed quick in her business and decisive with whom she'd sell her drugs to. She seemed always moving, as to not become too popular in any given area. Ingrid looked far ahead beyond the street's crest and saw men and women dressed in African tribal wear playing in a drum circle at the base of the great arch, the gateway to the west. A man dressed in similar attire walking toward the arch saw Ingrid's sparked curiosity.

"Do you know why they play inside the Gateway?"

Ingrid shook her head. They drove at the pace of his stride.

He smiled and said, "It is a portal to somewhere beyond the imagination of human beings."

"Take enough ecstasy and anyone can do that," Ingrid said, grouping him with the mannerisms of those around him.

"We stand apart from the inebriated coalesce," he said, looking around at everything. "We are the ones who taste clearly the elements of this universe, dire to gratify her ageless beauty, and perhaps evoke wrath, if it meant right. Were it not for man's sins, the gravity of the divine feminine age would not have sunk its teeth so deeply. Yet we see the burning pillars of man's heaven falling toward us like planes shattered by flak in the night. The Gateway is our cosmic point of origin, and we are its disciples. And in our archives these martyrs shall be known, for the one who yearns to bring back the sun even after the memories of our children have faded, shall know who to trust at the break of our pagan dawn."

He then continued to walk at the same pace but ignored their presence. With a wink at Ezra, as if he knew who he was but wasn't going to tell a soul, he dipped into an alley and walked toward the arch.

"We have to be careful, Ingrid," Ezra said. "We can't get our name out there. It could spread like the plague."

"Ezra… *we* could spread like plague," Ingrid said, only half kidding.

"What are you saying?" Ezra asked.

"Let's get a room first, then I will tell you," Ingrid said. Her body had been through so much. A warm bath was all she desired.

"Hey buddy!" Ezra yelled to a young man dancing with two girls. "Want your own room to party for a week?!"

"Yeah right," the kid said skeptically.

"All I got is cash and for some reason my card won't go through. I can't sign into a room under my name."

The kid stared at him blankly.

"You're probably a criminal or something."

Ezra got impatient. "Hey kid you just won the lottery. Do you want to take your gals and 5 Gs to spend a week at The Majestic? My wife and I lost our home to a forest fire and it's been a tough week. I'm just looking for some help."

The kid smiled and nodded rapidly. Ezra gave him the money and instructions.

"Two rooms, both under your name. Call them and set the reservation up and I'll give you the rest of the cash."

The kid made the arrangements and Ezra drove off.

"You're cruel, you know that?" Ingrid scoffed.

"I'm just using him as a temporary decoy," Ezra muttered.

"That's what I mean," Ingrid said. She was mad but knew it was a better option than living in a shack on the outskirts of town.

Ingrid and Ezra had heard on the radio that back in Montana, a wild land firefighter had found the van on the western flank of the fire's edge. The entire assassination operation was turned into a scandal with Ingrid's and Ezra's disappearance as the media's driving interest in their version of the story. Though nothing in the news mentioned anything of the involvement of corporate titan Cassandra Larson, she was still Ezra's primary suspect and he knew, based on some intelligence from his brother and a few others, that she currently presided somewhere in the city, likely high up in a plush sky room far above the infested surface. Perhaps she'd been waiting there anxiously for the couple's arrival, sitting on her white leather couch, her young yet scarred, skeletal hands pouring Cognac from her private cellar. The false sense of security from her agents matched her oversized ego. However the circumstances, both Ezra and Ingrid were totally unaware of how big their situation was about to become.

"There's a dark feeling in the air today," Ezra said as he stood on their hotel room balcony. His sensory cells pulsed, and his skin breathed in deeply the rising suns light. It was a late August morning and they had spent a few days resting in their room before making a plan. However, a heightened sense of urgency influenced by recent night terrors drove Ezra to want to start making moves. Ingrid had been awakened by the gurgling of the coffee pot and lay in bed staring serenely at her husband.

"You didn't feel it a few nights ago when we arrived?"

"No, I did not," Ezra said. He wore only some cut off black sweatpants and stood in a tree pose, balanced and unmoved.

217

"Something turbulent in me drives this anxiety. His presence is becoming stronger."

"Vishnu," Ingrid whispered, afraid to say his name any louder.

Ezra turned his head sideways and gave the slightest nod. He ended his morning yoga session and walked back through the sliding glass doors, closing them softly behind him.

"How do you feel this morning?"

"Better. I'm very sore," Ingrid said.

"Of course you are, dear. Today I will get you some things to help the healing process. I'll find my brother and get him to come here and assist us. He's stationed close by... a few hours or so. And you're sure you don't need a doctor?" Ezra said.

Ingrid smiled and nodded. "Just rest."

"So what did you discover that you wanted to tell me?" Ezra wondered.

"Well, a few days before the birth I stumbled upon something that made me think Michael would be born with your traits. That he'd be Sararan."

"But he's not. You saw him. You *birthed him*. Was he not human to you?"

"He is. But perhaps his dormant genes will engage at a peak physical age, when his hormonal shift takes place and he is ready for the transformation. Anyway, it's just a theory."

Ezra nodded but said nothing. Suddenly his phone rang.

"Hello?" Ezra answered.

"Ezra, hey, it's me, Gadreel. I'll make this short. Ed Curtis was killed last night. Someone took him out in a pretty seamless operation. Made it look like suicide. But we both know that's not the case. Whoever did it might be after you, too."

"What should I do?" Ezra asked.

"Speak softly and carry a big stick. Call me in a couple of days."

"Will do. Thanks," Ezra said. He hung up the phone. "Curtis is dead."

"Your old commander? Oh no!" Ingrid said, "I'm sorry, love."

Ezra shook his head and sighed. "Well this changes things. We need to execute this mission sooner than later."

"Will you need my help?"

"Yes. I'm not sure how yet, but I will when I get more information."

"I'm not sure how well I'll feel, but I'll do what I can."

"I will give you some pain medication, because as much as I don't want you to be hurt any more than you already are, I have no one else besides my brother to help us out, and he already has a job."

He walked over and poured some coffee for his recuperating wife before kissing her on the forehead.

"You've endured more in the past week than anyone should endure in half a century. I'll back a bit later today with what we need. And just so you know, there is a shotgun behind the bed frame, a pistol under the pillow, and a Kalashnikov in the closet, among other weapons you may or may not find hidden throughout the suite. Use them on anyone who walks through this door who isn't William or myself."

"Okay!" Ingrid said cutely as she snuggled back into her blankets.

She fell asleep again and dreamt deeply as if the conversation hadn't existed. But even if she'd only dreamt it, which could certainly have been the case given their ridiculous circumstances, she'd know that Ezra was approaching some distinct happening. Because like him, Ingrid understood the importance of dreams and symbols, that they themselves guided the listener like a maestro orchestrating fates from the subconscious realm. Ezra knew this truth far better than anyone around him. He saw animals as omens, war as divination, and words as guide tones to navigate the universes obstructions. Though love and fortitude formed the surface traits of his Sararan ascent, a myriad of dangerous variables hid beneath them. Hot blood and adrenaline from the chaos began to infiltrate his violent genes. By attempting to reject the body he'd been trapped in, Ezra paradoxically caught himself in the inertia of his own metaphysical evolution and was becoming more powerful each day.

Hours passed. Ingrid slouched on the bed watching TV with an opiate-infused coffee in one hand and an AK-47 in the other. The story on the news just so happened to be pertaining to Cassandra Larson and the rise of the private military industry. The news anchor reported as Ingrid turned up the volume.

"...and helping repeal the Patriot Act while she was in office. As former Vice President, Cassandra Larson was a key player in negotiations during the dismantling of the European Union, though many have accused her for favoring Northern European countries during the deal because of her political ties there. Larson allocated more immigration freedoms and tax cuts to Sweden than any other country in Europe. As of last week, Larson is now a major shareholder for the private military companies Titan Guard and P.A.I.N. Security. Her involvement in the last few years became more publicized after twenty-two contractors from the Swedish company Titan Guard were charged with war crimes after the deaths of over one hundred civilians took place near the Finnish border. Larson claimed the contractors acted far beyond her command or control, but an investigation into the operation is taking place. Miss Larson will be attending an open hearing next week for the justice department to discuss the power of such companies and how even the U.S. Military has been caught in skirmishes against these secretive and highly funded forces. Secretary of State Mark Shannon said, 'Now that these companies are working on U.S. soil, new policies must be written to limit their operational scope, because, in actuality they are practicing unrestricted warfare in unsanctioned zones."

Ingrid heard a knock at the door. She walked up to it and looked through the peephole. It was Will. She opened it.

"Hey Ingrid!"

"Hi William," Ingrid said, hugging him.

"How are you doing?"

"I don't really know," Ingrid said, backing up and showing her tired face to him. "Please come in."

"Ezra should be up in just a few minutes."

They walked back toward the living room and Ingrid poured a cup of coffee for the two of them.

"The room is nice," Will said, looking around at their top floor penthouse. Ingrid didn't bother commenting on the matter.

"Are you hanging in there?" Will asked.

"I've just been sleeping a lot since the birth."

"Yeah I bet you're pretty tired." Will shook his head.

"More like hiding in my dreams. It's easier than facing reality," Ingrid said solemnly, taking a sip of coffee then handing her brother-in-law a cup.

"Damn. It's been a rough go for you... How's Michael?"

"I just got off the phone with Lily a few hours ago. He's... he's fine," Ingrid said, beginning to whimper.

"Hey now, everything is going to be okay. Ezra and I are going to turn this around on them and expose whoever is plotting against you two. Then you'll be home."

"How?" she asked, sniffling.

Just then Ezra entered the room with an oversized duffle bag and said, "By being very quick about things."

"What's in the bag?" Will asked.

"We'll get to that in a minute. Ingrid, I have a hot job for you."

Ezra tossed a green prescription bottle to her. She caught it and sighed with relief.

"This operation is going down tonight. There's a big rave near the city center at Atlantis. Leonard Carson is planning to be in the VIP lounge. I want you to try and get some information from him."

"What for?" she asked.

"Gadreel thinks he's behind Curtis's death, that he was trying to silence anyone who knew too much about the company's plans. I need you to do this, Ingrid. You can dress up as extravagantly as you want. You'll be disguised as a raver. He won't even recognize you. Just find out what you can and leave."

"Why can't I stay here? Only the twerp knows where we are," Ingrid said, referring to the teen snorting moon rocks in a room full of escorts eleven stories down.

222

"He won't talk because Ezra gave him five thousand dollars. He'll talk if he gets a baton to the jaw," Will said, clicking a pen in and out, nervously.

Ezra looked down for a moment and spoke slowly. "Trust me when I say that Vishnu is near. It's my assumption that he's working with Cassandra and Leonard in their plot. You can never know what Vishnu's motives are until they are done."

"While you're at the rave, Will and I will coordinate and execute the killing of Larson. Leonard will receive the news soon after and likely leave. Then we will meet here and go to our next location."

"Where will you be?" Ingrid asked as she got nervous and popped a few of the pills.

"I will be high up in the abandoned skyscraper ten blocks south of her room. Larson will hopefully be in her home, on the top floor of the Echoplex Building, on the southeast corner. Will's post will be three blocks north of her in a gargoyle nest at the top of the old Church on 64th Street, watching the front doors. She never goes in any other entries. She likes to greet her staff and make her presence known. So if she arrives, she's dead. If she leaves, she's dead. If she hides, we wait."

"And where do I go after all this?" Ingrid asked.

"Back to this room. Take esoteric forms of transportation. Rickshaws. Party buses. Segways. Please be safe. You are in a fragile state as it is," Ezra said.

"What if you're not here when I get back?" Ingrid asked.

"Then check back in another 12 hours. Go somewhere non-exclusive," Ezra said.

Ingrid started hyperventilating as the reality of her involvement in an assassination set in.

"This is bigger than just us, Ingrid," Will said, reassuring her place there.

Ezra tagged onto his comment, "Cassandra Larson is a threat to our family... but also our country. That's why she didn't use her own mercenaries to capture us. She's a policy maker. She makes big-picture decisions because she now owns half of P.A.I.N. Security. But she made a huge mistake coming after us and not finishing the job. And it's the last mistake she'll make," Ezra assured her.

Ingrid opened the bottle and swallowed another pill before washing them down with some coffee.

"Don't forget to hydrate," Will said, worried for Ingrid.

"Don't you think you should be a bit easier on her?" he asked Ezra.

"Nothing is easy right now," Ezra said in a strangely stern voice.

Ingrid and Will nodded in agreement, realizing each of one them had their own fears, their own regrets, their own doubts. Suddenly, Michael was on each of their minds. His father's. His mother's. His uncle's. All of them prayed for their son and nephew, whose name had been drawn from the archangel. Michael was their driving emotional and spiritual force for everything they knew to be true and provided them strength when they needed it most.

"We end this tonight," Will said, getting excited. "Now, what's in the bag?"

Ezra unzipped the duffle and pulled out pieces of what looked like two enormous rifles, but they were more like small cannons.

"Are we shooting through tanks?!" Ingrid asked.

"No, just bullet proof glass," Will smirked.

"I suggest you two start getting ready," Ezra said, pulling off his shirt and lighting up a cigar. "We're going to hell again."

Ingrid's buzz dug in like a slow soul song persuading the senses. She went to the bathroom and began getting ready for the night. After a long shower, she fit herself with a zipped up, purple velvet coat stitched with white rabbit fur cuffs and hood. She wore the top of her hair back with the sides down which she straightened and laid over her psychedelic blue and green feather earrings. She lit a joint and smoked it while doing her face paint. She painted her neck and face deep ocean blue with prominent white streaks running laterally from brow to collarbone, touching it all off with silver glitter lipstick, purple and pink mascara, and a layered red, gold and white dot in her third eye. She licked the mirror in a strange daze of confidence and sensual power, giving in to the substance's numbness. She sucked the thick smoke from the roach and put it out in the sink then swallowed two more pills down with some water. She opened the door.

She walked into Ezra and Will putting on a different kind of makeup: their night camouflage and black face paint; a mixed look of homelessness and tactical advantage to hide their true aim. A cloud of smoke pursued Ingrid as she approached them.

"What time is it?" Ingrid asked.

"Nine," Ezra said.

"Is that weed I smell?" Will asked.

"When do I leave?" she asked.

"Right after we do."

"Which is?"

"Soon. You okay?"

"Yeah, I'm just... a bit soft around the edges," she said, laughing.

Will had an anxious look on his face. Ingrid turned the music up and began nodding to the beat.

"Oh hell yeah," she muttered.

"Don't worry, the adrenaline will sharpen her up and balance out the dope," Ezra said to Will quietly. "Grandpa told me that back in Vietnam there were the stoners and the alcoholics. The stoners were easy to spot because they didn't get down as fast if they got ambushed."

"What happened if you were both?" Will asked.

"You were dead."

Ingrid reached for a bottle of rum on the table.

"Ah ah ah! No you don't!" Ezra said, running over to her and grasping the bottle from her.

"Just a sip!" she begged.

"The prescription I gave you will do the job just fine," he said.

The brothers continued suiting up. Ezra secretly felt invigorated with the idea of going on a mission. He prepared the weapons. He programmed the radios to a hidden frequency. He sharpened knives that had been dulled from deboning elk in the mountains.

Will's phone lit up with a text message as he put on his vest.

"That's confirmation on our backup. Ten retired marines are standing by ready for us to make the call."

"Do they know they are participating in the assassination of a former U.S. Diplomat?"

"Affirm. They are just as eager to make changes as we are, and I found a loophole anyways – a way to vindicate us from any crimes. Look I did some research on this cunt-"

"Hey! I don't care if she did try to kill us, don't ever call a woman that!" Ingrid said, smacking Will on the back of the head.

Will looked at Ezra and shook his head.

"Like I was saying, turns out she broke off from a syndicate before she came to the U.S. She has relatives in Europe who are in prison for all kinds of offenses."

"Such as?"

"Tax evasion. Arms trafficking. Espionage. If we can find enough dirt on her, she'll lose her place in the company overnight. She could be a double agent for someone."

"She's probably a triple agent and working primarily for Vishnu. I'm beginning to worry she's bringing Zurvans into the country if she's been integrated into Vishnu's family."

"Vishnu has relatives?" Will asked.

"None of his blood kin are alive today. Vishnu's so-called 'family' of spiritual healers is really a band of former refugees he's adopted and turned into a terrorist network comprised of geniuses of the modern age. He seeks out the most downtrodden youth molded in the wake of war and he teaches them his path to enlightenment. I feel as though he and Larson are connected to this whole ordeal, so we got to be on-fucking-point if we face him. Take as many magazines for your carbine as you can possibly carry."

"We could take down Vishnu then too! Fuck 'em all!" Will said.

"You do realize he's killed Marines of all ages? And when I say that, I mean he's killed those in World War II, Korea,

Vietnam, and Desert storm. It wasn't until 2001 he began working with the U.S. government officially."

"Wait, what?" Will asked.

"He's over 150 years old... at least."

"That's not possible." Will shook his head, smiling as if it were a joke.

"It is possible. And he's a human."

"He was your comrade; why does he want to fuck with you?"

"Even comrades can be at war," Ezra assured him, wrapping a black scarf around his neck and down into his jacket.

Will thought about that for a moment and shook his head. "I don't understand Vishnu's deal. What's he trying to get at?"

Ezra took a deep breath. "As if being a world class assassin isn't enough, Vishnu has played the world leaders against each other in a blind game of chess, where only he knows who will become a captured pawn or a game-winning rook. Acting alone gives him an advantage in his murder spree. Most of his missions are completely unknown to even his most trusted combatants, thereby giving national agencies zero chance of picking up on his trail. And at the same time, he deploys thousands to help him. Without any overhead or long-term foreign contacts, he operates completely blacked out from the system. If humankind is bacteria, Vishnu is a virus, lying dormant inside the membrane of society until his sickness needs spreading. While killing the ideals of unified nations is a guilty pleasure, in his bare state he is a textbook sociopath, a professional and an opportunist. Hired every few years as a contingency resource by the United States or France to fund his cult's needs, he manages to stay in control through fulfilled contracts and outstanding marks with a new identity every few decades. But after years of floating over the world like a shape-shifting fog, not even covert warfare is enough to satisfy his cravings. Vishnu needs his life's work to bring a tremor every person on Earth will feel. Assassinating the Catholic hierarchy in Rome was just the beginning, and to strain the world's nerves into forced transfiguration, it will take more than splitting the high bishop's ring that will bring western civilization to its knees. That's his plan. That's his deal. I'm not sure how he's going to do it, but he wants me involved."

Will nodded. "I suppose it's time then," he said, pulling his gloves on.

Ezra handed Ingrid a small carbon blade. "Hide this somewhere accessible. It won't show up on metal detectors."

She took it and pulled him close and kissed him. The lovers pulled away and looked into each other's determined eyes.

"Be safe," she said.

"You too." he replied.

Clad in rags and urban warfare attire, and beckoning trouble in the most populated city in America, Will and Ezra walked down the hall as brothers in arms. Ezra signaled for Will to take a right down the intersecting hall toward the emergency exit. They did a quick radio check and went separate ways. Ezra followed the main hall for a bit longer. An old woman stared at him blankly as he walked by in his full kit.

"Police business! Just a false alarm, ma'am. Have a good evening," Ezra said, winking and adjusting his rifle strap.

He took a hard left and walked toward another emergency exit. As he walked outside, Ezra felt the moonlight graze his skin with its soft, diluted energy. It was soothing against his battle-ready nerves. Silently, Ezra climbed down the metal stairs and into the steaming city alleyway toward his objective: the skeleton of a 20th century skyscraper, gutted to its foundation by new tides of greed.

As the doors of the hotel opened, so did Ingrid's heart. She walked with a deadly elegance, a cocktail of narcotics brewing in her blood, her stride matching the vibrations below her feet. High rises towered over her, attempting to outshine the stars as a one hundred-foot neon Anubis walked between the building's light-window mosaic.

"What a time to be alive," she said to herself, gaining confidence with each pulsing bass beat.

She waved a taxi down and jumped in the back, her fingers grazing her knife.

"Where to?" the driver asked.

"Atlantis."

"You got it." he said, driving away quickly.

"You could have sat up front you know? Most people do." the man said.

She smiled and nodded.

"I appreciate the hospitality, but I need the space," she said, sprawling out on the seat like a cat.

"No seatbelt, huh? You must have nine lives." he laughed.

"I'm just waiting to be worshipped." she said in a relaxed tone.

"Oh yeah, by who?"

"Anyone who wants to live."

They drove a few blocks and pulled up to a bright red, neon arch that offered a stairway leading underground.

"Have a good night darling," she said as she slunk out of the car and the man sped away. As she walked up to the arch, two guards with hand-held metal detectors stopped her.

"Lift up your arms please, Miss."

She stood with arms raised and let them check her from head to toe.

"You're clear. The entry fee for this event is five hundred dollars."

Ingrid pulled a thousand-dollar bill from her blouse and handed it to him.

"Keep the change."

She stepped down below into the subterranean oasis where a throng of thrill seekers were dosing one another under a wide circular water tank full of rare ocean creatures: an Aquarius mecca suspended from the ceiling where the guests' acid-soaked eyes could watch schools of fish swarm and deceive predators while octopus tentacles wrapped around coral and changed color. The music blared loudly as Ingrid wove through the crowd of mermaids and other noble sea-dwellers. The beat slowly dissolved her. She became one with the crazed swarm of humans, dancing and sweating and forgetting her troubles in the heat of her movement. A woman with makeup like fish scales on her cheeks and luminescent yellow eyes twirled with her a moment and kissed her deeply, passing a paper tab from her mouth to Ingrid's and whispering something lasting into her ear. The woman spun back into the crowd and smiled as Ingrid licked her lips and smiled in return. As she swallowed the tab of unknown chemistry, she looked over the ravers' bobbing heads and saw the sign to the VIP lounge.

"Time to shake things up," she murmured as she swam her way through the crowd to the doorway.

The streets were oddly empty in that downtrodden corner of the city; Ezra found concealment easily. He'd seen random homeless people sleeping behind dumpsters or wandering about between the blocks that were usually filled with the noises of the city's quick pace. Will was having the opposite problem.

"Wolf-robe. Night Hawk."

"Go ahead, Night Hawk," Ezra said on his radio as he approached the base of the building he was about to ascend.

"I'm held up by a fucking space-hippy parade. I have one more street to cross and then I'm at the church."

"Fuck," Ezra said to himself. "Are you well-hidden for now?" he said to Will.

"Affirm," Will acknowledged.

"Just wait there for it to pass. You're too close to Cassandra's range of security to go cutting through and causing commotion."

"Roger that," Will said, sighing.

"Give me a shout when you're hunkered in," Ezra said, as he began climbing the stairs in the massive dilapidated building.

"Roger. Will do," Will responded.

Some of the tower floors were intact, but it was nearly possible to climb to the very top if one dared. Ezra went to a high story and had to balance on a zigzagging line of cracked I-beams that hung loosely above the shattered innards. He searched for a few minutes for a room that had trustworthy footing and a good view. He walked into a room with a large floor window broken out and a group of teens were laughing and painting graffiti. They all looked at him as if he were a cop.

"Whoa, man, is this a bust?" one of the long-haired hipsters asked nervously.

"This building is being demolished tomorrow morning, you know that, right?"

"Okay, man, no problem. I don't wanna be a fucking prisoner, man, no fucking way, man..." he said as his friends walked back to the stairs, quickly yet uncoordinated.

Ezra waited until the last of their laughs and yells could be heard before unzipping his bag.

He set up his rifle with perfection and ease, like a machine, like he had done so many times in his life. Everything slid into place with a small sound as Ezra used gravity instead of force to place the parts together. He loaded a magazine and extended the bipod. His breaths slowed; his heart rate increased. He laid down and looked through his scope, settling into a position that would allow him to keep still for hours or days, if need be.

Almost a mile away the lights of Cassandra's room had been dimmed, but her penthouse was easily seen as the curtains had been drawn up. Two men stood guard near her door, but Larson was nowhere to be seen.

"Night-Hawk. Wolf-robe," Ezra spoke into his mic.

"Go ahead," Will said.

"You get past that fuckery yet?"

"Not yet. It's near the end but it's taking a while. God damn wooks."

"Roger that. I'm at my post and have eyes on the room. Ready to engage."

"Like shootin' fish in a fuckin' barrel," Will said off mic, itching to get into position.

The VIP room was guarded with armed men when Ingrid approached.

"Sorry, Miss, this if for special guests only."

She thought for a moment. "My name is Ingrid Beller. You know, the scientist?"

The man tilted his brow. "I'll check."

He walked behind the door for a minute and came back out.

"You can come inside, Miss Beller."

She walked in and gasped. The subtle blue light and pillar shaped fish tanks held colorful sea creatures that swam around the room as if able to go beyond the glass.

"What am I seeing?" she asked herself. The acid pulsed through her veins as her body temperature rose and she began glowing like the lionfish beside her. Several wealthy stylish people sat about, conversing and drinking craft cocktails. A calming smoke hung in the air, something her nose could not rightfully define. Then she saw him. Leonard Carson. Billionaire, businessman and arms trafficking extraordinaire, dressed exquisitely and complacent of his predicament. He sat on a wide couch with his mistress and a few other women who laughed and jested with him. When his mistress and a few of the dancers walked to the bar, Ingrid moved in beside him.

"Hello Mr. Carson," she said as she sat and held out her hand.

"And who might you be?" he asked, kissing her knuckle.

"Ingrid Beller. You once employed my husband."

"Holy smokes, it is you! How very good to meet you, Ingrid. And where is your husband?" he asked in his slightly nervous, cocaine-infused state.

"Oh don't worry about him, he's out with some friends. I came here to have a good time." she winked.

"You're welcome to join us, of course."

"Thank you," she said as she crossed her legs and put her arm behind him on the couch.

"So what brings you to Atlantis? This is where people go to hide, usually."

"Hiding in Montana didn't work out so well, so I'm here."

"I'm sorry to hear that. But I can assure you, Neon City has everything you need to disappear."

"Want to disappear with me?" she smiled.

His face turned flush and looked to see where his mistress had gone but Ingrid had already gripped his hand and pulled him to his feet. She guided him down a hall to a small private room's doorway.

"You're a married woman, Ingrid," he said as she pushed him against the wall. He became red with lust, breathing hard and eagerly awaiting her next move.

"And you're a married man, Leonard. There's just one little thing I want to know before I suck your cock. Will you please tell me?" she begged.

"Yeah. Yeah. What is it?" he said, leaning down and kissing her neck.

"Did you have Ed Curtis killed?"

"What?" he asked, pulling away suddenly. "Why would you ask me that? Who the fuck do you think you are?!" Suddenly too angry to control his temper, he backhanded her across the face. She looked back with a frown and punched him in the nose.

"You fucking bitch!" he yelled.

He pulled her into the private room, shut the door and began strangling her in the dark, trying desperately to silence her screams. As she kicked and fought back, Ingrid was able to get her left hand on the carbon blade and stabbed him in the thigh.

"Fuck!" he yelled.

Ingrid rolled over and mounted him and began thrusting the blade into his chest and neck. Blood splattered her as he choked and hit her with his flailing arms, but it wasn't enough to ward off her maniacal acid frenzy. She saw his sour soul rise into the air and even though the blue demons scoured her, she let her burning heart clear the air, as she knew the emotions which drove her violence were noble and necessary. She stabbed him several more times just to make sure and sat on his chest like a ghoul in the pitch black, waiting until his breath and pulse had stopped. Panting, she sat for a moment and let her heartbeat settle.

"I just killed someone," she said aloud. But her adrenaline lessoned her realization and she knew that Ezra had committed the same act a hundred times over – though perhaps not so intimately. She stood and walked out of the room. A tall, rigid, blonde woman and several armed guards stood behind her.

"If you had committed murder anywhere else... but here, Ingrid? At least you silenced my only rival," the woman said. "You did me a favor. Now I'll get ALL the shares to the company."

Ingrid quickly reached for her radio mic. "Wolf-robe, Pavonis. She's here at Atlantis! The target is not on location!"

Cassandra laughed.

"Your transmission won't send from underground, but I appreciate the warning. I could have lost my head."

The guards tackled Ingrid and wrapped a black bag over her face as she screamed and kicked in the darkness.

A crackle came from Will's radio.

"What's that?" Will asked. "You broke off."

"Stand by," Ezra said, focusing in.

A blonde woman with a white dress entered the penthouse of the Echoplex. She threw her purse on the table before sitting on the couch. Another security officer came in from another room and handed her a drink.

"What is the wind like near you?" Ezra asked Will.

"I can see a flag about fourteen stories above and it looks like there are 10 mph gusts coming from the east in two to four-minute increments," Will answered.

"Is there wind right now?"

"Yes."

"Target confirmed. Standby," Ezra said, flipping off the safety on his gun.

"This is for trying to take my family from me you evil bitch," Ezra whispered to himself.

As the woman took a sip of champagne, Ezra double checked his angles and took a deep breath. Half in, half out. He squeezed the trigger.

Ezra's body leapt into the air from the tremendous explosion billowing from the end of the rifle. Through his scope he watched the bullet shatter the window and pulverize the woman's face. Pieces of her skull and brains splattered against expensive art prints and the eburnean furniture.

"Target is down!" Ezra said in his mic. "Standby for confirmation."

"Aha! Nice!" Will said quietly on his end.

Just then, as Ezra kept watching, he saw the security team leave the room without even looking at the body.

"Wait. Why wouldn't they at least take her with them? Unless..."

Ezra suddenly got frantic. He stood and kicked the rifle against the wall and screamed with the anger of a hundred heathens. After disassembling the sniper rifle and throwing his gear into the duffle he slung his smaller carbine rifle over his shoulder and ran as fast as he could for the stairs.

"No go, no go! Target was a decoy! I repeat, the target was a decoy! Get back to rendezvous point armed and ready! Acknowledge then clear channel!"

"Affirmative," Will said quickly before shutting off his radio.

Ezra started missing steps, then jumped staircases, then floors, until he seemed to be flying while occasionally grasping onto an I-beam or handrail in his quick descent. Ezra chanted all the while, "By falling, I am given wings. By falling, I am given wings."

He landed on the street into a tuck and roll and kept running. Over cars and trash bins he leapt, through alleyways and busy streets alike he ran. As fast as he came through a place, he'd be gone, as people saw only a shade interrupting their bright night of spectacle.

He entered the hotel's south entrance. Will was awaiting him behind a hedge grove.

"What happened, you killed the wrong person?" he asked, jumping out of the bush.

"There's no time for that shit. Get in there and mind your senses, we have to get Ingrid and leave," Ezra said, using his key card to get in.

A petite housemaid standing by her door jumped with shock and had an inquisitive look on her face.

"Excuse me, sir, are you two guests?"

"We were just checking out, actually," Ezra said, running up the stairs with Will right in front of him. The girl called the front desk.

Once on the floor of their room, Ezra looked at Will.

"Where are your men?"

"They wouldn't tell me. Their code name is Team Voodoo," Will answered.

Ezra switched on his radio.

"Voodoo, this is Wolf-Robe," Ezra said as Will mounted his gun on his shoulder and pushed ahead of Ezra as point-man.

"Go ahead Wolf-Robe," a deep voice said.

"When can you be at drop point Hotel?"

"Twenty-five minutes," the voice answered.

"Try to make it fifteen," Ezra ordered.

"We're already moving," the man said.

"Good, at least we have back up," Will said nervously.

"Will they shoot cops?" Ezra asked.

"I mean... if the cops shoot first," Will shrugged.

They got up to the top floor and snuck up behind the door of Ezra's room.

"Okay, time to go in. The door opens from the right, so I'll take the left side," Ezra said, hoping Ingrid awaited them alone.

Will turned around and nodded at Ezra, who nodded in return. He stood back from the door and kicked it with the power of a wrecking ball. The bolt snapped and the door swung open to an unbelievable scene.

"Put down your weapons and kneel. Hands on your heads. We can be civil," a familiar voice said.

Vishnu stood across the room with two handguns pointed at Ezra's and Will's heads. Next to him stood Shakti, her hands also wrapped around pistol grips, pointing them both at Ezra, her white kimono wrapped in bladed weapons and thick armor. Next to her stood the real Cassandra. She wore contractor attire with full armor, but without a helmet so that her long blonde hair draped over her shoulders. She licked her teeth and stared at Will with glacial eyes, her shotgun barrel pointed at his chest. Next to her stood two of Vishnu's apprentices: teen Filipino twins, near perfect in their synchronized nature and menacing visage. One of the girls held Ingrid close with a gun to her head. Ingrid was crying, still blazed from the heavy narcotics, acid, and concussion she'd received from the guards in her post-partum state. She'd been beaten and bled further by the arrival of the deadly entourage, her blue and silver face paint running in streaks with tears. Ezra's eyes razed in a sulphureous glow.

"Don't hurt her!"

"Kneel then," Vishnu said calmly.

"Down, brother," Will said.

They slowly put down their guns and knelt before the dark sage.

"Shut the door," he ordered. They did. Vishnu smiled widely as if awaiting that moment ever since he'd met Ezra.

"You fell for my trap," Vishnu said, "yet you are no fool!"

"I guess I am then, hm?" Ezra said angrily.

"But you wanted to be caught! I think you'd rather face this than live a life of false identity."

"And what am I facing? A coward who sends dogs to capture me and my pregnant wife?"

"That was Cassandra's doing, or as she's called among us, Sandraudiga. She got my permission to draw you to me, unscathed, by whatever means. And here you are, in perfect Sararan physique, in perfect hatred."

"That's not where the strength in my DNA lies! Love is the true driving essence!"

"I agree, Ezra! And I have more love inside of me than you could possibly imagine, which is why it will forever pain me to do to you what I must do in order for this world to overcome the evils of western fortune."

Ingrid cried and beckoned Ezra. "Please, Ezra. Save us. Whatever it takes."

"Self-preservation," Vishnu began. "Your wife knows the way. I'm offering you an everlasting life with your son and wife. This is your last chance to join me willingly, Ezra."

"Join what?" Ezra asked.

"Your blood in mine. Let us use the Sararan gene to cleanse the world of its most destructive species."

"Why don't you just go to Peru and retrieve the damn lichen yourself?" Will asked angrily.

"Unfortunately, we were unable to find the rare specimen, and we're running out of time. No matter. My source is right in front of us."

Ezra shook his head, "It doesn't work like that. You can't just put Sararan blood into you and become one," Ezra said.

"It might with a little faith and the right chemist. And I have one. Shakti is one of the best there is. Potions are her specialty."

Ezra bit his tongue enough to bleed and spit on the carpet.

"There it is. Take it."

"No Ezra. I need more than that. I am obtaining your blood tonight, with or without your consent. So what will it be?"

"I'll tell you the same thing I told the cock suckers that wanted it at homeland security. You are below me. I-"

Vishnu, Shakti, and Sandraudiga laughed. The pistol-wielding twins stood serious as ever.

Vishnu spoke while smiling, "Ezra. That is what I do love about you. It is as if you flew from the pages of a lost scripture; an angel's ghost, sent up from that universe of pain. This is who you are. You carry with you the pains of time and heartbreak concentrated in the Earths soil, even after gaining a new consciousness. See your true self, you will, both in the reflected image of your beloveds eyes before the fall, and of our shared visions of a new dawn. As a messenger for truth I know your intentions are sound, that you wish to bring balance back to nature. You've accomplished this in your own life, with your own family, but this planet needs more from you. In order for my life's work to be complete, I need more from you."

"Thus my destiny may be revealed," Ezra said, spitting.

"You are my sword, Ezra."

"No," Ezra snarled.

"Your fate no longer depends on the virtues you've lived by, nor the actions against the creatures who have opposed you. I control your fate now."

"No," Ezra said louder.

"Your destiny is to be my right hand until death."

"Never!" Ezra yelled.

Suddenly, the door was kicked open and bullet rounds poured into the room. Shards of wood rained on the kneeling brothers as a hail of lead and copper forced Vishnu's squad behind cover.

Marines wearing tuxedos and tactical helmets began moving into the room with sub machine guns blazing while the assassins shot back with their own arsenal that they'd stashed behind the furniture.

"Akuma no inu!" Vishnu yelled as he loaded his weapon, referring to them as 'devil dogs'.

Ingrid fell to the floor with a gun wound to the chest. With a haze of bullets above him, Ezra crawled over to Ingrid quickly and pulled her out of the room, getting hit with a bullet in the leg himself just as he rounded the corner to the hallway.

"Fuck! Shit! Fuck!" Will panicked in the hallway.

"Let's go!" Ezra yelled as four more Marines entered the room.

"You're wounded! Ingrid too!" Will yelled.

Will did his best to help both Ingrid and his brother down the stairs. A blood trail followed behind Ezra's seeping leg and he realized that Vishnu got what he came for after all.

"Son of a bitch," Ezra said, as they piled into an elevator.

"What if they... pursue us?" Ingrid asked in a universe of torment from all the trauma over the last few days.

"Are you kidding? My men are mowing them down right now," Will said.

"William, your men may not make it. Vishnu and his crew have gotten hit, but they won't be that easy to take down," Ezra said.

When the police finally got to the scene, they entered a room where ten dead marines lay about, their bodies perforated by hot lead, the room all but empty of any sign of the instigators presence. Someone heard a helicopter taking off from the rooftop a few minutes after. Downstairs, a nineteen-year-old was arrested for possession and harboring a wanted criminal.

Ingrid screamed and lurched in the back seat of Will's truck as they drove through the hotels parking garage.

"My shoulder!" she moaned.

Will sped out of the garage and turned away from the police brigade, weaving through traffic while attempting to evade them. Ezra ripped his scarf in half and began bandaging Ingrid's gushing wound.

"Where are we going, Ezra?" Will asked, trying to go as fast as possible without looking like he was leaving the scene of a crime.

"She needs serious medical help. There, there, Sweetness. Breathe with me," Ezra said trying to calm his devastated lover.

Her complexion was becoming a faint greenish hue, just like when the fungal sickness overtook her.

"I have a trauma kit in the back of my rig," Will said, "We probably shouldn't go to any hospitals."

"Fuck. I just don't know how to fix her without serious medical help."

"How bad is it?"

"It's getting worse. She's going out on me. Ingrid. Ingrid. INGRID!" Ezra yelled.

Suddenly the plinking of bullets hitting Will's tailgate caused them to duck and curse. Ezra let out livid scream and abandoned Ingrid's slouched pose. He went to the opposite window and rolled it down before pulling out his pistol and hanging himself half-way out the truck. Bright green lights flashed like a strobe as they sped down the busy street, passing cars and splitting lanes with the massive diesel. Every rear-view mirror they passed shattered from their charge. Sparks and glass shards splashed Ezra's face in a wake of metallic shrapnel. People on the sidewalks ran and shrieked as Ezra fired at the police car pursuing them. He blasted the passenger first and the window cracked, and the passenger cops arm dropped lifeless, his side arm skidding across the road and exploding into pieces. As the traffic loosened, Will hit the gas, and the furious diesel engine growled ahead. Ezra fired his weapon twice more into the driver's head, causing a wreck that stopped the pursuit of the other police vehicles behind them.

They escaped the city's madness and drove as far away from the metropolis center as they could. After a few minutes, Will pulled the truck over to what appeared as an abandoned house in a remote area of the suburbs. Helicopters hummed in the distance with lights scanning the ground with long probing beams.

"I'll head in and check it out. Get her inside, lay her down, keep her head and chest elevated," Ezra said.

Ezra used his rifle as a crutch and hopped up the steps on his shot-up leg. He opened the door to the old house. No one was home. He hopped to each room with a flashlight and found no one in the foreclosure.

Will carried Ingrid inside and he placed her in a bedroom close to the door. After laying her down, Will yelled in a random outburst of panic. Ezra shed a bloody tear but forced himself to hide it as he was in denial of the critical condition of his wife.

"Get the trauma kit! Are there any tubes in it?" Ezra yelled.

"Tubes?" Will asked.

"Go to the kitchen or something after you grab the trauma kit and find some tubing or a hose or something!" Ezra shrieked.

Will found some hosing under the sink and then brought the trauma kit to Ezra.

"Ever perform an inter-human blood transplant?"

"No. Obviously."

"Well you're about to with a Sararan."

Will looked into Ezra's eyes, helpless and frightened.

"I can't-"

"You will," Ezra said. "We don't have much time. Use that wall lamp to elevate the hoses. Cut the ends off of the hose and fix them to the syringes from the trauma kit."

Will hastily began to setup as Ingrid lay still as ever.

"Put some gloves on first, damn it!" Ezra yelled, "And hurry!"

"Ah just give me a second!"

246

Will was trying his fastest to do everything Ezra ordered but he was still shaking from the firefight. Ingrid's eyes were slowly rolling into the back of her head. The gloss in her pupils had faded. Her skin felt cold. Ezra put his head to her chest and felt her neck for her pulse. Her heart stopped.

"NO!" Ezra screamed.

Will stopped for a moment in case they were too late.

"HURRY THE FUCK UP! I'M NOT GIVING UP ON HER!" Ezra cried. Dark red tears dripped like a bloody fountain from Ezra's brilliant orange-red eyes, alight like the fire in his gut.

Will made the connections with tape, rubber bands, and a way to pump the blood using a turkey baster he found in the kitchen. It was improvised and barely functional, but he knew no other way.

"Now!" Ezra yelled.

Will stuck him in the arm with a large syringe and then put another in Ingrid's femoral artery.

"I'm pulling the clips!" Will warned, unclipping the flow of blood from Ezra's twelve-valve heart to Ingrid's failing one.

"Dear God, let Vishnu be right," Ezra said, praying.

Will stood in awe, covered in Ingrid's blood, his trousers wet with his own soiling.

"Come back to me, Ingrid. Let Vishnu be right. Let Vishnu be right about the healing powers of my blood," Ezra begged.

Ingrid lay on the bed, her skin losing heat, her eyes fading, and a silence suddenly filled the empty house, a terrible silence.

"Come back, Ingrid. Come back to your lover. I'm here, Ingrid. Come to me."

Still nothing. Will breathed quickly with eyes wide. Ezra squinted through the coagulated blood caked under his eyelids.

"Ingrid. You are my love, my light. Come back to me. This world needs you. I need you. Michael needs you," he said, almost whispering.

After a few minutes, Ezra's head drooped, and he wept a stream of crimson. He held the cold hand of his dead wife. Will looked on in disbelief.

"She can't be..." Will said.

Ezra cried and let his moans dissipate. They didn't move. Yet as the silence dragged on, a peculiar sound could be heard in the back of Ingrid's throat. Ingrid raised her hand, just slightly, and reached over to graze Ezra's blood-stained cheeks.

"My love?" Ezra asked, wide eyed.

"I am here," Ingrid said, wheezing. Color returned to her face, warmth to her hands.

She opened her eyes to show her new Sararan identity. Unlike Ezra's they contained small galaxies of white specks and blue nebula floating in a deep purple and green backdrop of space as if they had a whole universe in them. She smiled as the blood flow returned to her body. Her wound stopped bleeding and she breathed in deeply as her chest cavity popped open and her collapsed lung inflated. She rose from the dead an entirely different creature.

"Ha!" Will said, in disbelief. "No fucking way."

"You just saved a life, William," Ezra said looking deeply into the cosmos-like pupils of his beautiful, strong Sararan wife.

"Our love will offset the stars," Ingrid said in an eerie voice of fuzzy overtones, as if multiple voices of different pitches spoke at once. Will fainted, landing on an adjacent mattress. Ingrid smiled and leaned toward Ezra's bloodied face. She hesitated. Ezra looked into her eyes. She then kissed him more passionately than any human ever could.

CHAPTER 13
WINDS OF THE IMMORTALS

Will awoke in the decrepit house's bathtub. Ezra sat beside him, watching his younger brother like a father watches his child sleep. The dim light of early day entered through the old dusty bathroom window. A bucket of hot water steamed next to Ezra, who was clean and dressed in a prim black suit.

"Good morning, great protector," Ezra said. "You've earned your role as Godfather to my son."

"Holy fuck. That was a crazy night. I saved Ingrid! Fuck... I'm no longer in the Marines. And I'm probably wanted," he realized.

"Will, you'll always be a Marine. But you are probably wanted. Come with us to the mountains. You'll be safe there. We'll probably have to relocate to Canada."

"I guess I have no other choice," he said, anxious and at the same time, relieved.

"Tell you what, I'll buy you a helicopter and you can take Michael on flights over the Rockies."

"Where on Earth do you get all the money for this shit?" Will asked, shaking his head. "Seeing how I'm a criminal now, I guess I don't have many other options. How is your leg?"

"Oh it will be fine. A few more hours and I'll be one hundred percent," Ezra said, standing up from his chair.

"So it's over?" Will asked.

"What's over?" Ezra asked.

"Vishnu! The fucking double agent Cassandra… that fucking… cunt bitch!"

"I don't know. Vishnu is going to do something with my blood, though I can't imagine what. I'm afraid he will do something globally impacting with it."

"Is there anything he might have said to hint to what he'd do?"

"He may have in the past, but my memory is elusive. Or he's become a Sararan, and he's already clouding my thoughts."

Will stared at his brother then said, "We need to get back to the mountains. This lifestyle of yours has become extremely hazardous."

"I agree. First clean yourself up and come downstairs. I have a fresh set of clothes for you."

"Where is your newly mutated wife anyways?" Will asked, taking the bucket of water and dousing his head as the steam rose like a specter being pulled from his body.

The morning sun crested over the city's towering range and a healed, stronger, and smarter Ingrid walked across the lot of a motorcycle dealership. She came in the door with such a precise way, not even the brass bell hanging above the door rang. A salesclerk jumped up from the computer screen in which his eyes had been glued as Ingrid's voice boomed through the hall of bikes.

"Hello sir, I'm on a tight schedule and I am here to buy the three bikes out front. The black, the red, and the white one."

The man was speechless.

Ingrid had cut her hair in a short fashion—the bottom of her sheared black strands following the angle of her jaw line. She wore green cut off cotton gloves, a black cashmere turtleneck and tight black leather pants with knee-high military boots and large round green-rimmed sunglasses hiding her deep Sararan eyes.

"Uhhh... you're wanting all three?" the clerk asked, bewildered.

"Yes. Post-haste!"

"And you have auto-insurance, a license, and a motorcycle endorsement?"

"Nope. But I have a hundred thousand dollars in this bag," Ingrid said, holding up a satchel and smiling.

"I can't sell you these just because you have a lot of money-" the man hesitated.

"Why not?" Ingrid asked, getting impatient.

"Well because there are laws and regulations!"

Ingrid put her hand in her pocket and pulled out her lipstick, twisting it up and lining her heart shaped lips.

"I mean... you can't just walk in here and expect to-"

Ingrid pulled the man's tie close to her face and kissed him on the lips.

"You're wasting my time, fool," she said, pushing his body against the wall as the sedative from her skin penetrated his system. He slouched like a sack of potatoes against a shelf of old auto reports that buried him with a clatter.

"Now where did that mechanic go?" Ingrid asked herself.

"Can I help you ma'am?" a man walked in and shouted from shop door.

"You may!" Ingrid yelled, smiling and walking to come meet him.

"Yes! What can I help you with?" he said as he walked over to Ingrid.

Ingrid reached her arm out and touched his neck with the tip of her finger. The man fell into her arms and she laid him down on the floor. She got on her radio.

"Wolf-Robe, Pavonis."

"Yes dear," Ezra answered.

"Get a cab. Once I find the keys I want to be out of here," she said.

"Were you bad?" Ezra asked.

"The worst," Ingrid said, smiling savagely.

As the potent new DNA code assimilated with her body, Ingrid felt how relaxing and invigorating it was to be a confident and powerful Sararan. All the troubles of childbirth, abandoning Michael, and the physical torments she'd endured in the dreadful city was cause for her own rebirth. She felt more able to protect and nurture her family than she could have ever imagined. As wise as she'd become, she was not so complacent that she believed Vishnu would leave her and Ezra to live their lives peacefully. Ingrid knew too, that some kind of closure with Vishnu's cult was crucial to her and Ezra's freedom. Ingrid, however, was no longer scared. There was a great fire in her chest. The mutation had brought out the lioness in her, and she saw no foe that couldn't be compromised by her and her husband's thirst for vengeance. She was eager, unstoppable, and her imagination allowed for some formidable of attributions. Ingrid became the first Sararan female, with twice the evolution rate of a male, a vastly deeper insight into the divine, and with increased access to the more powerful feminine energies she'd beckon from the sun and the subatomic universe. Mastering the periodic table through application became

Ingrid's first goal. She'd clean up pollution, bring species back from near extinction, and alter the structure of life, if need be. Though set to use her new body for good intentions, she'd have no idea how dangerous such a craft could be implemented whether in her own hands, or someone else's.

Ezra and Will arrived at the shop minutes later, freshly shaven and well-dressed. Ingrid stood on the front lawn using a large tool to unlock the bikes from their pedestals. She put down the tool and walked over.

"Black," she said, handing a key to Ezra. "Red," she handed a key to Will. "And mine's white," she said, putting on a matching white helmet.

"We're missing Death," Will said, referring to the modernized four horseman motif they seemed to be following.

"Do you know how to drive one of these, Will?" Ezra asked, starting up his engine.

"Bro, I'm a pilot. I can drive anything."

Will started up his engine and revved it a few times.

"Just like riding a bike," he said.

Ingrid led the group out, with Will in the middle and Ezra covering the back. They sped off, ready to break down the confines of everything that had hindered them in the past.

On the morning of August 31st the trio escaped Neon City and sped west. The sky was mostly clear, yet the smoke of many forest fires hundreds of miles away caused a haze on the

253

western horizon. Ingrid was the most focused. She had been tracking the celestial bodies since she was a teenager, and knew that in a few hours, five planets were about to align in one of the most significant astrological events in decades. Ezra's thoughts of the future, however, were being charged by the fear of Vishnu and feeding into biblical form as he began seeing patterns between his fate and Christ's, and how it had been nearly exactly two thousand years since the messiah's death.

It was near midnight when the smoke lingered thickly, and their headlights took shape in the grayish white air. The trio stopped at one of Ingrid's relative's cabins in Rapid City South Dakota. Will needed the rest, and the couple needed to be alone for a while. Ingrid found the keys to two of the cabins. Will went straight to his bed, exhausted from the long ride. Ingrid and Ezra, however, had other plans.

"Get down," Ingrid said, roughly pushing Ezra onto the bed the moment they entered their room.

She unzipped her leather jacket and threw it on the floor while kicking her boots off.

"I don't know what it is," Ezra said, "But something about you has really been turning me on lately."

"Shhh," Ingrid said as she took off her belt and whipped him in the leg.

She began tantalizing him and touching him with static fingertips. Ezra bit her lip and licked her neck as they fell into one another's cravings. He crouched and began kissing her vagina, forking his tongue like a snake's and wrapping her clitoris in its cleave. Her legs squirmed, her thighs becoming wet.

Ingrid's blue and green nebulous eyes lit the room like projectors and the lights fed the ceilings a celestial glow. Then she dominated him with arm clenching vigor. The way Ingrid pleased and punished Ezra's body that night made him yell with multiple orgasms, and they made love through the night, over and over as Ingrid's powerfully seductive energy won her male mate, so that he was winded like a cheated antelope. By the time they had climaxed into the early morning hours, some sun-healing was needed for both of them.

"Holy..." Ezra said, panting as he lay back down on the sweat-soaked sheets.

"Unholy," Ingrid said as she kissed his chest and laughed a vile laugh. "Let's do it again," she teased.

"I don't know if I have it in me."

"Oh, I think you do," Ingrid said as she went down on him.

This went on and on as Ingrid's highly charged cells were in need of the kinetic forces to expend her radiating passion.

The next morning, they stopped to get fuel in Grand Rapids. Will sipped an orange juice inside the station waiting in line for the cash register with Ingrid. He looked up at Ingrid with a confused expression.

"Why are your eyes blue with white lights and Ezra's are dark red?"

"Because the process of Sararan assimilation is individually customized to its generic model. Anyone with the mutation would have their own eyes, their own mentality, their own strengths and defenses," Ingrid answered.

On the television behind the cashier something drastic was happening,

"Turn up the volume, would you please?" Ingrid said to the cashier.

A news anchor's voice increased in volume, as the woman turned up the TV.

"The cause of the massive blaze in Yellowstone Park, Wyoming, has been found to be human related, but it doesn't stop there. The suspected arsonists have trapped themselves inside the park where authority figures are unable to get to them by ground. The group is composed of individuals affiliated with the terrorist organization identified as the Zurvan Elite. The group allegedly has already killed four park rangers and shot down a National Guard helicopter containing five individuals. All five national guardsmen were killed in the crash. Authorities are calling on the military for help and are raising the national terrorism threat level to orange. All park entrances and exits are closed, and airports nationwide are on standby..."

"Jesus Christ," Ingrid said. "It's Vishnu."

"I get that part but what is he going to do?" Will asked.

They paid for their fuel and walked outside hastily.

Ingrid told Ezra what they saw. Ezra thought deeply for a moment.

"What is Vishnu's 'life work' he spoke of?" Ingrid asked.

"I'm trying to think. He was never that specific. He'd never tell a soul his end game."

"Let's assume he's already inserted the Sararan gene into himself. What would he want with Yellowstone Park?"

Ingrid and Ezra's eyes suddenly widened.

"What? What is he doing?" Will asked.

"We have to get to that fire now!" Ezra said as he and Ingrid mounted their bikes.

"What's going on?" Will asked impatiently.

"Vishnu hasn't been training for two centuries for nothing. He's going to use the Sararan blood to fulfill his Hindu name. He's gone completely mad," Ezra said, starting his engine with a loud rev.

"So? Isn't it just another forest fire!"

"No, it's not. That's a distraction and wall of defense so he can prepare!"

"Prepare for what?" Will asked, starting up his engine.

Ingrid turned to him and lifted up her helmet visor. "He's going to try and awaken the caldera beneath him and cause a volcanic eruption to destroy nearly all life on Earth."

With that said, Will suddenly felt hurried as well. They roared their bikes back onto the freeway and shot westward, toward the inferno set alight by Vishnu's long-awaited fury.

Thick clouds gathered in the west as the fire sucked in a storm cell, feeding off of its energy and gaining strength with pyro-cumulous buildup. Miles of dark grey clouds billowed over the mountains as the plains steepened into the foothills that turned into Wyoming's Rocky Mountains. It was a hot morning, though the sun could not be seen behind the immensity of smoke and clouds that hung above them.

Ezra roared his bike through the deep forest highway, the three of them passing fire engines and government vehicles that drove both to and from the incident. They whisked past roadblocks, causing firefighters to get on their radios and report the unexpected visitors.

When they arrived a few miles from the fire, a small contingency camp had been erected in a large field. Ezra spotted a helicopter about to take off from a refueling station at the edge of the field. He pointed in that direction and then turned toward it sharply.

They rode through the camp with their engines blaring, startling firefighters and causing a sheriff standing next to the command center to pull out his pistol and chase them on foot. When they got close to the chopper, a group of helitack firefighters waved them to step back, which Will responded to by pulling out his side arm and pointing it at them.

"Step away! You don't want to get shot today!" Will yelled.

They obeyed without resistance and ran back toward the camp. Will put his gun up to the pilot's window and knocked on it with the barrel. The pilot and co-pilot opened the doors and ran out with their hands raised.

"Let's go!" he yelled to Ezra and Ingrid.

Ingrid got in the co-pilot seat as Ezra jumped into the helicopter's open bay. They lifted off as Ezra racked the slide on his pistol. The sheriff fired fifteen desperate shots, with only a few hitting the bottom of the ship as it rose into the air.

Ezra's hair whipped with the lurch of the helicopter's rising winds. He knelt down and examined the bucket on the end of the large rope that was connected to the bottom of the bay.

"Disconnect the bucket, Will!" he yelled.

Will looked around rapidly then found the toggle. He flipped it and engaged the switch. The cable and bucket unhooked and dropped below.

"High speed, low drag," Ezra muttered.

The ship sped off toward the smoke. A massive wall of torching trees burned in front of them. Canopy winds pulled the flames from one tree to another, lighting them like matches with big whooshing waves as the flames engulfed the crowns.

"Look for an open area! They probably did a back burn and are hiding out there!" Ezra yelled. He rested the gun on his knee, watching the beautiful spectacle of mother nature's reincarnation as they flew over the fires edge. Smoke billowed up into his eyes, though he could see through it without wincing. The heat became that of a warm oven, and spark trails followed the tailwind of the craft.

Ezra looked over to the other side of the chopper.

"There! By those pools!"

Boiling geothermal pools dotted the blackened area. It lay about a quarter mile away from them, and Ezra could see figures standing by the pools. "There it is: Vishnu's intended point of entry!" Ezra yelled.

"Be on the ready, they have already used anti-aircraft munitions once today!"

Just as he had warned Will, the National Guard helicopter could be seen burning in the fire below them.

"Fucking terrorists," Will said.

"Come around from the other side and try to drop me off in a hurry. I can jump from at least thirty feet. Just keep moving!"

"Copy that! Then what?!" Will asked.

"Circle the area while I improvise!" Ezra answered. An air attack spotter plane could be seen flying high above the incident like a buzzard.

Will followed his brother's orders and did a large loop around to the blind side of Vishnu's area where a small hill rose behind the robed master. Will turned around and dropped low, speeding up as he did so.

"Get ready!" Will said. Ezra braced himself and aimed his weapon downward. Ingrid pulled out a large revolver and opened her side door. She clicked in her seatbelt and held steady, her sunglasses falling off onto the charred earth below.

Will was only a few hundred yards from the clearing.

"Steady!" Ezra said.

The clearing came into view. One of the mysterious young teenage girls was standing in the middle of the clearing with an assault rifle pointed at them.

"Steady!" Ezra said, watching the girl closely.

Will pulled up just as they flew above the girl pointing the gun at them. Ezra shot, but she pulled her trigger a nano-second before he did.

Ezra's braced arm half exploded in a blast of metal, blood and bone as the bullet separated him from his only grasp onto the ship. He fell to the ground seventy feet below, yelling all the way.

"Ezra!" Ingrid shrieked. She began shooting rounds at the girl as a rocket suddenly whizzed past the cock pit.

"Shit we're taking fire!" Will yelled. He strafed right and kept moving while looking for Ezra. Another rocket came from the black edge of the clearing, this one getting close to their tail rotor.

"Ezra is on his own! We'll get shot down if we stay any longer!"

"Fuck!" Ingrid yelled as she watched her husband stand up after the disastrous fall. They fled the scene, with two more rockets nearly hitting the helicopter as they escaped.

Will landed the ship back near the fire's edge, where a hand crew was clearing dozer line for a fuel break. Ash fell in the breeze. The oncoming flame front picked up its pace. Ingrid exited the craft and looked into the mesmerizing burning flames before her. She began walking toward them.

"Ingrid wait!" Will said, leaving the helicopter still running while he ran out to stop her.

Ezra used his stub to get back on his feet. He screamed in anger and pain. Around him, steam rose from the boiling pits and mixed with the smoke in the air. Swarms of fire beetles bit Ezra like demon wasps, their gnawing like small embers burning against his skin. Bullets whizzed past him and plinked off of rocks right by his head, some hitting his arms and shoulders in bloody spurts. He looked up at his perpetrator. The young girl stood firing the weapon and walking toward him. She stood a few hundred paces from Ezra but that did not stop him from leveling his pistol and firing the long shot, taking two more bullets in his side as he did so. His first bullet hit her abdomen, and she dropped instantly from the hollow point .45 round bursting through her flesh.

Looking to his left, he could see Shakti walking next to the un-burnt tree line behind the fire's origin. She dropped the rocket launcher to the ground and picked up her katana sword. Walking quickly to Vishnu, she kept her eyes on Ezra without distraction.

Vishnu's pose was a determined one. He faced Ezra, sitting half-lotus in white robes next to the natural cauldron of that mouth to hell.

"Put down the gun, Ezra," Shakti said calmly, stepping in front of Vishnu on the other side of the pool, her katana held up battle ready.

Ezra spat and held up his pistol.

POW! POW!

Both shots were redirected by Shakti's blade as she swung them with preconceived motions.

"You cannot stop us!" Shakti said.

Ezra fired three more shots, each one ricocheting from the perfect movements of Shakti's steel. Vishnu opened his eyes slowly. His irises were a moving current of white water and deep blue oceanic catastrophe. Ezra wondered if he was Sararan or a totally different mutated organism altogether, *beyond* Sararan.

Ezra tried firing again. His gun jammed. He threw the pistol down and dropped to his knees in defeat.

"Why must you do this?" he asked Vishnu.

"You know why, brother," Vishnu said, with a demeanor suddenly as compassionate as the Buddha.

"But this can't be the only way," Ezra said, sobbing crimson tears.

"I have been waiting for this moment all my life, and I want to make sure that one day, no one has to go through what *they* went through."

Vishnu took a deep breath in and spoke a quiet mantra to himself. He pulled his knees up to his chest and ever so gently rolled head-first into the boiling hot water. The reflection of the dark grey clouds in the water danced within the ripples made plenty by the suicidal sage.

"His death, like a star, will end in super nova," Shakti said, sheathing her katana.

"NO!!" Ezra screamed, bleeding and wailing in agony.

"Go to your lover, fool," Shakti said, walking over to where her own helicopter was entering the clearing and chopping the ash filled air. Steam from the pools swirled around her. Shakti picked up the wounded girl and placed her in the ship.

"Oh and Ezra!" Shakti yelled over the rotors, "you might want to hurry back to your lover. Hell is coming to us this time." She laughed sadistically. The helicopter took off, speeding away from the scene.

Ezra started trotting for the charred forest, stepping into hot spots and stumps still burning with immense heat. He began running faster and faster, getting furious, and using his charged cells to sprint through the blackened wood and callous his skin.

Ingrid was waiting on the other side of the fire and felt Ezra's presence within a few hundred feet of the flame's edge. Even at that distance, the heat was singing her hair.

"Ingrid, stop! It's too dangerous!" Will yelled. "You two come help me! It's an emergency!" Will told a couple of strong-armed firefighters.

Ingrid's eyes watched for any sign of her beloved as she stepped forward.

Ezra peaked the top of a hill and felt the orange death in his face. Flames swirled around him creating fire whirls, great tornadoes of embers that danced and spat fuel in all directions. He felt his skin shed in thin layers as he singed at its boundary, for his enemy's skin was also being ripped from his body as

Vishnu dove down into the boiling water at the helm of the world's deadliest hatch. Ezra took a deep breath and ran into the inferno. His skin ripped from him and his hair singed to nothing. His clothing burnt to a crisp in the two-thousand-degree furnace he'd thrown himself into. Burning while healing, healing while burning, he ran on, ducking under burning branches, hopping over scorching logs and running through winds of nothing but red embers, ash and flames that reached the sky.

"I can see him!" Ingrid said loudly. "Ezra!"

The furnace beckoned death. It raged with a wailing roar and threw ash all around. Suddenly a burnt and faceless zombie of a person stumbled into the head of the fire.

Will and the other firefighters ran to pull Ingrid back from the oncoming fire, but she began running toward Ezra's failing body, which could not keep up with healing his seared flesh any longer. He slowed to a walking pace and looked out and could see the clearing, just barely, through a distorted view. There his wife stood, waiting for him.

"My love," he whispered to himself.

"Ezra look out!" she screamed, as she watched a massive tree next to him snap at its base.

Without the strength to move nor the senses to hear the snag collapse in the midst of such turbulence of wind and flame, Ezra succumbed to nature's wrath. The six-ton snag fell like a whistling tower, crushing him into nothing.

Ingrid let out a scream like the clap of a bomb. She began crying hysterically, and let out another scream, knocking Will and the firefighters onto their backs from her explosive vocal cords rippling through the grasses. Another shriek hit the air hard enough to change the fire's course. She inhaled and screamed once more, the loudest and most powerful of them all, as a shockwave exploded from Ingrid's mouth, tipping the helicopter onto its side and shattering the ship's propellers into countless pieces that flew haphazardly in all directions. The fire retreated. The grass laid flat. Will and the firefighters flopped across the field like playing cards, and on that day, Ingrid was born a Goddess, having broken the sound barrier with her broken heart.

Will re-entered the camp in chaos and placed Pavonis' limp body on the back of his motorcycle, speeding away from the incident. He knew that every moment passed meant Vishnu neared the main chamber of the Caldera. He sped east, hoping the way they came in would be the same way they could leave. Faster he went. 90. 100. 140. 170 miles per hour, zipping by the parked government vehicles on the straightaway.

Pavonis grasped onto Will without any strength in her body to do much else. Her grief enveloped her as she envisioned Ezra holding Michael as a toddler. She saw them playing in the field by the cabins. Michael jumped into Ezra's arms, and Ezra spun him around in the air, smiling and laughing. Ingrid kissed her son and took him to the flower garden where he picked up a daisy. Michael went to hand Ezra the flower, but Ezra's hand fell away. Pavonis opened her eyes.

With an intensity unmatched by any event on Earth since its last great extinction, a sky-cracking shockwave bore up into the atmosphere behind them, carrying a climbing column of ash and molten rock with it. The column iced out in minutes and collapsed on itself, shooting rocks the size of houses and toxic gases in all directions. Pieces of Earth fell all around them, and Ingrid shielded them with a force field of dispersing atoms. The rocks and boulders pummeled the force field as her and Will managed to escape the initial blast radius. Boulders turned to pebbles turned to dust until behind them only a black cloud could be seen growing like an ink blot in the sky, its explosive energy grumbling and snapping in a violent upward thrust.

Will's bike sped out of the forest, but they were far from safety. All Will could do was speed northward and eventually round back west, hoping to meet Lily and Michael before it was too late.

Finally away from the foot of the super volcano, Will raced along an eastern highway in Montana when he arrived at a military roadblock in the middle of seemingly nowhere. Only rolling hills and dull yellow grasses stretched in all directions. Several trucks including two armed Humvees with mounted guns stood in the way.

A Marine held out his hand for them to stop.

Will stopped the bike and the soldier looked at Pavonis' eyes as she tipped up her visor.

"We got a bogey!" he said.

Everyone put their weapons against their shoulders and pointed their guns at them.

"Hands up! I said put your fucking hands up!" the captain yelled.

Will put his hands up, but Pavonis remained still. She slipped off her helmet and let it fall to the ground.

"Alpha-One, we have Juliet in sight. Standby for confirmation of submission," the captain said on his radio.

"You, lady. Is your name Ingrid Beller?"

She moved not a muscle and stared at the man blankly.

"My name is Pavonis," she said, completely still.

"We're not the ones who caused the eruption, sir. We were trying to stop them-" Will argued.

"Hey cunt! Get your fucking hands up!" the officer yelled at Ingrid.

Pavonis stood up off of the bike and spit, staring at the captain.

"Get your fucking hands up or I'll shoot!"

Suddenly, the clouds behind her gathered thickly in a spiraling vortex. Pavonis looked up, her eyes glowing blue and green. To everyone's astonishment, she began to levitate off of the ground.

"What the-" the captain said as the hairs on his arms stood up straight. The dark clouds popped and trembled.

BOOM. Lightning, summoned by Pavonis' nervous system shot down with a hundred spider legged bolts, crushing and incinerating the blockade. The blast threw Will from the bike like a rag doll, though he was the only survivor of her surge. As the smoking ground became wet with light rain drops, she picked up Will and walked north, leaving the bodies of the Marines where they lay. She stepped aimlessly into the featureless landscape of endless coulees; widowed, without child, and holding onto nothing but her wounded brother and a stark premonition for the post-eruption world.

A few hundred miles to the east, Lily had heard the news of Yellowstone erupting and was just getting finished packing her things into her car.

"Last but not least little one!" Lily said as she put baby Michael into the basket woven by his mother's hands. She carried him out to the car and strapped him into the car seat.

"We have a long ways to go, Michael! But you know what? We're going be okay! You'll be seeing your folks in no time, I'm sure!" she said optimistically. Lily was going to where she always thought she'd go in such circumstances: the far lands of the Northwest Territories, close to the Alaskan border.

That night was clear, despite the raging storm of fire and ash that loomed toward them from the south. As they drove further from the volcano, Michael's still adjusting eyes could make out the auroras far above him in the night sky. Perhaps his first sight was that beautiful luminosity. The face he thought to be his mother was the face of the celestial map above him, like his mother's nebulous eyes looking back at him.

On the Oregon coast, where tall rocks jutted from the oceans gnashing like great black teeth, Shakti stepped out of the helicopter, took off her boots and dug her feet into the wet sand. She breathed in the cool air. The sea's mists cleansed her ashy face as she beckoned her apprentices.

"What now, Master Shakti?" the girl asked, taking off her flight helmet.

Shakti smiled at the thought of being called master.

"Now we execute The Prophecy in full, Mayari."

"Administer this to Tala," Shakti said, handing a vile of blood to her.

"It's the hybrid, formulated with genetically modified amino acids, a dash of DMT, and shards of steal from Vishnu's wakizashi blade."

She grasped the vile and looked at it.

"Will there be no ceremony? No proper ritual?" she asked.

"There is not always time for such nuances, my skilled apprentice. After this, however, her whole life will become ritualistic. As will yours."

She poured the liquid into her sister Tala's wounded side. The dying twin looked up inquisitively, her eyes connecting with her sister's in a dangerous lock as their altered states gave shape to Mayari's servitude and Tala's ascension.

"Now take some yourself," Shakti ordered. "The transfiguration of my heirs into Lords will be my hundredth birthday present. This concoction is ten times more complex than the Sararan gene. I named it after Aradia, the female messiah of The Old Religion, who fought the evil masculine forces of Rome."

The girl was nervous but did as Shakti said and sliced her hand open before pouring the hybrid formula of dark blood inside her.

"My sisters, you will be the most feared beings in the world, and someday, the galaxy. You will be the only Aradians created after Vishnu. You will take care of your master's orders, and you will become masters yourselves. You will move mountains. You will empty seas. You will kill many men. And you will continue Vishnu's dream of paradise," Shakti said.

"We will be... engineers," Mayari said, smiling slightly, feeling the substance shred her identity and redefine it, causing euphoria and sudden introspection.

"An appropriate term for an organism so perfectly suitable for both destruction and creation. Welcome to the land of the setting sun, sisters. This will be your new kingdom," Shakti said, grazing Mayari's soft hair as she stared into her eyes, which were becoming chrome and reflective with each passing second. She then looked at Tala, whose eyes projected memories like windows into a troubled mind. The Aradian dynamic was complete, one that reflects and one that absorbs. Twin Aradians; twin Goddesses.

"What shall we take with us, and what shall we leave behind?" asked Tala.

Shakti looked at Tala and said, "We as a trinity will continue to erase countless lineages, but we must filter not the weak but the unwilling. And the stars will scatter. And the mountains will belch blood. The beasts will roam prolific. And the golden sun dial of our prophecy realized will phase out evil men until we meet God at its singularity."

They watched the sun as it sank beyond the mighty Pacific one last time before disappearing behind an ash cloud that blanketed itself over the globe, thickening like a black curtain and blinding the world of its own reflection.

Working vicariously through his perfectly manipulated apprentices, Vishnu's master plan had finally set the stage for humankind's cataclysmic fall. And though the U.S. military complex was ready for almost any kind of war, nothing could have prepared them for the fight against the Aradian women of the east. Western powers simply weren't used to fighting in a world choked in smoke, without proper communication,

271

resources or social stability. But like all Vishnu's apprentices, Tala and Mayari were war refugees. They were *born in a world choked in smoke*, forged by its heat like a sword in the blast furnace. Breathing fire like dragons, no form of torture could be greater than their adolescence spent in the blaze of the Vietnam war's napalm swirling hell. They had been raised in bomb craters and sustained on only rice water. It was only fitting that decades after Tala and Mayari inhaled the toxic invasion of the west, these twin sisters would spread terror in a tidal wave of violence to follow the volcano's wrath. Vishnu gave them the power of immortality, as it would let them exhale their hatred onto the world in ways that made people wish they'd been devoured by the caldera itself.

Violence and darkness and all things dread crept through the world, a malignant shadow, like a mind-sick mother suffocating her children in the night, where small screams kept soft in the lupus hour are fed to the mouth of silence and nothingness under tear stained sheets. What appeared to many as Armageddon became the beginning of a far more horrific and surreal nightmare for the unlucky few survivors, who through their enduring found only ranges of death and waste in their escape from the immense chaos of it all. Only months post eruption, the carcass laden lands stank a thousand regrettable smells, until the rivers dammed with the bile of poisoned fish and fowl, and lakes steamed with acidic trash, and clouds coagulated indefinitely with their nauseous churning, and new borders were drawn with rows of crucified families, each corpse more tortured rotten than the last. Outcasts of savage tribes roamed the blue-grey abyss more bone than skin, naked, wearing only antique gas masks and hoisting headless toddlers on spears like flags of a brute land; a planet lawless and unforgiving, containing those who remained virtuous and those who did not, children of a common womb feeding from the shriveled bosom of Earth's vessels until only the maggots on their lacerated feet were left to ingest beyond the prospect of cannibalism.

The last gasp of man's might met its bitter end with winter's frost. Everything and everyone was now at the mercy of the Immortals and their moonscape disciples. And yet beyond the horizon of the fallout's settling, some new divine wind awaited to insult the Zurvan takeover. A whisper wheezed through the arctic canyons a tender agony. A child's cry. Abandoned but not forgotten. Hidden but not forsaken. Deep in the woods he cried. Awaiting his mother. Awaiting his destiny. Awaiting his transformation.